Dead Man's Gold

First published in 2016

Mendus Harris

ISBN: 978-1539659006

Harris has worked as a geologist all over the world, and in his debut novel he uses his knowledge of the mirky business of gold mining in West Africa to tell a story that is exciting and yet believable. His imagination works in harmony with his powers of observation to create a compelling story of greed and murder three miles down.

Dead Man's Gold is an engaging and atmospheric thriller, with a strong sense of place and vividly drawn characters. A rollicking good read!

Andrew Williams
Best-selling historical crime author

Dead Man's Gold

Mendus Harris

DEDICATION

To Rachel.

CONTENTS

PROLOGUE

Edryd (Ed) Evans looked left and right through the windows of the YAK 12A aircraft as it flew low over the lush green jungle vegetation. He was nervous, the clouds had been thickening up ahead for the last thirty minutes to form a bruise-coloured barrier that stretched left and right to the distant horizon. At the current rate of travel (very slow) they would reach the edge of the cloud-front in less than twenty minutes.

The pilot, a tall and wasted Russian who had come to West Africa in search of warmth and a fortune, had suggested that they were at least an hour away from their destination. 'Add thirty minutes to that', Ed thought, trying to shut out the smell of homemade vodka that permeated the cockpit.

A faint flash of light up ahead made him focus more intently. It emanated from one of the darker clouds. He leaned over and knocked the pilot on the shoulder and pointed, "thunder and lightning storm," he shouted. "We must go back."

But the Russian indicated the fuel needle on the

dashboard, it showed they had less than a quarter of a tank left. "Can't go back," he shouted.

A griping feeling entered Ed's stomach. He thought of Alice at home in Liverpool and her last words to him as he left, "Promise me you'll not take risks." As he'd boarded the train to London he'd had every intention of obeying, but by degrees his resolve had crumbled. The gold mining company were willing to pay him a substantial fee if he would cooperate; so much money that he could even retire, buy Taid's old farmhouse in the Welsh Marches, persuade Alice to move in with him.

When he'd arrived at the airfield cut in the jungle and discovered the plane in which he was to be transported across enemy territory (as the locals called it) belonged in a World War II museum of rubbish Russian aircraft technology, he should have walked away. He cursed his weakness, his bravado, his impatience.

The Russian had been sober when they'd been introduced, he'd come across as competent and stoic. It was only when they were cruising at altitude that Ed had caught the first whiff of alcohol. He'd initially thought it was some kind of fuel additive but then the sun shining through the cockpit window had glinted off a bottle. Next time the Russian had tried to take a swig Ed had leaned forward and grabbed it from his hand.

As they approached the cloud bank the plane began to bounce violently. Shutting his eyes, Ed tried to make himself relax; he half thought of sinking the rest of the Russian's vodka, but he'd need his eye-sight if ever he survived the coming ordeal.

A loud clap of thunder made him look up in time to see a fork of lightning flash past the starboard wing. His stomach lurched as the aircraft plummeted toward the ground, its wings bending under the tremendous strains exerted by ferocious down-drafts. Then they began climbing again, up through turbulence that was the equivalent of an atmospheric waterfall, engine labouring against impossible forces, trying to break free of the vortex in which they were caught. With visibility close to zero another source of anxiety seized Ed; somewhere around here the land started to rise into mountains, in fact it was probably the influence of the elevated forest that caused the storm.

For ten minutes that felt like a lifetime, the pilot struggled to hold his aircraft against forces that threatened to pull it to the ground. Ed's insides felt like they were haemorrhaging, he was sure their fragile craft would start disintegrating. Looking down he searched for features to judge their height, he saw vague shadows a few metres below that didn't look like cloud. With a great yell of terror he shouted at the pilot that they were heading straight for the ground. The pilot pulled back on the joystick but there was nothing he could do except straighten the nose as the wing tips and the propeller hit the top of the tree canopy.

The world froze and Alice's face swam in front of him, her eyes alight with promise; he could see his own desire reflected there. Then the nose of the aircraft dropped and the world was filled with leaves, flying wooden splinters and glass. He threw his head forward and pulled a massive rucksack onto his back. The flimsy wooden boards of the YAK began to disintegrate, sharp branches scraped at his shirt, ripped holes in the rucksack fabric. A human scream erupted that quickly died to a horrible wet gurgle as the tattered and torn chassis came to rest with a sudden and violent jerk.

For thirty seconds he waited, listening to silence erupt into a cacophony of complaining forest animals.

Unbending, he saw the pilot's head thrown back, caked in blood that still trickled from a massive wound in his chest where a long, splintered branch had entered.

The aircraft was stuck half way up a large silver tree, thirty feet from the ground. Slowly undoing his belt buckle he shifted his weight to test stability. The tree swayed a little and then stopped. Standing, he looked down and realised that beyond the dead pilot there were a series of branches that would take him down at least twenty feet.

Leaning forward he carefully swung his right leg over the front seat, brushing the head of the dead pilot, then waited until he was certain that the aircraft was stable before moving to his left. To his alarm a branch bent, then snapped, and the floor of the aircraft fell half a metre. Heart in his mouth, he waited, ready to leap to a nearby branch if required. The aircraft vibrated alarmingly before stopping its downward motion.

The escape branch was just a small jump away, he could easily make it. Without daring to think he threw himself into nothingness and grabbed madly, feeling his hands clutch the smooth bark. The branch bounced but held firm and for a split second he felt the elation of escape. But then there was a much louder snap and he sensed the aircraft start to move. Turning quickly he saw one of the torn metal struts roll around, there was no time to pull himself away, the metal slashed at his face, gouging long, deep marks in his cheek.

The chassis continued its roll, crashing into the branch that was his last slender hope of survival. A scream of frustration left him as he scrabbled madly, but his hands were now slick with blood, he lost his grip and followed after the remnants of YAK 12A bouncing off broken branches and clinging to hanging vines. Somewhere close to the ground he lost consciousness.

When he opened his eyes again it was dark, pain emanated from every part of his body, in particular his ankle. He was being carried on a primitive bier by men dressed in shorts and shirts, each with a foot long machete strapped to their belts. They were moving fast along a poorly-defined path, away from the aircraft and its signalling distress beacon that was his last chance of easy rescue.

AT THE LOMAX MINE

TWO YEARS LATER

Edryd Evans was dreaming of Taid's old kitchen with its smell of age-old dampness, the aroma of wood smoke from the fire, the scent of hay and sheep seeping through the cracks in the door and window frames. In his sleep, he sniffed the air around him, finding more hints of the smells that had been part of his childhood, like dried sweat off tweed jacket, wet dog, the greasy smell of a slow cooked mutton broth bubbling on the Rayburn, the herbal fragrance of old fashioned tobacco. He saw Taid, his grandfather, with pipe in his mouth puffing like an old tramp steamer, a blue haze drifting out into the gathering gloom. Beside him stood Greg Boston, a tall boy with curly blonde hair and a trademark grin.

A loud yell very close to his ear caused him to wake suddenly and a feeling like vertigo took hold of his senses as he emerged from the comforting world of Taid's Welsh Borderland farm. A violent shaking motion threw him forward causing him to smacked his nose against something soft. Darkness turned to painful light as he opened his eyes onto a world that was entirely different from the one he was expecting. There was no old Rayburn sitting comfortably to one side, nor any smelly, decrepit armchairs or rustic kitchen table. He saw a large African woman dressed in gold and black who was rubbing her arm and looking at him reproachfully.

"Sorry," he murmured, quickly looking out of the window to see children running away and heard scolding shouts from fellow passengers and the bus driver.

Thoughts flooded into his mind as though an interrupt signal had triggered the re-introduction of his real world self. He was on a bus travelling along a bouncy road somewhere in West Africa. The last time he'd been vaguely aware of what was going on around him was somewhere on the outskirts of Accra.

Outside the window were streets full of market stalls and neighbourhoods of shacks. Bare mountainsides and tall chimneys appeared above corrugated iron roofs. Ghana was a relatively prosperous country but the ubiquitous use of corrugated iron still indicated poverty to a western mind. A sign went past the window, 'Welcome to the township of Lomax, home of Lomax Gold Mine'. Clenching his hands, he dug his hard-bitten fingernails into his palms until the shock of being forced from one world into another subsided.

It had been his agent, John Williams, curse his wrinkled Australian hide, who had phoned to ask if he was interested in going back to work in West Africa. "It's a simple job, right up your street, auditing exploration drilling at Lomax Gold Mine in Ghana. Lucky Lomax himself has asked for you, chose you straight from our catalogue of exploration geologists."

"Chose me?" Ed had replied. "Lucky Lomax?"

"Don't let it go to your head. The man may be as rich as Croesus but he's basically a stuck up pommie bastard, born with a silver spoon stuck right up his arse. Some men are born bastards, others have bastardom thrust upon them. Lucky Lomax comes into both categories. I tried to put him off, told him you weren't available, been ill and such like but he and his little sneak thief Jeremy insisted that I contact you. You'd be replacing Greg Boston. He's apparently done a bunk and they need somebody quickly."

"Done a bunk?"

"Well, more like vanished." There'd been an awkward pause on the end of the line. "Weren't you two friends, once upon a time?"

"What happened to him?"

"Dunno, but it's a bit unusual for a geologist to go missing in Ghana, it's one of the more civilised places. Take my advice and don't go near the place, bound to be something nasty and underhand if that lapdog Jeremy's involved. You've never met Jeremy, got the tan of a high class tart and walks around like he's got big ben between his legs. I'd say your mate Greg's got himself mixed up with a bad lot."

But Ed had accepted the job, perhaps because he felt a grain of loyalty to Greg, his friend from childhood and once Taid's trusted young farm hand. More probably it was the money and the thought of spending winter away from the Welsh hills. Even now, he couldn't say exactly what had motivated him to sign the terms and conditions.

There were many reasons why a man might disappear in West Africa, particularly a gold explorationist like Greg. He could have met a local woman, been kidnapped, got drunk and wandered into the forest. He might have got himself involved in a tribal feud over digging rights and got his throat cut. All of these things were possible, except that Greg was experienced and more than capable of keeping himself out of trouble.

On the way he'd visited Alice, Greg's wife of nearly two years, who'd been surprisingly sanguine about his disappearance, almost like she'd expected something of the sort to happen. She'd reluctantly surrendered some of Greg's correspondence, full of gossip and background about the Lomax mine. From these, he'd been able to develop useful character sketches of the people with whom he'd be working. A man named Paul Forge who had an obsession with trilobites; James Allen, described as a joker.

Interestingly, it was two Ghanaian geologists, Bismarck and Kojo, who Greg liked most. He described them as genial, good at their job, and totally unlike their fellow countryman, Chiri, the Exploration Manager, who was nothing short of psychotic.

Apparently, Lomax township had been built unencumbered by planning regulation, plumb line or set square. Most of the buildings, constructed of wood, mud brick and corrugated iron, were concentrated around the entrance to the Lomax Gold Mine, the town's main employer.

Tension rising in his chest he wondered how he would live for the duration of his stay. Hopefully better than last night - no air conditioning, and a diesel generator that ran all night outside his bedroom window. When he'd arrived on the scheduled flight from London, there was no agent to guide him through Customs and Immigration, or escort him to a waiting limousine. When he'd emerged from the airport, it was into a throng of taxi drivers. Somebody had grabbed his hand, and another his bag. A fight had broken out. A hand had reached around and tugged at his bag, and this time it had been an urgent pull that was difficult to resist. Either he lost his bag, or he followed. He'd been thrown into the back seat of a small, dented taxi emblazoned with the words 'God is Love'.

But all that had been yesterday, a fading memory. This morning, after a night's sleep, he'd woken up refreshed and had even enjoyed mounting the bus that would take him to the gold mine where he would spend the foreseeable future.

He pinched his nose and then absent-mindedly ran his finger up and down the crooked bridge, feeling the protrusions that were souvenirs from his rugby playing days. He'd taken up the sport after joining the army as a gangly youth. It had no doubt helped his rapid rise out of the ranks. By his mid-twenties his horizons had expanded sufficiently to consider a proper education. So the lad from a poor council house in Garston, Liverpool, went back to his home city to study geology.

He'd decided on the subject because the army was always in need of men with an engineering or scientific background and geology seemed to bridge the gap between them. Besides, he'd been mad about fossil collecting whenever he stayed with Taid on his hill farm.

After a year, Greg had turned up at his door and proposed that they both share Ed's flat. It had been several years since Ed had clapped eyes on Greg and he had grown from Taid's troublesome farm hand into a tall, rangy blonde who could sweet talk birds from trees.

"I've been accepted onto the same course as you," he'd said and grinned. Ed had been delighted, and over the next few years they both developed a degree of notoriety around the university.

At the end of the course, and now approaching thirty,

Ed had been uncertain what he wanted to do for the rest of his life. It definitely was not the army. Too much water had flowed under the bridge.

Somebody suggested he contact John Williams Consulting in London, a firm who specialised in recruiting geologists and engineers for gold mining and exploration. Ed's experience in the army made him ideal and so he was offered a six-month contract working for a large metal mining company in West Africa.

There followed several years of contract work in which Ed spent a good bit of his time in West Africa. At Ed's suggestion, Greg also took a contract after he graduated, and they worked together from time to time, continuing to share the flat back in Liverpool, although they very rarely coincided. Concerned that the flat would deteriorate in their absence, they advertised for a lodger who would look after it while they were away. Alice, Greg's future wife, was the first to apply.

Ed finished rubbing the bridge of his nose and instead started to clench his fists again. He sucked on the memory of Alice like a sore tooth.

Outside, the ramshackle corrugated roofs and narrow passageways that led off into a maze of back streets was a familiar scene to somebody like Ed who had spent the best part of ten years working in West Africa. In the past, he might have found the prospect of arriving in a new town and a new mine interesting, even exciting. But rather than the thrill of the unknown rattling through his chest, he now merely felt sick with apprehension.

The bus had stopped and people were rising from their seats. He could see a large gate emblazoned with, 'Welcome to Lomax Gold Mine; A Lomax Enterprises Company'. Tall watchtowers and military-style scout cars could be seen beyond a three-metre high razor wire fence that stretched off in either direction.

Dismounting the bus, he grabbed his rucksack before looking around. There was a market which was exactly as Greg had described. Bread sellers hawked their small loaves from large baskets slung on the front of bicycles. Craft stalls decoratively displayed intricately-carved stools and face masks that had inlaid metal and different woods. Speakers blasted out the stallholders' favourite music; there were arguments aplenty to be had with customers, or other stallholders. Even away from the market stalls there was restlessness. People ran, shook their fists, rode on badly maintained motorbikes. Bashed old taxis with religious slogans chugged past, avoiding potholes and kicking up clouds of dust. Most market stalls were owned by women with babies slung across their back. They shouted and harried their menfolk who stood around talking. Children ran about in rags, barefoot, shouting at each other, provoking disapproving glowers.

Ed imbibed the scene, as Greg must have done when he had first arrived on the gold mine service bus. He could imagine Greg gazing in fascination at tables where fly-struck meat was exposed to blazing sunlight.

Approaching the checkpoint beside the mine gates, he showed a letter with an authorisation stamp. The duty guard examined it carefully before escorting him through a small entrance and into a wooden shelter which had the look of a bus stop.

"You wait here. Mr Kojo wants to speak to you," he said.

Putting down his rucksack, Ed looked around. He had entered an area of functional efficiency in which roads were tarmacked and Toyota pickups were parked in ranks, engines running so the drivers could benefit from air conditioning.

Close to the gates a set of steps led up to wooden walkways where men in smart green uniforms bustled to and fro between offices. They knocked on doors and disappeared.

Further along the tarmacked road, brick buildings clad in white plaster, with ornate black ironwork had floor to ceiling glass doors that opened onto verandas. They looked more like colonial residences. It suddenly struck him that the Lomax Mine and its precursors must have been running a long time.

High on a hill overlooking the mine, surrounded by slopes of pristine forest, was the most splendid villa of all. Three storeys high it had huge bay windows and massive iron verandas. This must be the Mine Manager's residence, or somewhere the owner, Lucky Lomax, stayed when he visited. Lucky Lomax was counted as one of the richest men in the world.

Closing his eyes he saw cold, grey clouds full of lightning and a drunken Russian pilot struggling to maintain control against violent down-drafts. After the crash and the fall from the tree in which he'd fractured an ankle, he'd been found by a group of local tribesmen who'd been out spying on one of their many enemies (loggers, Maoists, anti-government rebels). They'd taken him back to their village where his ankle had been mended and his facial injury healed with an infusion of bark and leaves. When they realised he could not offer them guns or technology to make themselves a more effective fighting force his position began to look perilous.

They would not return him through rebel-held territory and so despite his injured leg he'd decided to take the long way home, travelling north through the mountains, then west, and down to the coast where he was finally able to contact the British Embassy.

He'd not forgotten how his employers had denied they'd sent him into the region, nor the embarrassment of the embassy officials as they loaded him onto the plane back to London. Worse was to come when he returned. Alice had married Greg.

Cutting himself off from them both, he'd used most of his money to buy Taid's old place up in the Welsh hills. Taid was long dead, the property virtually derelict, so when Ed moved in he spent a couple of weeks making the place habitable, installing a bed and ensuring that the worst of the Welsh winter weather had to try harder to enter. Then, when he felt settled, secure and alone, he had subsided into torpor.

He had visions of hiding in a hole while gangs of rebels patrolled the area. Plenty of time to contemplate what one man can do to another.

He'd begun to emerge into consciousness, like an amphibian rising from the water and wondering if it's possible to live in air. At last he'd woken to the smell of disinfectant and not to rancid milk, cauliflower and mildew. A neighbour he hardly knew had come to his rescue. She had been kind in a matronly way, kept an eye on him, talked to him as if she knew what he was going through.

****

After five minutes, the guard returned and gestured to a row of white pickups drawn up in a large car park nearby. "Mr Kojo's at Lomax 'A'".

Ed's eye wandered down the line of waiting trucks, wondering which had been sent to collect him. At the far end was a less modern-looking vehicle which was revving its engine loudly. Limping, he saw that this was also the only pickup that had a driver that was awake. He climbed into the front seat and smiled at a figure dressed in an open-necked Hawaiian-style shirt, chunky gold jewellery and dark glasses. "Mr Kojo, please, Lomax 'A'," he said, shutting the door. The driver tilted his head in acknowledgement and then manoeuvred out of the compound gate, past the scout cars and Kalashnikov-toting guards.

The road through town passed dilapidated shacks crammed into higgledy-piggledy rows. Women swept red dust from front steps in an effort to maintain appearances. At other doors, people looked out at the traffic or talked animatedly with neighbours. Children were everywhere, dancing to avoid the mud and water sprayed by the vehicle.

Before long he was able to see the tall watchtowers and the barbed wire of the mine's defensive zone protruding above the corrugated iron roofs. A large gate announced, 'Welcome to Lomax 'A' Shaft'. Instead of the elegant villas with steps up to busy offices, there were single storey prisoner-of-war-style wooden huts arranged in long rows on the top of breeze blocks.

The guards on the gate, young enough to be in school, nervously fingered the trigger of their Kalashnikov assault rifles. Their thin straggly limbs and boyish good looks contrasted with the strong, broad shoulders and weathered faces of the miners who milled around close-by. In his correspondence, Greg had referred to these guards as lads with Kalashnikovs. They were poorly trained and ill-equipped to deal with the needs of the mine.

Their passage through the gate was blocked by a morass of moving bodies. The driver beeped the horn and several hundred African faces, black as iridescent charcoal stared at them resentfully. Ed suddenly felt conspicuous, like a fox surrounded by a pack of hounds.

Once past this knot of men, the Lomax 'A' winding tower came into view. Its massive iron latticework glowed in the afternoon heat. Atop the tower was a motionless spoked wheel from which dropped thick iron hawsers. Greg had waxed lyrical in his correspondence to Alice about conditions at the bottom of the Lomax 'A' shaft. In the 'Deeps', ventilation was so poor you gasped for breath, and the walls bowed and exploded into the passages because of the weight of overlying rock. Worst of all was the dreadful, sapping heat that caused a man to collapse.

The driver stopped at one of the huts and pointed to a door which had the words, 'Manager of Geology'. "Mr Kojo, here," he said.

Like all mines Ed had ever visited in Africa, if there were any black professionals employed, they tended to be on the geology side rather than the engineering side. Geologists kept the mine working, did the measuring, sampling and analysis; they reported their findings to the engineers, who took an overview and made the most important decisions. Kojo, as Manager of Geology, would be the most important African in the mine, but in the overall scheme he would still be junior.

Kojo turned out to have normally proportioned limbs and face, but an enormous belly; the physique of a pregnant woman. His was a splendid office, air conditioned into an uncomfortable state of frigidity. He was overjoyed that Ed had arrived safely. A grin or a laugh was never far away from Kojo's lips. Ed understood why Greg had held this man in such high regard and affection.

"We have a problem," he said over a freezing Coke. "Our exploration department needs some help. They are struggling…." Kojo continued his monologue as Ed listened with half an ear, trying not to shiver. "There have been a number of unfortunate exploration decisions which have resulted in the mine losing some ground on its competitors. Mr Lomax is extremely angry, and he wants some answers." He paused to drink some Coke and to give a smile. "You will be working with Paul Forge in order to check that work is being carried out in accordance with accepted procedures."

"What's your best guess for what's gone wrong?"

Kojo smiled again and then shrugged his shoulders. "I think we've got a case of bad communication between departments, particularly between Forge and our Exploration Manager."

Ed grimaced at the layers of meaning in Kojo's words. Senior African managers like Kojo had to navigate through a minefield of local cultural sensitivities and the brutal economic realism of white mining engineers. He guessed that at that moment Kojo was unsure about Ed and 'there is a communication problem…..' was as far as he would venture. According to Greg's letters, Forge was a menace.

"So where would you like me to start?" Ed asked.

Sitting back in his seat and steepling his hands, Kojo pretended to consider Ed's words. "I think," he said eventually, "that you should work with Forge straight away. You should look at the drilling."

"And to whom should I report?"

Again, there was a pause. "To me," he said eventually. "And of course, to James Allen."

"Okay then," he said. "I suppose I better go and meet with Paul Forge to start with before dropping off my belongings."

Nodding his head, Kojo leaned forward. "Paul Forge is trusted by the Mine Manager and he has strong connections within Lomax Enterprises." His manner became intense. "All the data is held in the DataMine system, of course. But Forge has been here a long time, before we had DataMine." He leant back in his chair but continued to maintain eye contact. "He knows where gold is, and he knows where gold isn't."

"And what about data collected before the DataMine system?" asked Ed.

Kojo looked surprised at Ed's prescience. "Forge is gradually transferring it. But he likes to maintain his own paper library." He hesitated and licked his lips.

"What d'you mean?"

Again, Kojo hesitated, and this time looked up at his ceiling, unwilling to look Ed in the face. "I know for a fact that data has been sent to Forge electronically but has never found its way onto DataMine. When I challenged him he initially denied all knowledge, but then said he'd done some analysis and found the data to be untrustworthy." After sipping some more Coke, he added, "It wasn't."

Opening his mouth to ask why no one had kicked Forge out and got somebody else in, Ed decided to ask a different question. "And you've reported it further up the chain, and they've decided to employ me in order to audit Forge's data?"

For the first time Kojo looked sorrowful. "Clearly I don't want our conversation to go any further." He stood up and reached across the desk to shake Ed's hand, a beaming smile on his face again. "I've booked you a room in the contractors' compound, and Frank will be your driver for the rest of your stay. You go and introduce yourself to Forge and then head back to the compound."

"Where is Forge's office?"

"In the geology and drilling section at the main gates, top of the flight of stairs."

Ed nodded his recognition. "And what about the villas opposite?"

"That's engineering."

After many smiles and handshakes, Ed found himself outside Kojo's office, in the searing heat and sunshine, looking around for Frank and the pickup. It had been a strange meeting, Ed was to do exactly the same job as Greg Boston, but there had been no mention of Greg or his disappearance.

He found Frank parked in the shade of one of the wooden huts. The engine was running and the windows were rolled up. When he opened the door a near-arctic blast of air met him. Frank gazed through bleary eyes before sitting up resentfully and bringing the back of his seat into a more upright position.

"Back to the main gate, I'm to visit Paul Forge and then go to the contractors' compound."

They made their way past the huge A frame of the Lomax 'A' shaft winding tower, it seemed that Frank had decided to take the road through the mine and avoid the town. The pickup met smooth, tarmacked road and sped up. They travelled for a further five minutes through pleasant grassed areas and open parkland which had been developed into a nine-hole golf course. Sprinklers threw water onto greens, and several men in uniform raked leaf litter from fairways.

Back at the main gates, the scout cars hadn't moved, and the guards, noticeably older and more heavily built than those at the Lomax 'A' shaft, gave them a cursory glance. Frank pointed to offices at the top of the long flight of steps: "third office from the right."

Ed reached into his rucksack and produced a canvas bag he used as a briefcase and then he opened the door. A furnace-like breeze rushed into the cabin and made him gasp momentarily. "I won't be long," he wheezed before slamming the door shut.

Looking around, he glanced at the smart colonial villas, which he now knew to be engineering offices, before he addressed his attention to the wooden offices where he was destined to spend the foreseeable future. They were painted green and had large windows that looked out over the main gate and the town. He hesitated and looked once again at the steps that led up to the offices. Then, nodding his thanks to Frank, he limped off.

By the time he reached the top landing and found the drilling room, he was dripping with sweat. He knocked and entered to find two white men, one broad, fat and bald, the other small and thin. They both gazed at him with a complete lack of curiosity. "My name's Ed," he said, extending a hand to each one. "I think I'm expected." No reaction. He sensed their antipathy, bordering on hostility.

"Paul Forge," said the fat one eventually, in a high-pitched Cockney voice. He had a bushy moustache, cold blue eyes and wore the uniform of the mine, khaki green with yellow trim, spotless and ironed to within an inch of its life. "I keep track of the drilling." He swept his hand to indicate the wall behind his desk. The entire length of the room was dominated by neatly stored and meticulously labelled volumes. In front of each gleamed a beautifully polished and lacquered fossil trilobite. Momentarily mesmerised by the delicate thoracic sections and compound eyes Ed didn't immediately realise that Forge had continued to talk at him. "This is Dave Smith, my assistant…."

Much smaller and thinner, with round spectacles and a Roman nose, Dave's Adam's apple stuck out of a long thin neck. His clothes were crumpled and his thick blonde hair unkempt. His blank expression and open mouth made him look soft and pliable, unlike his boss.

A third desk was placed at the far end of the room, underneath a set of windows that looked out into vegetation. Ed's eyes lingered over a picture frame turned to face away from the room. Then, turning back, he caught sight of something strange on Forge's desk.

Amidst yet more carefully chiselled fossil trilobites was one that was bashed and dusty, like an ugly duckling in a gaggle of swans. He recognised it, not just the form but the actual specimen. He remembered collecting it on a day out to the Welsh coast with Taid. He had presented the fossil to Greg, who had been overjoyed and even given it a name, 'Taid's trilobite'. It had been the start of Greg's interest in geology, an interest he had followed up until two weeks ago, when he'd vanished.

Forge's blue eyes were blank and impassive. "I collect trilobites," he said. "It's my passion." He paused for a fraction of a second. "I'll take you to see Kojo, the Manager of Geology."

"No need," replied Ed. "I've seen him already. Is this my desk?" he asked, pointing to the one with the picture frame. A nod of the head indicated that this was the case. Ed stalked across the room and rounded the edge of his new desk. Sitting down on a bare, three legged stool he glanced at the picture. A dark haired freckled woman of about thirty was holding a drink, and a man with blonde frizzy hair and a thin face had his arm around her. The background was blacked out, and it looked as if they'd been making a night of it. In the corner of the photograph was a comment: 'To Alice and Greg. Good luck to you both'.

The faces in the photo were familiar, but to find them here, in such a strange office, gave him an odd feeling. It was like he was seeing them anew and from afar, like a part remembered dream or premonition.

"Your predecessor, Greg Boston," a voice said. Forge was looking at him, his cold blue eyes searching.

"Oh?" said Ed, trying to sound relaxed. "What happened to him?"

A shrug before turning back to the document he'd been studying. "Disappeared one night. Probably went off with some seamstress to Nigeria or wherever. We're not allowed to clear his desk, orders from the Mine Manager himself." Forge's profile was cartoon-like, bent over, eager, the light from the computer on his desk lit up part of his facc to reveal a glistening scalp.

Ed grabbed the picture of Greg and Alice and pretended to put it in a bottom drawer, but secretly stashed it in his canvas bag. No need to open Greg's drawers until he was alone.

Forge ignored his farewell when he left, the figures on his computer screen had too much fascination. On reaching the bottom of the steps he stood on the smooth black tarmac of the mine road next to Frank's waiting pickup. With a look back up at Forge's office, he climbed into the passenger seat. Frank revved the engine and they bombed out of the gates, past Kalashnikov-toting guards and blue-painted scout cars and onto the rutted dirt road that led north, to the contractors' accommodation block..

BISMARCK AND ALLEN

Early the next morning, Ed woke to the thrum of his room's air conditioner. It whispered, almost inaudibly, like somebody close at hand trying to wake him. When he opened his eyes, the magnolia washed walls of his room looked fuzzy through the gently rippling mosquito net. There was a beer bottle on his bedside table that glinted luminous green from the sunlight streaming through the room's tiny windows. The atmosphere was frigid and dry as a bone.

Hobbling unsteadily, he crossed to the air conditioner and turned it down, then looked in the mirror. Too many beers in the compound bar last night had given him a cotton wool brain and bags under his eyes. On the other hand, he'd met quite a few contractors, and all had their favourite stories to tell about Lomax Gold Mine. Some were interesting, others less. Nothing had been said about Greg and his disappearance. It was almost like he'd never existed.

Breakfast in the compound dining room was lonely and consisted of pineapple and toast. After a while a large pot of tea arrived, brought by a pretty African waitress who said her name was Moonlight. He folded a generous tip underneath his plate, poured a cup of tea and looked around at the other inmates, most of whom he had met in the bar last night. They were South Africans, Canadians, New Zealanders, Australians and British. A post-colonial mishmash. They sat in groups, or individually, with the simmering distrust of people who live and work together too closely. All were middle aged men who had been swept from the technical departments of multinational corporations during the periodic purge of staff. They were doomed to roam the earth on six month contracts, cursed by their estranged families when they returned home, destined to be outsiders for the rest of their working lives. To Ed they were warnings of what he might become, like his own Jacob Marley. He referred to them collectively as "Faces" because he could never distinguish one from another, and never had a head for names.

In one corner were Manchester Navvies, ugly and coarse. There were ten of them, bricklayers, sheet metal workers and scaffolders, probably from across the northwest of England. Their lack of education meant they stuck out like a sore thumb amidst the other contractors. They had not yet learned how to live in a society where patience was prized and cooperation could be guaranteed with some well-placed dollars. One face in the bar had joked that they moved around the mine like a fat and unfit army in enemy territory, spurning everybody, whether African, European or Antipodean.

Ed averted his eyes and looked in a different direction. On the other side of the room, several tables had been pushed together to accommodate a group of South Africans. Silent and watchful, their faces were prematurely wrinkled and creased from repeated exposure to strong sunlight.

Here was a place where there was no such thing as society, just individuals loosely bonded together. He fell to thinking about what Greg had said about this place in one of the last emails he sent before disappearing. "Some have come to get rich, others are running away, and a few have come to hide." He wondered how Greg saw himself in this context.

He pushed back his chair and stood up.

Outside, in the unremitting heat of an African morning, he stopped to watch sprinklers whizz as they watered the immaculate lawns. There was a large bar with tables covered by a tarpaulin gazebo. The entire area had been a hive of activity last night when the contractors stopped work and started to play. There'd been many women – seamstresses – from the local town.

Staff busied themselves collecting debris and setting up for the forthcoming night's festivities. Hummingbirds buzzed gently over flowerbeds and around the heads of the staff, darting to and fro like overactive moths. Beyond the tall razor-wire fences that bound the edge of the contractors' compound, he could see vast hills devoid of vegetation; the accumulated detritus dug from cavernous holes within the earth. In the foreground, heavy diggers moved like grumbling, smoke-emitting monsters, shovelling yet more earth into piles. In the far distance were jungle-clad mountains, their tranquil tops blanketed in wispy, white clouds.

Frank was in the pickup at the front of the main compound building, asleep. Ed banged on the window and was greeted by a resentful red eye. Undaunted, he opened the door and climbed in. "Drilling office please," he said.

Adjusting the angle of his seat, Frank put on his dark glasses, pulled down the trim of his Hawaiian shirt and then made certain his medallion was centred. "You mean Mr Forge?" he asked.

"Correct."

The pickup reversed in a cloud of dust and sped out of the gates and onto the mud track that wound its way through Lomax township. But before entering the town, Frank took a right turn and shot through a set of gates. They were past the guard post before the lads with Kalashnikovs knew what was happening. For several hundred metres they followed mine roads that skirted open pits full of mining equipment. It was Ed's first glimpse of the open cast operation of Lomax Mine and he could tell that it was a magnitude greater in size than anything he'd ever witnessed. Frank took a left turn onto a road that led into tall scrub. From here, Ed could see nothing except nascent growth of jungle until the road started to descend and Lomax 'A' shaft with its winding tower came into view.

Coming through the main gate, and making their way towards the shaft, were hundreds of miners, all cheek by jowl. There was a hum of conversation as the pickup passed, and many pairs of eyes turned. Past Lomax 'A' shaft and Mr Kojo's office Frank put his foot down so that within only a few minutes the drilling office and the blue scout cars of the mine militia came into view. Frank threw the truck into a vacant parking bay and then turned and peered at Ed through his dark glasses.

Ed grabbed his canvas bag and leapt out, shutting his door noisily and walking quickly to the foot of the long stairs. The climb to the top was no easier than the previous day when he'd been covered in sweat after the first few steps.

On arrival, Forge was present but his assistant was nowhere to be seen. "Morning," Ed said cheerily.

No response. The atmosphere was just as chilly as the previous day. He advanced across the room to his desk, ignoring the waves of resentment that emanated from every fibre and knothole of the office. Settling himself down on a stool, he looked around.

His gaze took in the shelves of drilling information behind Forge.

"Kojo wants me to look at the drilling," he said, rising and walking across the room to stand next to the shelves of bound volumes. "What's Lomax 'A'?" he asked, looking at the labels.

A frown reached Forge's face, which quickly turned to resentment and then contempt. He put down the mug of coffee that he'd brought part way to his lips and then looked up. "It's the main shaft."

"Do all of these volumes with Lomax 'A' on the binding come from near the shaft?" There was a quick nod of the head and a return to his coffee. But Ed had not finished. "Do you have a map showing the locations of the drill paths, by elevation?"

A long slow sip and a smack of the lips was the only reply. Forge's attention had returned to the list of figures on his computer screen. Shoulders tense, print-outs shaking in his hand, it was clear that he was getting himself worked up.

"Sorry, Paul. Do you have plans showing the drilling at each elevation?"

There was no ignoring Ed this time. The bulbous, bald head didn't bother lifting itself from the figures. "I'll need authorisation for you to see that data."

Insides knotting in frustration, Ed retreated. "I'll go and get it," he said striding to the door and throwing it open, feeling heat flood into the room. Should he slam the door behind him? Or should he leave the door open, thereby forcing Forge to rise from his desk and shut it himself. He shut the door quietly behind him. Perhaps it was best not to antagonise so early in their relationship. See how Forge would respond to a straight bat.

Forge's assistant, Dave, was coming up the stairs, mouth gaping and lower lip jutting. When he saw

Ed, his face flickered with recognition. "Remember me?" Ed asked. A slight nod. "I saw you in the bar last night, but you were busy with your lady friends." Dave smiled again and pushed past to get into his office, but Ed caught his shoulder. "Where do I get permission to see the drilling data?" The lower lip jutted in confusion.

"What about Kojo, would he be the best?" An expression of relief crossed Dave's eyes and he nodded. "Where would I find him this time of day?"

For a moment, Dave's look of confusion returned. Then, like clouds clearing from the sun, his face lit up. He pointed along the walkway at a set of steps. "Up there," he said, "turn left, first door on the right. If he's not there he's in a meeting or gone back to Lomax 'A'.

"Thanks," said Ed and let go of his shoulder.

Dave entered the office and went straight to his desk and sat down. Forge did not look up.

Marching angrily along the wooden boardwalk, Ed thumped up the stairs to Kojo's office door. But Kojo was not in his office, so he knocked at the next door and asked where he could be found. He was apparently in an exploration drilling meeting.

Cursing, he stomped back to the drilling office to find nobody at home and the door locked. Frustrated, he wandered away. It would be too easy to interpret Forge's behaviour as obstructive and mendacious. Perhaps there was a room where he could keep cool. In the offices along the walkway there were men who might take pity on him.

A shout and cheerful laugh and the sound of a door slamming came from the office adjacent to Forge's. He looked through the window to see three African men grinning at something. One of them glimpsed his face and gestured to his fellows. Knocking on the door, Ed entered without waiting for a response. The room temperature was neither too hot nor cold but, like porridge in the fairy tale, was just right.

"I'm Ed Evans, Greg Boston's replacement."

The man who had originally spotted him in the window had large, mended glasses that were attached to a loop of string around his neck. The frayed ends of the string stuck up above his ears giving him the appearance of an owl. He was dressed in the mine livery of green with yellow trim. Several pencils and pens projected from his shirt pocket.

"Bismarck," he said extending a long and delicate hand. "And this is Joe and Kwame."

Ed shook Bismarck's hand and found it comfortable and warm. "I was wondering if there's anywhere I can sit until the drilling office opens again."

Bismarck indicated a desk at the far end of the office. "That was Greg's."

"Greg's?"

Bismarck gave a big grin, "He found the drilling room too cold." Joe and Kwame smiled and exchanged knowing glances.

"If you folks don't mind, I'll stay for a while."

Bismarck shrugged and all three turned back to their work. Ed could sense a disappointment that their fun had been disturbed. He made his way over to Greg's desk and sat down on a stool.

So this was Bismarck, Greg's friend and colleague. Surely he would have an opinion about what had happened to Greg.

Silence descended on the office, except for the whirr of the air conditioner and the tick of a cheap clock on the wall. After fifteen minutes, when the silence had become unbearable, he decided to strike up a conversation. "Huge amount of miners at Lomax 'A' this morning," he said. "Took us a while to get through."

Bismarck looked across at his two companions and then turned back to what he was doing. "Day of action today," he said. "I'd say three quarters have stayed away."

"Day of action?" repeated Ed. Bismarck was unwilling to elaborate. He resolutely put his head down and stared at the report that was open on his desk. "What d'you mean day of action? Why?"

Bismarck glanced across at his fellows again before answering. "Troublemakers trying to disrupt the production of the mine." He reluctantly pushed his chair away from his desk and decided to explain. "Those men you saw today were Liberians, strike breakers, they'd work for next to nothing. The majority of Ghanaians have stayed away because Lucky Lomax sacked the leaders of the miners' union." He leaned back and picked up a small slab of stone and twirled it in his hands. It glistened silver and gold in the office light. Then he placed it back on the desk. "Herman the Helmet," he began. But whatever he was about to say was drowned by Joe and Kwame who both gave joyful hoots of laughter.

Bismarck grinned, embarrassed by the sudden outbreak of mirth amongst his colleagues. "Herman's the leader of the union. Some people call him Helmet because of the shape of his head. The miners'll stay away today, but they'll be back tomorrow."

A clear whistle from either Joe or Kwame caused Bismarck to look away and drop his head back to the report on his desk. Looking around in surprise Ed realised the three were exchanging words in low whispers without looking at one another. Then they fell silent.

Six faces appeared at the walkway window. They were blank and expressionless, like jailers examining the condemned. One of the men, large with prominent cheek scars, opened the door and stepped across the threshold. He stopped and surveyed the room and then he walked straight up to Ed, eyebrows narrowed in suspicion. "Introduce me, Bismarck." His voice was deep and resonant, used to giving commands.

"This is Ed Evans, Greg's replacement," said Bismarck in hushed tones. Then to Ed he said, "This is the Exploration Manager, Chiri." Chiri nodded his head at Bismarck's explanation, as if he approved.

"Where is Forge? I want to discuss a matter with him."

"He's in a drilling meeting with the Mine Manager and James Allen," said Bismarck.

Chiri snorted and turned to his men. They had all invaded the office and made themselves comfortable around the room, leaning against walls or perching on desks. They eyed each other, Joe, Kwame and Bismarck with interest. Ed was forcibly reminded of cats in an alley way.

"Let's go." Chiri strode from the room, followed swiftly by his subordinates who jostled and pushed each other in their effort not to be last out. The sound of their boots stomping along the walkway gradually diminished, and then disappeared. Kwame rose and gently shut the door.

There was an uncomfortable atmosphere, like the

shocked silence after a gun has been discharged in a confined space. The three men talked quietly in their own language, incomprehensible to Ed; he felt their unease. Greg's correspondence to his wife had mentioned Chiri, of course. He had referred to his strange cat-like followers as 'acolytes'. Now Ed had seen the man and his entourage close-up he was able to appreciate Greg's apprehension. There had been nothing remotely warm or hospitable in the dark, darting eyes, only cold calculation that had made Ed's blood freeze in his veins. He had been measured for something, or perhaps appraised in the way that a chess player might assess the strategic worth of pieces on the board.

For the next few days Ed got used to the routine. Work was organised into shifts, meals arrived every day at the same time, and there was no requirement to carry out any domestic chores. Initially, he worked with Paul Forge and his assistant Dave Smith on the mine drilling. It became clear that Dave's jutting lower lip and vacant expression were not an affectation brought on by too much time spent in the bush of his native New Zealand. It expressed a real sense of bewilderment, at a world he barely understood.

Forge, on the other hand, had an overweening urge to control and micromanage everything, including what everybody should think and feel in a given circumstance. He spent time pointing out ways that Dave could improve. Dave would listen, occasionally producing a small giggle of amusement.

There was something deeply miserable about Forge. Perhaps it was the way he sat in his air conditioned office without speaking, unless he wanted something. He used his strong Cockney accent to make his voice harsh and unpleasant. He sucked happiness from a room. Ed would have much preferred Greg Boston's old desk near Bismarck, but Kojo would not hear of it.

Forge would occasionally fulminate about Dave's compulsive use of the local seamstresses. These women were from all over West Africa and moved about the contractors' accommodation block in ravening hordes. As well as the native Ghanaian women there was a group from Mali, and another group from Liberia, and yet another from Nigeria. Dave preferred the Nigerian seamstresses.

He was not the only contractor who indulged his fancy. But where Dave differed was in the sheer immoderate scale of his excess. He was the seamstress' creature, rarely more than several feet away from his favoured grouping at any given time, usually with his mouth open and staring into space.

Keeping his ear to the ground, listening for rumours and gossip of Greg's disappearance, he heard the name of James Allen. Greg's correspondence had been full of this man. Initially, he'd been enthusiastic about the 'comic Irishman'. But the comments became more guarded after a while. 'Allen never knows when to stop', or 'Allen is too nosy'.

Kojo talked of Allen with excitement, and looked forward to the moment he and Ed would team up. Forge, on the other hand, went pink when his name was mentioned.

Some of the contractors in the bar were wary. "He's Irish American, has a strange Irish sense of humour. Rips at something like a terrier at a slipper; ask Paul Forge. He's careless choosing enemies, but he's assiduous in his choice of friends. He can read people like a prize poker player on a Mississippi river boat. He advises the mine management on exploration strategy." Ed pictured a man seven feet tall with ginger hair, a searing dry wit and a passion for cruel practical jokes.

When they finally met it was at the compound bar. He was shorter than Ed expected, and a good bit older. Watery brown eyes, like a highland stream, revealed a soul of sharp curiosity and good will.

"You'll be Ed," he said with certainty. "You're this clever dick everybody talks about. I like clever dicks. I've heard of you from Forge and Smith. They couldn't stop gushing with admiration and compliments. Some days I can't get a word in edgeways when those two get together. It's like a stream of consciousness with those boys. Like a day in the life of Leopold Bloom."

"They're not God's gift," Ed started.

"Tellin' me. That Forge is like a rat with his bum up a drainpipe. And lover boy," he pointed with his thumb at Dave who was at a table surrounded by seamstresses. "He's barely sentient. Just a life-support for a prick." He waved his newly-bought bottle of beer at Dave, who looked back vacantly, mouth open. "Will you look at that mosquito trap?"

The rapid fire comments were maintained for the next ten minutes, each person in the mine had their character read. Kojo was a good guy, Chiri the Exploration Manager was a prick, Forge was a sociopath, Smith was a simpleton. "And what about you?" he said finally. "Are you any good? D'you know your stuff? Are you one of us or one of them?"

Ed could think of nothing to say that would match the quick-fire patter. He stuck out his chin and looked Allen in the eye. "What about you?" he said defiantly.

"I'm one of a kind, one of my own kind. You'll like me." Ed found himself laughing. "You've been summoned by Kojo," Allen said suddenly. "There's a meeting tomorrow at the mine exploration offices out in the jungle, Chiri's lair. It's full of his acolytes pacing around, silent and watchful. I hate the place, and I work there. Beats me why they should bother building such a large facility deep in the forest. So expensive to service and maintain. Kojo says the offices were constructed to demonstrate to the Galamsey that the mine's remit runs throughout the area and not just the bit around the town. It's a symbol of the mine's dominion, like those fortresses built by the British Army in Ulster. Be careful when you come out."

"Galamsey?" asked Ed, trying to keep up. This was not the first time he'd heard their name mentioned. "Exactly who are they?"

"Illegal miners. They live in the forest and keep to the old ways, hacking and burning, planting crops and prospecting. They're African Hillbillies. Many still carry on with the old Voodoo religion. They've been getting bolder over the last year, invading the mine and stealing ore from the open pits. Bismarck reckons they must have somebody in the mine that's coordinating their attacks. There's a lot to what he says. The Galamsey always invade at times when the ore is being lifted and transported."

***

Ed reflected on Allen's words the next day as Frank drove him along the dusty-dry Exploration Office road. It cut through forest that was dark and full of shadows, even now when the sun had climbed to its noonday zenith. Bird song and zicada croaks mixed with other less obvious sounds like calling monkeys.

Forests were not his favourite places; too much to dazzle the eye, like an over-rich pudding. Line of sight narrowed with distance giving him a claustrophobic tremor, of snipers' bullets that could ricochet. He was happier in open landscapes where the horizon expanded with distance and it was easy to see approaching trouble.

As the jungle grew ever denser so did his sense of unease and the feeling that there were pairs of eyes in there looking back at him. But then they emerged into the shining daylight of a forest clearing. Through the sudden glare he was able to make out barbed wire fences, large gates, armoured cars and watch towers; it was a military encampment within enemy territory. The gates opened as they approached so that there was no need to stop and they zoomed past armed guards into an area dominated by low wooden buildings with corrugated roofs.

The pickup skidded to a halt enveloping everything nearby in a swirling mist of red particulate material. Ed threw open his door and jumped out. The blast of heat was overwhelming, as if he had been doused in a hot bath. Picking up his bag he looked around, sniffing the iron from the top dressing of the road, mixed with diesel.

The neighbouring vehicle was bright-white and brand new; looked like mine management were here as well, probably Kojo. Beyond, steps led up into a dark corridor in which one of Chiri's acolytes stood, barely visible in the shadows.

After a last look around, gazing hard at the grass savannah that stretched beyond the defensive fence, he put his head down and walked at a sedate pace. The next few hours might be interesting, but more likely they would be a complete waste of time, and boring beyond hope.

"C'mon Ed," came a cheerful Irish voice from somewhere behind. James Allen appeared, like a jack-in-the-box, from behind a pickup parked beyond Kojo's. He bounced up and shook Ed's hand vigorously, then led the way up the stairs. He rocketed up the steps into the exploration building causing the acolyte to move.

Following in his wake Ed saw him disappear to the left, through a doorway marked Conference Room. Beyond was a pleasant quadrangle dominated by grass and lined by wooden walkways. Men in green with yellow trim stood about talking. Faces appeared at different windows, curious about the new man who had arrived.

The conference room was long and narrow with rough wooden floor boards and green plasterboard walls. Light from the grassed central courtyard streamed through large plain windows. An elegant polished table filled almost the entire space, leaving room for chairs but nothing else. On the walls, air conditioning units shivered at maximum.

Allen had taken a place next to Kojo at the head of the table; they murmured together in voices too low for anybody else to hear. On the far wall, Chiri perched with three selected acolytes, their eyes swivelled as Ed entered but then they lost interest and looked away.

On the other side of Kojo from Allen sat Paul Forge, his head down writing notes. It must be an important meeting to force Forge out of his office, thought Ed. There were rumours he never went underground, and rarely into town.

The scraping of Ed's chair along the floor brought Kojo's attention to his presence. He produced a beaming smile and a wave before putting his head down again with Allen. After a minute more, Kojo stopped talking to Allen and sat back in his seat. "We're ready to start," he said to Chiri.

As the three acolytes levered themselves away from the wall Chiri chose the closest chair and sat down, body rigid, like he was barely touching the seat; hands were brought to rest on the table, fingers interlaced. After the acolytes had slouched from the room, Kojo nodded to Allen.

"James Allen will give a presentation, and I hope that we can then have a discussion about his main findings. I need to emphasise that nothing you hear in this meeting should be mentioned elsewhere." A hand gesture indicated that everything was fine for Allen to start.

Allen rose, smiling first at Ed and then at Chiri (he completely ignored Forge). A rolled-up map was ostentatiously produced from a long, brown cardboard tube. He flourished this at Chiri, and then at Ed, before unrolling it on the table.

The air of theatricality was enhanced as he produced a series of weights from a bag on the floor. The last to emerge was a transparent block containing an exquisite fossil trilobite. Placing this on the corner closest to Forge, a faraway look came into his eyes, as if he had spotted some important memory, or the face of a long forgotten girlfriend.

"I found this in a shop in New York," he said suddenly, looking down at the trilobite. "I couldn't believe it. A trilobite unique to the Burgess Shale, Hanburia." His delivery was absent minded, as if he was telling himself.

The fossil was coloured black and projected in three dimensions from a shale substrate. Ed eyed the specimen sceptically. He had seen many trilobites from the Burgess Shale, and they were exquisite etchings, like a hallucinating artist had got to work with a knife and some graphite. He had never seen one protrude in three dimensions before.

Forge's eyes were fixed and unblinking. Desire emanated from him like the haze around a smoker. It was so pungent that Allen need not have looked at him to know the effect he was having.

Kojo and Chiri sat inscrutable, looking directly ahead, embarrassed. Then Kojo coughed. "Very interesting, perhaps we could get on with the meeting."

Allen came out of his trance and looked around, like he had just remembered where he was. He gave a contemptuous glance at Forge before turning and nodding apologetically.

The map which Allen stood over showed all the exploration prospects the mine had sold in the last few years. It had off-loaded parts of its concessions to a small exploration company, Tremendous Resources of London, in the hope that they might prove more successful at finding gold. This outfit had paid peanuts for prospects where Chiri's team had reported negligible gold mineralisation. They had gone on to find sizeable deposits, bigger than the mine had anticipated.

Throughout Allen's monologue Forge's face was intent and eager; he barely took his eyes from the trilobite. Not even to do the job of keeping the minutes.

When Allen finished his talk, a heavy silence settled on the room. Kojo had his head down, taking notes, Chiri stared off into space, as if the meeting had nothing to do with him, Ed twiddled his thumbs, head down in case he caught anybody's eye and was asked to voice an opinion.

"And what's your best guess for why this has happened?" Kojo asked Allen.

Allen looked across the table, focusing on nothing, he gave a slight shrug of the shoulders before answering. "I've analysed the data and on chemistry alone the mine took the correct decision to sell."

"So what did Tremendous Resources do that we did not? How come they were successful?" asked Kojo.

"Perhaps they trusted more to their geological instincts than we did. They were less bound by the fear of failure and so they were able to take risks."

Silence while Kojo took notes. "And what's your opinion Mr Evans?" he asked eventually.

Ed snapped out of his trance and his head flew up to find both Kojo and Allen looking him straight in the face. Chiri's gaze was across the room, as if he could see something of far greater interest through the hut's windows. Ed thought he'd play safe and agree with Allen.

"I can understand the emphasis on chemistry. Mining engineers and investors like numbers, not geologists' hunches based on years of experience. On the other hand, small exploration outfits like Tremendous Resources are free to spend money how they see fit, follow their instincts and see where they lead."

This comment seemed to please Kojo and he nodded sagely, making a further note in his book. "So you are in agreement with Allen that the source of our problem is procedural and not technical."

Having no idea about the difference between procedural and technical, Ed nodded his head sagely.

Kojo finally turned to Chiri. "Anything to add?" he asked.

Chiri shrugged his shoulders and said nothing. Kojo persisted. "How are we going to ensure that the next lot of concessions we sell does not contain the jewels?"

This, Chiri could not ignore. "When me and my men have the money and the equipment we need," he said glibly. It was a rehearsed statement that fell from his mouth with practiced intonation.

Kojo turned to Allen. "What do you think we should do?" he asked.

"Recruit the men of Tremendous Resources."

A shocked expression came to Kojo's face. "That won't be necessary," he said quickly, pursing his lips. "Far too radical." He continued to make notes in his book, assiduously avoiding the gaze of Chiri.

A loud bang made everybody jump. The main door flew open letting in a blast of hot, moist air and one of Chiri's acolytes entered at a run, approaching his master. There was some urgent whispering and Chiri stood up. "There has been an incident with the Galamsey. I must go quickly."

Kojo looked relieved, Allen looked amused, Forge looked down at his notebook rather than at the fossil trilobite. It looked like Allen, with his comment about replacing the exploration department, had seen to it that there could be no realistic debate about what to do next.

Chiri ran from the room out into the sun-lit courtyard. His banging boots could be heard on the wooden walkway receding into the distance, and then he was gone.

Allen stood up and cleared away the map before flamboyantly removing the fossil trilobite from Forge's sight. Forge's eyes followed it, like a dog's following steak. Eventually the fossil disappeared into Allen's bag and Forge turned reluctantly to his notebook.

"We have to go," Kojo said as both he and Forge stood. He nodded to Ed and then Allen, face wreathed in a beaming smile. Then they too were both gone through the door.

'Was that it'? thought Ed. The meeting had started slowly and then finished in the blink of an eye. There had been no collective discussion and no conclusion about where to go next. On the other hand, he had also come to understand that he was another pair of eyes watching Chiri and the exploration department. Perhaps Ed had just witnessed something important that would eventually explain why Greg had vanished.

The incident with Hanburia had been interesting as well. "What's the thing with the fossil?" he asked Allen as he fastened his bag.

The impish glint returned. "Forge is a mad fossil collector. He spends his leave searching for the best specimens. But none of them are as good as my trilobite." He shrugged his shoulders. "Keeps me amused."

"Kind of cruel, don't you think?"

"Forge knows nothing about trilobites. He collects them, but he doesn't study them or do anything except show them off. In my book, he's fair game." He picked up his bag. "Like some shit coffee?"

They walked out of the conference room and made their way along enclosed wooden walkways that skirted around buildings. At no point were they exposed to the forest outside the perimeter fence, and the watchful eyes of the Galamsey. Eventually they arrived at an isolated part of the complex and Allen kicked a door before peering inside, as if checking that this was his room. After a few seconds he seemed satisfied that it was empty, and he entered.

There were maps on the wall, and reports on a bookcase, but nothing to indicate if Allen was married or had children. "Two coffees, Adzo, my love," he shouted before sitting down behind his desk. "Well? I want to know what you made of that meeting."

Ed tried to think. "I'm a geologist, not an investment strategist. You tell me what was going on."

"You first."

Ed screwed up his face, afraid to say something that would seem stupid. "Chiri's no good at his job and you're trying to get rid of him and bring in this Tremendous

Resources."

Allen smiled. "Is that what you saw?"

The door opened and a young woman in a tight black skirt and a colourful orange and yellow blouse entered carrying a tray of coffee. "Thanks Adzo, my African beauty," said Allen standing up and taking the tray.

Adzo smiled, looked at Ed appraisingly and walked out.

"You'll need to be careful," said Allen. "Some of these women have a way of capturing a man. And I'm not talking about Smith's seamstresses." He took a sip of his coffee and grimaced. "Around here, when you marry a woman, you marry her family as well. They'll see you as their cash cow, to be milked 'til you're dry."

He returned to the topic of the meeting. "The last thing I want is a competent Exploration Manager. There'd be no job for me as adviser to Kojo."

"Why don't you try for Chiri's job?"

"Dead Man's Shoes."

"What d'you mean?"

"Chiri's of a higher caste than Kojo, and he has many more friends in high places in Government. There's no way Kojo could sack him; it'd be like sacking minor royalty in Britain. And what's more, neither could any of the senior engineers. The only way you'd get Chiri out of here is in a box, or into a more senior position. I suggested Tremendous Resources because I like to pull Chiri's plonker from time to time, it keeps me amused."

"Like Forge and the fossil?" mused Ed aloud.

"No, that's more to do with dislike. Kojo and I are best mates, and Chiri tolerates me so long as I don't shake too many trees."

They sat in companionable silence for a few moments, sipping the bitter coffee concoction. "Talking of dead men's shoes, I wonder if you have any idea what happened to my predecessor?"

Allen hesitated and then averted his gaze and looked at the ceiling. "Is he dead?" he said eventually. "I never heard that."

"Forge thinks he disappeared with a seamstress to Nigeria."

Allen smiled. "Is that what he said? Forge has an unhealthy obsession with others' sex lives. It's the habit of those who have none." He paused for a moment and thought. "When he disappeared, Greg was working on a new prospect named Rusty Lion, about ten kilometres from here, deep inside bandit country. Kojo's just asked me to carry on the work he was doing."

"And what exactly was that?"

"Peer over Chiri's shoulder and make sure he's doing his job. I'm going out there this afternoon to visit a new part of the prospect that Chiri's drilling. Rumours have reached Kojo's ears that more gold mineralisation has been found."

"I'd like to have a look."

Allen shrugged. "All right. It'll open your eyes and make you realise you're living in Africa and not the Wirral."

Ed laughed. "No chance of that."

***

They found Frank in an office full of secretaries, his medallion swinging madly on the end of his gold chain as he held court. He muttered a few words under his breath and shook his head when they told him where they wanted to go.

The journey was through pristine forest in which,

every now and then, small settlements appeared. Men and women stared from beneath ramshackle roofs and barefoot children ran alongside their pickup shouting words that were incomprehensible. Both Ed and Allen were too engrossed in the passing scene to say anything, and the silence grew until it became a barrier between them.

After thirty minutes, they left the last vestiges of recognised road and entered a track that had been driven into the forest. It was made of leaves, small twigs and the splintered remains of logs, crushed into submission by bulldozer tracks. Trees lay on either side, toppled by the passage of heavy machinery. Up ahead a group of men emerged from the flanking forest, each held a bush knife that was tilted upward and held away from the body, their expressions hidden in shadow. Ed looked side-long at Allen and was reassured that he was calm and comfortable.

Soon they emerged into a wide-open clearing of flat brown earth where Frank skidded to a halt. Close- by was the remnant of a shack, its corrugated iron cladding strewn across a wide area. A pile of rotting vegetation heaped to one side testified that the clearing had once held a crop. A solitary drill rig stood a little way off, like a statue of liberty, its tall arm thrust vertically into the sky. A sign declared that it was owned by Lomax Gold Mine and that this was part of the 'Rusty Lion prospect'. Chiri stood close-by, surrounded by his subordinates.

At the forest margin, men, women and children shook their heads and eyed Kalashnikov-toting guards mutinously. Allen glanced at the gathered crowd, and then at Ed. "Chiri's not big on PR," he said.

The lack of vegetation concentrated the sun's energy into an inferno that made Ed feel light-headed. He steadied himself and, picking his way across the broken, bulldozed ground, followed in Allen's wake. He could see bits of metal, splintered wood, cloth, broken glass and china scattered around. A small stool ornament, no more than ten centimetres high, had been embedded in the soil by caterpillar tracks.

"Look at this," Ed said, detecting the beginnings of anger and shame. He nudged the stool with his toe. It had the quality of a prized possession, a family ornament that had been passed down the generations.

Chiri nodded at him and gave a sullen, cheerless smile that emphasised the ceremonial cheek scars on his face. "It is the symbol of the false god of the local tribe," he said.

There seemed little else to be said, there was no point haranguing him when he was surrounded by his acolytes. Allen walked off to the drill rig and Ed decided to follow. They spent the next few minutes in silence looking at rock chips, but Ed's mind kept being drawn back to the small wooden ornament, crushed by the track of a bulldozer. He thought of tanks and an occupying army.

"I know what you're thinking," said Allen, still looking at a chip through a magnifying lens.

Silence.

"You're thinking that these are simple agrarian people living a blameless existence as subsistence farmers. Well they're not, these are the Galamsey. This area was not cleared at random from the bush. They're better gold prospectors than me, Chiri or his acolytes will ever be. The crop and the shack on this spot were put here for a reason."

"Does that give the mine the right to bulldoze them away?"

"The mine owns the mineral rights here, not the

Galamsey," Allen explained patiently, still examining rock chips from a long trough. "This is a cat and mouse game. The Galamsey don't have the money or the technology to get at the gold, but they can claim compensation for loss of the crop and the homestead."

He turned at last to face Ed and smiled. "I once suggested to Kojo that they should employ the Galamsey to look for gold. They don't need expensive, state of the art equipment and they can live for days in the jungle, living off rats' urine, spiders and beetles. No need to fund expensive expeditions."

"What did Chiri say to that?"

"Never told him. Wouldn't want to yank his plonker too hard in case it came away in my hand. He hasn't much of a sense of humour. Take that remark about the false god. He wants to make it clear that he's above all that, it's part of a past that he wants to forget. You'll find Kojo and Bismarck would refer to a sub-god. Hedging their bets, you see."

He returned to examining the rock chips. "Once again, the Galamsey are spot on," he said with satisfaction. "This isn't the only clearing they've made in this area. All of them have this type of mineralisation. There's loads of chips being sampled now, so we'll know any day if we have a minable gold deposit."

They decided to return to the vehicle in order to make notes. Most of the crowd had dispersed from the edge of the clearing, and there was only a single boy left to stare at them resentfully. Allen regarded the boy for a while, taking in the ragged clothes and the lack of shoes. He leant across to Frank. "Ask him if he can get his older brother or father to clear snakes from the trenches in the jungle. I'll double the money for each snake they find."

Frank reported back quickly. "He says he can do it

himself."

They wandered over to the trenches where Allen gave instructions, by means of a stick, which piles of leaves needed a thorough poke. The boy found two Green Mambas which he expertly threw back into the forest. By the end, Allen was suitably grateful to hand over his entire wad of notes. The boy turned and walked off, the wad clutched tightly in his hand. There was a confident, almost arrogant, step to his stride.

After a quick inspection of the trenches, they made their way to the pickup. Chiri must have seen them emerge from the forest because he made a bee-line across the clearing, followed closely by his acolytes. He planted himself to the fore, blocking their path, chest stuck out like a leader of men, an expression of glee on his scarred face. "I hear Dave is no longer part of your team. There's a rumour that he has over-exerted himself."

A chorus of sniggering broke out and Chiri looked around at his adoring fan club before producing a particularly malicious smile. "Mind you, not a bad way to go."

"What d'you mean?" Allen said. "Dave looked quite OK in the bar last night."

"I have my sources," said Chiri, "And of course I can be relied upon to keep quiet about such things and so I am trusted."

Ed wondered if the acolytes could be trusted as much as Chiri.

"That's as may be," said Allen, "but I have no idea what you're talking about."

Satisfied that he'd made his point, Chiri walked back to the rig. His followers trooped after him, stumbling over the broken ground. Allen looked at their retreating backs. "You notice they left in the same order as they arrived?" he said. "Bismarck told me the closer you walk behind him, the higher you are in the pecking order. Apparently he likes to swap his favourites around, play divide and rule."

They climbed into the pick-up, glad to be out of the searing heat of the clearing. "What was he trying to say, about Dave?" asked Ed.

Allen shrugged. "Something or nothing. Chiri knows things much quicker than anybody else. He and Forge are similar in that way. Information is power on this mine, Ed, and those who hold it tend to keep it close to their chest."

Ed arrived back at the accommodation compound tired and troubled. He let himself into his room and then collapsed on the bed. He needed a drink now, but not beer from the bar where he might have to engage in conversation with a Manchester Navvy or one of the Faces. He delved into a wardrobe and reached into the recesses of his rucksack where he knew there was a bottle of scotch.

He poured himself a measure and then lay back on his bed, glass perched precariously on his chest. He thought about what he had learnt since arriving at Lomax mine. Nothing very definite, he concluded, except there was plenty of temptation in the compound bar at night. And Greg had form in that direction.

He remembered that when he had first started seeing Alice, he had warned Greg. 'You're none too fastidious when it comes to the wives and girlfriends of other men, so stay away from her'. Greg had smiled before replying. 'I like my women more sporty Porsche than family Ford'.

The point being that it was the competition and challenge that mattered to Greg. He wouldn't have been interested in the seamstresses who inhabited the bar.

Forge's comment about him disappearing across the border was simple spite and said more about Forge than about Greg. James Allen was also blithely uncaring about Greg; strange for a man who was interested in anything and everything about people.

There was a knock on the door, which made him jolt in surprise. He got slowly to his feet and went to answer; it was James Allen, his eyes dancing and gleaming, ready for the night ahead.

When they arrived at the bar, the sun had disappeared and the area was now lit by low luminosity bulbs which engendered a feeling of gloominess in Ed; "They attracted nothing but insects," was Allen's comment as they walked together. A constant throb from a generator gnawed away inside Ed's head.

Allen greeted each Face at the bar as if he was a long lost buddy. Leaving Allen to press the flesh like an award winning salesman, Ed bought a couple of beers and sat down at a table which was furthest from the centre of attention. There was no sign of Dave Smith, but his Nigerian girlfriends were in full view, they had attached themselves to the Manchester Navvies. His eyes lingered on the group before looking away quickly in case he was spotted staring.

Allen advanced from the bar with two beers in his hand, smiling his Cheshire cat grin. "I saw you got two beers so I thought I'd join ya." He sat down heavily on an adjacent stool. "Don't fancy yours much," he said looking at the Manchester Navvies.

"Horrible," Ed said nodding, taking a swig of beer.

"Still, I don't suppose sewing earns much money. Girl's gotta live somehow."

They both drank in silence for a few moments until Allen let out a breath of air in satisfaction. "They do serve a good drop of beer here."

"What were your mates saying?" asked Ed, indicating the group of Faces at the bar.

Allen smiled. "Galamsey raided the open pits today, set fire to equipment and cursed the ore body."

Ed raised his eyebrow in surprise.

"Voodoo sacrifice. Chicken and snake guts everywhere. It don't half spook everybody when they see signs of the old religion. And several o' the lads with Kalashnikovs had paraffin poured on them as well, as part of the ceremony." He paused to take some beer. "There's no knowing what's prompted this. Tensions between the mine and the Galamsey are always bad but I get the impression that things are building up quite nicely at the moment. "

"What d'you mean?" asked Ed.

Allen shrugged. "There's fat heads on both sides who'll not back down. Bismarck says we shouldn't worry until the sound of war drums begin sounding across the jungle."

There it was again, the name of Bismarck. Ed wondered how and why this man's influence extended well beyond his lowly rank and status. He pictured the man with his mended glasses and the climbing rope around the ears. He had the aura and manners of a university professor.

"Of course it doesn't take long to guess the names of the fat heads," continued Allen. A sudden expletive escaped his lips. "And here comes a prime example."

Ed followed Allen's line of sight to the bar where a large, balding man had detached himself and was making his way across to their table. His awkward stance, level stare and sickly glow gave him the appearance of a zombie. "Forge's double," Allen whispered under his breath.

Ed could see what Allen meant, particularly as the figure drew closer. The same cropped hair and the neatly ironed green suit with yellow trim. When he sat down he turned out to have the same sort of London accent. "Well, well," he said. "If it ain't me old Irish buddy, and he looks like he has a mate."

"Ed Evans, this is Jon 'Golf Club' Stone. A truly unpleasant man."

"There's no need to be so disagreeable, Allen. We all have jobs to do, and mine happens to be less cushy than others."

"What do you want, Golf Club?"

"Just a chat. I hear you've got friendly with Greg's replacement." He directed his toothy grin at Ed who noticed gold fillings. "I hope you don't lead him astray the way you did young Greg."

"If this is a bit of chit chat, then I don't want to know. Why don't you take your horrible carcass somewhere else?"

Ed felt embarrassed at Allen's unpleasantness. He looked quickly at Golf Club and saw that he was not particularly upset. On the contrary, Allen's words pleased him. "I just wanted to convey a bit of gossip. Word is that Dave Smith's shagged his last seamstress."

There was glee in the telling, and Allen reacted badly. "Is that it?"

Golf Club continued grinning. "Not quite so lucky as Greg." He looked intently at Ed. "He disappeared without a trace. Probably slipped across the border into Nigeria with a bit of skirt."

A bottle slammed down on the table. "So help me God, Golf Club, if you don't shut your horrible mouth and remove your disgusting, scaley body from my sight

I'll smash you across the head with this bottle."

Golf Club made to say something more, but Allen stood up threateningly and held the bottle of beer by the neck in the fashion of a club. "See you 'round, Allen," he said standing up and backing away.

"Not if I see you first."

Golf Club turned his back, but only after he had taken a few steps and was satisfied he was safely out of range. He lurched back to the crowd of Faces at the bar who swallowed him whole.

The expression of disgust on Allen's face remained. "The less time you spend with that man the better. He's Forge's only friend. They normally drink together up at the golf club bar at the mine. I wonder why he's decided to come here tonight?"

"To see if Dave's about?" Ed looked around the bar in case Dave had appeared while they'd been pre-occupied. "He isn't here. Is that odd?"

"Definitely unusual for Dave to be absent," Allen said, also looking around. "I can't see his special seamstress either. The one he drips around with much of the time."

"Do you think Greg disappeared with a seamstress?" Ed gazed intently at Allen. Such a lot depended on the answer.

Allen's eyes narrowed. He sensed that Ed had more than a passing interest. "Not that I know about," he said slowly. "You'd normally have to drag him into the bar to have a drink. Mind you, I don't live here so I couldn't monitor his movements or the company he kept. It's only the likes of Golf Club and Forge who believe everybody down here're up to their hilts."

"What did he mean by you leading him astray?"

"He meant warning him away from the likes of Golf Club. Golf Club has his gang, deeply unpleasant to a man as you might expect. They gather around the golf club bar and pretend Britain still rules the world."

Ed nodded. Greg would have had no time for fat men in ironed uniforms. He wouldn't need Allen to warn him away, the whole set up would have made him sick. "What's your best guess for what happened to him?"

Allen's eyes roved around the bar before answering. "I was drinking in here with him the night he disappeared. He was fine. No indication that he was about to do a hop, skip and a jump. The next morning somebody came into my office asking if I knew Greg's whereabouts."

"There must have been something odd, surely?"

Allen narrowed his eyes. "Why the interest?"

"I'd like to know. Wouldn't you if you knew your predecessor had disappeared in mysterious circumstances?"

Silence.

"There was a spate of air conditioner thefts the night he disappeared."

"Was his stolen as well?"

A sharp nod of the head. "But that's not strange. If you leave your air conditioner off when you sleep you're asking for trouble. I did the same once when I lived in the compound and the next morning I woke to see one of the guards gazing through the gap in the wall. Gave me a hell of a shock."

SOME NEWS

When Ed's pickup arrived at the mine offices the next morning, there were an extra two blue armoured scout cars parked close to the entrance. Lads with Kalashnikovs stood at regular intervals along the road, fingers on triggers. Their needle-sharp eyes were focussed on an orderly queue of men, women and children which snaked for quite a distance from a door marked 'Compensation'.

"Galamsey," hissed Frank.

Nodding, Ed looked more closely at the queue, hoping to see the boy who had cleared snakes from the trenches the previous day. His casual glance was returned by gimlet-like stares so that he was forced to avert his eyes. To cover his discomfort, he decided to interest himself in sorting out his briefcase.

Climbing the wooden stairs, he mused about Dave Smith and decided that he would not be surprised if he was sitting at his desk in Forge's office, staring into space much as usual. But when he opened the door only Forge was present.

"Shut the door, you're letting in the warm air," he said,

lifting his head in annoyance.

"Morning," said Ed in a cheery voice that belied his real feelings. He cast a side-long glance at Dave Smith's empty desk before walking across the room. No point asking Forge about the whereabouts of his assistant. Even if he knew, he wouldn't say.

On Ed's desk was a black notebook. He stared at it for a few seconds wondering about its significance. "What's this?" he asked eventually, looking across the room.

Instead of ignoring him, Forge chose to snap back, "Greg's notebook. I'd have thought you'd have recognised it."

Amazing, thought Ed. Forge had actually relinquished a source of information voluntarily and without a forensic cross examination. "Dave had it. Chiri found it amongst his belongings and wanted you to have it." Forge added.

"Dave had it? And where is Dave?"

A shrug of the shoulders and a sip of freeze-dried coffee. "No doubt his battery hens have been keeping him up until all hours."

"Shouldn't we ring the compound and ask them to knock him up? I couldn't raise him this morning."

Forge tried to smile, but only succeeded in grimacing. "You have things to do. In thirty minutes, John Price, the Manager of Engineering, wants a word. And then you need to meet Bismarck."

"Will you contact the compound about Dave then?"

"No." Forge picked up the sheet of figures again, his duty to help others discharged.

Slightly disconcerted at Forge's willingness to pass on messages, Ed pulled the notebook toward him and flicked through. He wondered what had given Chiri the right to search amongst Dave's belongings. Hunching over the book and placing his hands on his temples, he began to read.

It was a record of what Greg had been doing during his time at Lomax Gold Mine, written in his careful, almost copperplate, handwriting. On most of the pages there were descriptions and drawings of drill core mineralisation, on some there were observations of rocks in the underground or in the open pits. Several had illustrations of ore bodies, beautifully executed to emphasise important features.

On the last few pages were comments in a much rougher scrawl, including numbers and jotted references to conversations, most of which were illegible. There were also several doodles which showed a woman with a distended face and narrowed, mean eyes so that she looked wolf-like. Ed remembered that drawing sketches of people was one of Greg's party pieces, people would queue up to sit for him. This woman had been drawn wearing a nurse's uniform, straight dress with apron, and she had her hair tied back. It was undoubtedly Greg's wife, Alice. Shocked by the caricature, he went to the office window, ignoring the watchful presence of Forge.

But even in the full glare of daylight there was no way he could change the wolf-like hunger in Alice's eyes to anything more human. Feeling his heart thump in his chest he made to return to his desk, but then he hesitated. In the light from the window the scrawls and jottings made sense. Bernie, 2pm, Monday; Bernie, ring 10am, Accra. Meet Bernie golf bar 7.20pm. In all, there were fifteen appointments with Bernie.

Looking at his watch he realised that he needed to go to his appointment with John Price. It was less than five minutes' walk from Forge's office door to the Engineering Services villa, but he supposed that Forge might have been less than honest about the actual time of the appointment. He better arrive early just in case.

Cursing Forge, he marched down the steps and crossed the perfectly tarmacked road. Despite his anger, he noticed the road extended for a further hundred metres, past several more colonial-style offices before disappearing into native forest. Allen had said that some of these buildings were where certain favoured employees were housed, including Forge and Golf Club.

At the Manager of Engineering's villa, a man dressed immaculately in the mine livery led him down a dark corridor lined with flowers and beautiful native art into a reception room where an explosion of light burst through floor-to-ceiling glass doors. Light silk curtains flapped in the balmy breeze and revealed snatches of a beautiful balcony. Bunches of orchids sat on mahogany tables and there was a wooden floor that had been waxed and polished to perfection. Here was more art, including a life-sized stool of Chiri's false god.

He was about to take a seat on one of the many silk embroidered chaise longue when a woman of about sixty, grey-haired and dressed in an expensive summer frock and pearls, swept into the room from the balcony and held out her hand.

"Mr Evans, I'm John Price's wife, Miriam."

She sat on a chair, as if riding side saddle, and then fixed him with sharp green eyes. Ed was being appraised. "You've heard of all the recent unpleasantness where all those lorries were set on fire?" she asked suddenly. Her accent had a distinct Ulster twang.

He made to open his mouth, but Miriam looked up before he could start speaking, "Ahh..." she said, and motioned to a man with a tray of tea, who placed it on the table in front of her. "Do go on, Mr Evans."

"Well," he said awkwardly, uncertain what to say. "It's

the first time I've ever heard of Voodoo, chicken entrails and snake heads."

"I haven't heard of any of that, only about the lorries, and the guards," she replied. "Of course Voodoo still has a strong hold over the minds of people around here and I daresay the Galamsey use it as a way of intimidating the people who work at the mine." She stopped and appeared to consider her next statement. "I rather think, though, that they've gone a bit beyond using chickens and snakes this time. To pour paraffin over defenceless people in some sort of heathen ritual is beyond barbaric. Did you know, Mr Evans, that there is a movement to bring back British rule? You can see why when this sort of behaviour is allowed to go on without being challenged sufficiently."

Ed started to get a prickly feeling at the back of his neck. An attack of anxiety.

"You may have noticed that John and the Mine Manager have stepped up security?" she asked.

"Yes, I saw the armour at the front gate."

"I think that shooting a few out of hand might serve as a warning to the rest. I always maintain that if we'd done more of that in Northern Ireland we wouldn't have had all the trouble in the first place."

Not for the first time since coming to the mine Ed was lost for words. He was saved the bother of replying as Miriam ploughed on. "John tells me you were a military man."

"Army, once upon a time."

She looked satisfied that she had met a soulmate, and her face assumed a serene look. "My father was Captain of Destroyers during the war. He'd sail the Atlantic convoys, and the Russian convoys."

"Wow," Ed said, glad that they had moved onto a more comfortable subject.

"He was one of the only men to be both a Captain in the Royal Navy and the Merchant Navy. And when he came on shore, he became a Commander in the Ulster Constabulary."

Ed stuck out his lower lip in a sign of appreciation. "Very accomplished."

"And your career, Mr Evans?"

"Nothing so spectacular. Army was my ticket out of Liverpool. Gave me an education, gave me a family for a few years. Then we parted company."

She nodded knowledgably. "Of course, it's not for everybody, long periods away. It's similar to the life of an engineer or a geologist." She took time out to sip her tea and nibble a biscuit. There was silence, except for the swish of silk curtains in the balmy breeze, and the tick of a large ship's clock on the wall.

"Have you met Mr Allen?"

Ed nodded his head, his mouth still engaged with the tea cup. He was becoming dizzy with Miriam's swerves in conversation.

"What d'you think of him?"

A mouth full of hot tea gave him some time to consider what to say. "He's a livewire. Seems to know the ropes. Why d'you ask?"

Miriam considered her words for a few moments. "There are mainly two sorts of people in the mine. Some come for a short time and then scuttle home, considerably richer. Others come to hide."

"You think he's running away from something?"

Miriam smiled and bowed her head graciously. "Mr Allen never goes back to America or Ireland, nor does he have people to stay. He is a man who is alone, and apparently without family or friends. Does that not strike you as odd? I think he's here to hide."

Ed took a sip of his tea and nodded.

Once again there was a swerve in the conversation that put him completely off balance. "I gather you're not married, Mr Evans? I married quite late on. I thought I'd be alone for the rest of my life, but then John came along." She sipped some more tea and nibbled the biscuit again. "Do you have a girlfriend?"

Ed did some mental hopscotch. She was coming too close. Was she aware that he knew Greg, that they had shared a girl once upon a time? "I had a long term partner. But we're just very close friends now," he lied. He realised that Miriam's mental gymnastics was getting him to say things he would normally have kept quiet.

"What's her name?"

"Alice."

"Lovely name, I always thought. I called my third daughter Alison."

Ed felt he needed to shift her away from Alice. She was far too nosy for her own good, and he was likely to end up being rude and offensive if she prodded too deeply. "What's your theory for why James Allen's here?"

"I think he's an IRA man."

Ed choked on his tea and biscuit crumbs went flying as he started to cough uncontrollably. Tears came so that when he looked up at Miriam he could not read her expression. He wiped his eyes and got his coughing under control, hitting his chest with his fist.

Miriam sat ram-rod straight, still riding side saddle, poe-faced. She was not pleased.

"You may scoff, but my father was killed by them. I've made a study of those mad dogs and I know one when I see one. You, as a former military man, should be on your guard."

"Why?"

"The man claims to be Protestant. He told me he 'kicked with the right boot'. There are only a few Protestants in Belmullet where he was said to be born before emigrating to America, and I know them all, personally. There are no Allens."

"But," protested Ed, "does that make him a terrorist, or just a liar?"

"Why's he here? Why isn't he who he says he is? My husband thinks I'm paranoid and won't have any discussion about it. But I'm certain…"

"Sorry to keep you waiting," came a clipped male voice from the door. "Any tea there for me, Miriam?"

It was her husband, John Price, in mine uniform. He was about the same age and size as his wife, with a grey moustache and shiny, bald head. He looked a genial old buffer who would be more at home propping up the bar in a Home Counties' pub than running engineering in a large gold mine.

"Plenty," Miriam said and began to pour.

"Terrible business the other day, Mr Evans, terrible indeed." He took a sip of his tea. Miriam got up and walked out of the room saying that she would leave them to their business. Ed was now disappointed to see her go. He wished he could explore her suspicions of James Allen.

"I've called you here to say that we've had a bit of bad news concerning Mr Smith."

Ed had to do a mental re-adjustment to determine the identity of Mr Smith. And then he remembered that Dave's second name was Smith.

"Oh?" he was suddenly a bit wary.

"There was a bit of a ruckus the night before last at the compound. I guess you heard nothing of it. A local woman was discovered running down the hallway, stark naked and screaming. When the security guard went to investigate he found Mr Smith spread-eagled on the bed, dead as a door post."

He paused for a while and took a sip of his tea.

Ed was too stunned to take in what he was saying. Dave was dead, and he had only seen him a couple of nights ago in the bar. They had laughed at him for his strange ways.

"We've tried to hush it up. It's not good if the manner of his death gets around; it could always get back to his family. I believe he had a wife and child back in New Zealand."

"A wife and child? Dave said nothing about that, and the way he carried on I assumed he had no family."

"Yes," agreed Price, "but there it goes; how men can do the dirty on their wives and family. There are a few engineers from Britain and New Zealand and Australia and places who have gone native and live with assorted seamstresses in the town. Don't know what the life expectancy is for them, but their life at home must have been miserable for them to give everything up and live in those dreadful corrugated iron shacks amid the filth and squalor." He sipped his tea absentmindedly before continuing. "The standard procedure in these circumstances is for the manager with direct responsibility to write to the wife. I guess that means Forge. But he's refused to do it."

"Standard procedure? Does this happen a lot then?"

"Not a lot, no, but it has happened before. Anyway, Forge says he's no good with letters and thinks James Allen, our Irish man of mystery, would be the best man for the job. But Miriam is dead against this idea, and I must say I agree with her. He's far too unreliable. Kojo thinks you should write the letter and James Allen should advise." He stood and walked to the threshold of the room. "Time is money."

"But I've been here less than a fortnight," Ed complained. He stood up. "There must be somebody better qualified. Can't you order Forge to write the letter?"

"I'm ordering you."

He began to walk down the dimly-lit corridor to the front door. Ed followed, his mind spinning again. "I hardly know the man," he said. "What should I write?"

Price opened the door and turned. "That he was a good sort who was loved by everyone. Tell her a cheque will be in the post for last month's work."

"But…"

"Make it good, and don't mention the seamstresses." The door slammed.

Ed made his way back to Geological Services, his mind picturing Dave in the bar with his strange staring expression, and enormous, protuberant Adam's apple. He had been such a figure of fun for everybody, and his death had a certain amount of dark humour, although at that moment Ed was finding difficulty appreciating it.

He wandered back across the road and climbed the wooden steps in a daze and stood at the landing looking along at the Drilling Office. Forge would be sitting behind his desk sipping an endless cup of coffee not caring less about his assistant's death. He felt a seam of anger split him. He would march down and enter the office and demand that Forge do the decent thing and write to the widow. How dare he push his responsibilities off on somebody else, he needed to be confronted.

Picking up his feet, he marched along the landing, stomping the boards as hard as he could. Through the office window he saw Forge sitting at his desk gazing at the computer screen. A door opened and Bismarck, with his mended glasses and climbing rope around his ears, came out onto the landing and beckoned to him. Ed hesitated, glanced through the window at the back of Forge's head and then reluctantly dragged himself away. "What?" he said testily.

"Kojo wants me to take you to see an ore body. He thinks it would be an excellent idea."

"I just need to have a word with Forge, tell him where I'm going and things."

But Bismarck was most insistent, like he sensed what was on Ed's mind and wanted to prevent the confrontation. "You're upset; we all are."

Ed was surprised. "Upset at what?" But then he realised that the whole story must be on its third or fourth round through the mine by now.

Bismarck pressed on. "Come into the office and we'll get ready to go."

Reluctantly, Ed followed him inside. He gazed again at the office and its décor; with its pictures of wives and children, pieces of childish art, African carvings and curios, it was much more homely than either Forge's or Allen's offices. The place was almost cluttered.

His eyes lingered on a single photograph in which Bismarck stood against distinctly European-style Gothic architecture. Finely cut lawns stretched off into the distance. "Trip to Britain a year ago," said Bismarck, noting Ed's interest. "I had a guided tour around Cambridge courtesy of Mr Lomax."

Ed nodded and turned his attention to the different rock specimens that were spaced around the room. Beside the radio handset holder was a familiar lump of rock shaped like a pack of cards. He walked over and picked it up. It was Taid's Trilobite.

"A gift from Greg," came a voice.

"I saw it on Forge's desk the other day," Ed said putting it back down on the shelf.

"He took it for his collection," Bismarck explained. "But then he returned it yesterday for some reason. I didn't notice it had gone until he brought it back." He picked up keys from his desk and moved to the door. "There's an ore body in the open pits that's not being mined at the moment so we can look at it in peace without getting in anybody's way."

They headed out of the door and down the steps, into a waiting pickup. Bismarck quickly reversed, and then headed down the perfectly tarmacked road past the villas of the Engineering Services. They turned right and plunged onto a levelled dirt track that bumped through scrub and trees along ridge.

Gradually, the scrub died away to reveal a two-kilometre-wide zone of orange-brown devastation spreading away into the distance. Ed had rarely seen destruction on such a scale in his ten years as a mining geologist. Several sizeable hills must have been removed in a bid to extract the last drops of wealth, like greedy corrosive maggots chewing their way through an apple. Far below him, in the depths of the open pits, massive haul-pack lorries, dwarfed to the scale of ants, scurried around and produced a blanket of thin particulate mist.

Bismarck gunned the engine and then set off in a cloud of dust and exhaust fumes. Half an hour later they reached an area that stood like a green island out of the red-brown earth-sea. A side track led to a series of two-metre-high benches that had been cut into the hillside. The edges were rounded and deeply incised by intense tropical weathering.

Donning plastic helmets they stepped out of the

vehicle into an excruciating haze which made Ed squint and gasp. Below and to the west, massive haul-packs trundled in and out of open pits that projected out into the surrounding jungle.

"It's a satellite ore body," said Bismarck, pointing to the pits. "Found last year. They'll take it out and come back for this in due course." He pointed to a metre-wide vertical zone of smashed black rock sticking out of the bench in front of them.

Ed looked at the ore zone, and then up the hill where there was nascent growth of small bushes through which saplings were starting to sprout. It would all soon be gone, he reflected, blown to smithereens and then carted off in a lorry as big as a house. At the top there was a line of mature trees looking down disapprovingly at the scene, sensing that they were next.

Part way up the hill bushes moved as if small animals were making their way through the undergrowth. Then a human head popped up and looked about. Ed nudged Bismarck, who looked up. Realising he'd been spotted, the man ducked his head down and the bushes went still.

Disconcerted, Ed started examining the ore body. He confirmed the presence of graphite and pyrite and then turned his attention to other parts of the bench wall where there was some strange yellow and red material. Bismarck was looking at exactly the same area, his face suffused with anger.

"Galamsey," he said. The strange patch looked stringy and was covered in a black coating of buzzing flies.

"Voodoo," he confirmed.

As Ed gazed more intently he could clearly distinguish the head of a cockerel, its empty eye sockets staring at nothing. A vague sizzle indicated that the sacrifice was being cooked on the hot rock.

Bismarck shook his head. "Many of the miners are superstitious. I am not superstitious. Such things are ridiculous. Greg found them quite amusing and we laughed together quite a lot." Bismarck's statement gradually trailed off as his eyes fixed on something over his shoulder. Turning, Ed saw a thick plume of black smoke rise from just beneath the edge of the bench.

"Trouble," said Bismarck.

As they ran across the broken ground a fireball appeared above the lip of the bench. Stopping dead in their tracks, Bismarck held out a warning hand. "Careful," he said starting to creep forward.

On reaching a position where they could see down to the pit with the satellite ore body, they found one of the massive haul-packs on fire in the middle of the road. Twenty metres away figures leapt from a second flaming lorry which moments later exploded so that the massive machine rose into the air.

A hundred metres away a group of twenty or more mining operatives traipsed up the road from an open pit while a horde of other figures danced amidst abandoned digging equipment. More fires started to flare and echoing explosions reverberated across the landscape.

Bismarck went to find radios while Ed continued to watch the mob celebrate their victory. Miriam, were she here, would have had a simple solution to stop it happening again.

Bismarck came back. "We need to get out of the area," he said. "Security knows of the attack and they're sending scout cars and reinforcements. Looks like the Galamsey have kidnapped guards and stolen their guns."

"What about them?" asked Ed, pointing to the gang of miners approaching from the abandoned open pit.

"Can't be helped. Job for security."

They sped away from the scene, conscious that they should get as far away as possible. Bismarck explained that he wanted to avoid the mine on the way back, in case they bumped into more Galamsey, or the mine militia. He headed to the nearest exit, which turned out to be a small gate occupied by a few guards who were apparently unaware of the fracas happening only a matter of ten minutes from where they stood.

When they entered the town and its narrow streets, Ed looked out of the window and gazed at the small corrugated shacks which were covered in a thick film of dust. Women in threadbare nylon clothing shouted at children who played around the edges of muddy puddles. In this part of town, the sewers ran down the side of the street past people's front doors. "Not a bundle of laughs when the monsoon rains arrive," he remarked to Bismarck.

"Looks unclean, but it's not a bad place to live," said Bismarck smiling.

"Looks like any other place in West Africa to me."

Bismarck turned his head slightly. "You cannot have been to too many nice places, then."

"I'm sorry, Bismarck. I've only ever visited gold mining towns."

"I'm not offended," he said smiling, seemingly unconcerned. "Don't forget I have visited England and I know how other people live."

"Where did you visit?" asked Ed, glad to be off the subject of West African towns.

"Here and there, but what was most memorable was the visit to Lucky Lomax. He lives in an amazing place. Each room has a toilet with its own crystal washing basin, and the taps are all golden. They say he has a yacht in which he sails the world's oceans. They don't call him

Lucky Lomax for nothing," he paused. "But you must have actually met him?" he said, his voice betraying his enthusiasm.

"I deal with him through John Williams Consulting," said Ed, shaking his head. "John operates from a small office in London; no gold taps or crystal washing basins. He rang me up and offered me the job. I hadn't had any other better offers at the time, so I said yes."

Ed's lack of connections was clearly a disappointment and Bismarck lost no time in expressing his opinion. "Greg said that he met Lucky Lomax several times, and he was once invited to stay with him, as I was. Greg was hand-picked by Lucky Lomax."

Ed coughed slightly. "It's the fashion to employ the best agents at the moment. Saves time and energy."

Silence again while Bismarck digested the information. "But your agent works in a small office, how can he be the best?"

"Never judge a book by its appearances," Ed sighed.

They were now approaching the main gates of the mine, and Bismarck decided to concentrate on navigating through a crowd of miners. It was clear what Bismarck thought, that Greg had charm and an ability to ingratiate himself with the powerful whereas Ed was no more than a simple agency monkey. Could Bismarck really admire Lucky Lomax so much when Ed knew for a fact that he bled this mine dry but had rarely set foot anywhere near the place? His workers were treated dreadfully, and paid a pittance, while he lived the life of Riley in his Surrey mansion.

'For what shall it profit a man, if he shall gain the whole world, and lose his own soul'? It was the only bit of the Bible Taid would quote in English. Ed had dismissed it as the ramblings of an old man trying to justify his own poverty. Except Taid hadn't lived high on an impoverished Welsh hillside his entire life. He had travelled in ships overseas, fought in wars, lost friends. He'd lost his closest brother, Edryd, in a mining disaster in Gresford.

Bismarck expertly manoeuvred the pickup into a spare parking place, then he turned to Ed, his face suddenly sharp and eager, almost piercing, the soft and cheerful smile had gone. "Your name is Ed, which everybody around here thinks is a shortened version of Edward. But I know your real name is Edryd." The change in Bismarck's attitude was startling. The mask of simpleton had gone and had been replaced by something altogether more aggressive.

"So?"

"I knew Greg well. We were good friends, as much as we could be in a place like this. We talked about friends and family."

Silence.

"Greg has gone away. I suggest you do as well. This is not a safe place. Especially for a man like yourself who has been ill."

Ed seized on the admission. "Where's he gone?"

Bismarck got out of the pickup, slammed the door shut then set off up the stairs.

"Where's he gone?" Ed repeated getting out of the vehicle. But within a blink of an eye, Bismarck had reached the top of the stairs, turned left and run along the walkway, out of sight.

Never mind. Bismarck had shown some of his hand. There would be moments over the next few weeks when he would be able to corner him and carry on the conversation. He walked swiftly up the stairs and along to the Drilling Office. Forge was nowhere to be seen.

Bismarck's office was also empty.

A loud voice hailed him and he turned to see the broad smiling face of Kojo standing at the end of the walkway. Ed returned the smile. "Couldn't let me into my office could you? Forge has been a bit reluctant to issue keys."

Belly bouncing good naturedly, Kojo marched along the gangway, a bunch of keys clanking on a wire. "Of course," he said. "So many offices, and so many keys. We should have had the locks done on a similar design so there would be a master that opens every door." He shook his head, "But I don't suppose that would be very secure."

He found the key he required and the door opened with a quiet click.

"Thanks."

"I'll get a key made for you as soon as possible," he said and then made to turn.

"Could you have a key made for Bismarck's room as well please?" Ed asked. "Greg had a desk in there. It'd be good to work with Bismarck as well as Forge. It seems he has a lot of knowledge."

Kojo thought about his request for a few moments and then nodded his head. "I'll see what I can do." Then he was gone down the walkway.

Moving quickly to Greg's old desk he started to pull open drawers. This was not something he had wanted to do while Forge and Dave Smith had been in the office. The less they knew or suspected about any relationship he had with Greg, the better.

In the top drawer was the usual bric-a-brac of pencils and pens. He pulled it further out to check there was nothing else. At the back was a Gideon Bible. He threw it straight into his bag. The second drawer had photographs of rock, and there was also a rock specimen. He dropped both into his bag, and then he turned to the third drawer. This was the one he was most determined to investigate.

Filling most of the space was a strong box with an old fashioned combination lock. Shaking it he found to his disappointment that it was empty except for something loose and metallic which rattled around. Putting it in his bag he sat back in his seat. If Forge came in now, Ed would simply walk past him with Greg's belongings in his bag.

His mind switched to focus on Dave Smith and the letter that he would soon be forced to write. Eyeing Dave's desk, he cautiously stood up. As Ed had the responsibility of writing a letter to Dave's widow he had every right to search his personal belongings. And if Forge objected, he would get a blast of invective.

The top drawer contained nothing at all, the same with the second drawer. But the last drawer had a few odds and ends: a key, an A4 diary, another Gideon Bible and a memory stick. He deposited Dave's few belongings next to Greg's, and then sat down again. The key looked like it would fit one of the room locks in the contractors' compound, perhaps even Dave's room. He took it out of the bag and found it was almost identical to his own room key.

Allen was waiting for him in the bar when he returned to the contractors' compound. He was sitting at a table by his own in front of a large bottle of beer, running a finger through the dew that had formed on the glass. A few seamstresses stood at the bar next to a contractor who had just come off shift but otherwise the place was deserted.

Buying two more ice cold beers he approached Allen's table and was greeted with a smile. "Heard about your excursion today in the open pits."

"How?"

"Met Bismarck in a meeting with Kojo."

"Did he say anything else?"

"Nothing. But I suggested he take you to the Deeps tomorrow for a look-see. He agreed. You're to meet him at the shaft tomorrow morning at nine."

Ed wrinkled his nose. "Thanks," he said without conviction.

"Anyway," Allen said, leaning across conspiratorially. "I've been hearing some disturbing rumours."

"Oh?"

"Dave has done a runner across the border to Nigeria. Golf Club caught up with me at the Lomax 'A' canteen."

Ed shook his head. "The story is more bizarre even than that, and I can guarantee he hasn't gone to Nigeria."

Allen looked around the bar and surrounding areas. "Go on then dummy, what's your story? And where is lover boy?"

There was no way of breaking the news gently. And what was the point? "He's dead."

"Dead? You're kidding me," he replied, waiting for the punch-line.

Ed told him what John Price had said that morning while Allen listened with increasing amazement. "He has a wife and child? The stupid, stark-starin', mad bastard," he murmured. "You're going to write to his widow?"

"I'll have to," replied Ed. "It's the decent thing to do apparently, and standard procedure."

"Those seamstresses might have poisoned the poor bastard."

"I don't think the mine would be in the slightest bit interested. Dave's a dead body and they need a quick and easy burial. There's no coroner and no police force to speak of, except those lads with Kalashnikovs."

"What're you going to say in the letter then?"

"Don't know, I never had to do one before. I wonder how close they were? Can't have been that close, he spent the last three years shagging for New Zealand; she'll probably be glad to be shot of him." A thought occurred suddenly. "He was quite popular with the lads in the geology office, I could put that in. The trouble is we only shared an office for a few days, and he was never one for saying anything about himself."

Allen looked up to the tarpaulin ceiling of the bar and began to dictate his thoughts. "What about, he was popular and well-liked by everyone and that he was a strong supporter of the local sewing industry." He looked down, smiled, and then started to giggle.

"Come on, be serious," said Ed. "The man has died and I have to write a letter to his grieving widow. For God's sake, his child might read the letter when it's old enough. It might well be an important family memento for the child about its father."

"Lighten up, his death was as comical as the man was in life. She'll probably be glad to be shot of him, and the child'll be a darn sight better off without him. Having that monkey staring at you over the breakfast table as you're growing up would be bound to leave mental scars well into adulthood. Perhaps you should put that in the part of the letter marked 'positives'." Allen paused and took a mouth full of beer and began to orally compose the letter.

"Dear Mrs Smith: Dave, your loving and attentive husband has lost his life as a result of a tragic mining accident in his bedroom. However, all is not lost for you. You should make lists pointing out the negative and positive aspects of Dave's demise. On the one hand you have lost a man who was a source of income and support for yourself and your child. On the other hand, you've managed to rid yourself of a strange bespectacled individual with a mad stare and prodigious sexual appetite. Find yourself another man is my advice. Regards, Ed…etc etc."

Ed was unsure what to make of Allen's casual black humour. He knew what Miriam would have said. Despite himself, he began to laugh at the grotesqueness of the situation.

While Allen bustled off to find food, Ed was left to contemplate Dave's extraordinary behaviour. He wondered about the woman who was unguarded enough to accept a marriage proposal from Dave Smith. Perhaps in reality Dave was a warm and dutiful husband. He shook his head. It must be difficult for a married man, stuck out here in the middle of West Africa. Ed wouldn't know because he wasn't married, nor was he likely to be in the near future. A vision of Alice shot through his mind, it lingered for a moment before it vanished. And what about Forge? He must have known about Dave's death when Ed had burst into his room that morning, yet he had chosen to pretend he knew nothing. It was the casualness of the lie that bothered him.

Back in his room half an hour later he retrieved the strong box that he'd found in Greg's bottom drawer. Gazing at the old fashioned combination lock on its top he was reminded of old films where robbers would use stethoscopes as they turned the dial. Ed did not have a stethoscope, nor did he have equipment that would force the lock.

Sitting on his bed he noticed there were no marks to indicate an attempt to force an entry. He gave the spin wheel an experimental twiddle and concluded it was certainly well made and it would have taken some serious cutting equipment to open.

Turning to the other items, he considered the meaning of the Gideon Bibles. Strange that both Greg and Dave Smith should have one each. He let Ed's book fall open on a page and found a series of under-linings.

Romans 5:8

But God commendeth his love toward us, in that, while we were yet sinners, Christ died for us.

He searched through the rest of the Bible, and discovered other passages had been underlined. They were both from the book of Matthew.

Matthew 6:20

But lay up for yourselves treasures in heaven, where neither moth nor rust doth corrupt, and where thieves do not break through nor steal.

Matthew 28:18

And Jesus came and spake unto them, saying, 'All power is given unto me in heaven and in earth.'

Greg was not religious. True, he would accompany Taid to the local Tabernacle chapel in the village when demanded, usually on Christmas and Easter and some other important church dates, but that was hardly being observant. Since Taid had died and Greg had been forced to move away, he had not bothered going to church at all.

Perhaps he had undergone a religious conversion whilst in Africa. He must have been under terrible pressure before his disappearance. Had he found comfort in the words of the bible? Or maybe this was not his bible, but belonged to somebody else. He turned to the inside of the front cover to see if a name had been written. 'To my good friend Greg'.

On impulse he opened Dave Smith's bible at exactly

the same place. The same message, 'To my good friend Dave'. Same handwriting. He rifled through it and found that a few verses had been circled in heavy biro.

Matthew 7:7

Ask, and it shall be given you; seek, and ye shall find; knock, and it shall be opened unto you.

1 Peter 5:8

Be sober, be vigilant; because your adversary the devil, as a roaring lion, walketh about, seeking whom he may devour.

Romans 12:14

Bless them which persecute you: bless, and curse not.

Apart from the preference for Romans and St Matthew, there seemed little in common between the quotations. The quotation from Peter could be about any number of people Ed had met.

Shaking his head as if there were moths or flies fluttering around his brain space he realised he was entirely missing the point. Dave's behaviour was hardly consistent with having an actively religious outlook. There was something meaningful in these books that was beyond their religious purpose.

He put the bibles down and looked at some of the other items he had thrown into his bag during the time he had spent in Forge's office. His eye fell on the key.

Letting himself quietly out of his room a minute later he remembered that Dave had had the room at the far end of the building closest to the barbed wire perimeter. Turning, he made sure there was nobody else around, then he set off at a brisk walk. Dave's room was number five. He checked the numbers on the doors as he approached the area; ten, nine, eight…

At number five he checked over his shoulder again, wondering about any secret cameras. With a shake, he let himself into the room and turned on the light. Dave's clothes, bags and other belongings were scattered everywhere, his bed overturned and mattress propped against the wall.

As he advanced into the room, he realised that the air conditioner must be off because the atmosphere was stuffy and fetid as if it had been depleted of oxygen. There was a horrible smell which immediately put an old soldier like Ed on guard.

Inching his way cautiously toward the upturned bed, he found the mosquito net was ripped and Dave's linen had been tossed across the floor. This chaos and awful smell was not what he had expected.

Then his eyes caught a strangely shaped black stain on the iron bed stead, it had wisps of fibrous material that did not look as if they belonged. As he drew closer, his mind realised that he was seeing tufts of blond hair. The breath caught in his throat as he saw a great tear-shaped reddish stain on the mattress. The bed sheet cast carelessly in the corner of the room was also stained red.

Sniffing the air again he recognised that slightly sour-sweet smell that arises from the stale sweat of fear and the decomposition of blood products. It was the scent of violent death.

The carapace of the air conditioning unit lay on the floor leaving a square hole in the wall.

He needed to get out of the room and quick. Stepping briskly to the door he took a peak through the spyhole to make sure that nobody was outside.

A woman looked back at him, her features distorted by the lens so that she had the appearance of a creature from another planet. "I know you're in there. I saw you looking, and I can see a light under the door."

Cursing his stupidity, he rested his head against the wall. The woman continued, "If you don't open this door I'll start screaming and I'll bring every security guard in the place here."

With sudden resolution, Ed threw the door open and recognised one of Dave's seamstresses. Startled at how quickly her demand had been answered, she stepped back a pace. Grabbing her arm, he pulled her into the room and then threw her down in a chair. "What the hell's going on here? Why has this place been turned over? Is it your lot looking for valuables and money?" He loomed over her and saw discomfort and anxiety in her eyes. "Tell me what went on here," he insisted. Panic was making him angry and upset.

Grabbing her by an arm he drew her further into the room. "Dave was murdered. He didn't die on the job. Somebody ran him through with a knife and bashed his brains out."

The seamstress stared in shock at the chaos.

"Was it you lot? Had he been planning to transfer across to another gang and you decided to do him in rather than let him go?"

She turned on her heel and tried to get out through the door, but Ed was quicker and stronger and got there first, he slammed the door shut. "What's happened here?"

Tears were coming to her eyes. "Let me go," she said suddenly. "I have seen enough." Her voice had lost the strident tone and she was now speaking in a hoarse whisper.

"What have you seen? What happened to Dave?"

"He is dead," she said. "And my sister Anna is dead as well. They must have killed both of them."

"Where's Dave's body? Where will they have taken

it?" And then, he had a flash of understanding; the mine militia, the only real police force in town, would have the body. They would be disposing of the body as well, as soon as possible, if not already. It was they who ordered that the room should not be made ready for a new guest but to be kept locked. And who gives the militia instructions?

He looked down at the weeping woman. "Anna was Dave's special?" She nodded. "And nobody's seen her lately," he said to himself. Probably dead or being kept out of the way until the dust settled, he mused; the play thing of lads with Kalashnikovs; or acolytes.

Feeling sorry for his rough treatment he opened the door and let her go through, then watched her hurry down the corridor. She would tell her friends what she had seen and it would spread like wildfire around the compound and town. He should have bribed her to keep his name quiet.

GOING UNDERGROUND

Frank found a route through the morass of miners at the Lomax 'A' gate and located a parking place close to the series of long wooden huts that served as offices in this part of the mine. Already there were hundreds of men congregating around the base of the Lomax 'A' winding tower and soon there would be waves of hundreds more arriving.

Bismarck appeared and indicated a door marked 'equipment' several sheds down. "Be there in a minute," he called before disappearing again. Ed tried the door indicated and entered a cold and partially whitewashed room in which a surly man with cheek scars stood at a counter. On a series of shelves behind him were hard hats and miners' lamps.

"Underground," said Ed and Cheek Scars scuttled off into the back returning less than a minute later with red overalls, a hard hat, a lamp and a belt. Handing them over, he shoved a careless finger at a semi-private area off to the side where Ed could change. As he donned the overalls and looked around for his belt and lamp, Cheek

Scars decided to speak.

"You a contractor?"

Ed nodded and looked up and smiled.

"You got any mugs and tee shirts?"

"Sorry, I'm a company of one. I can't afford to have all that."

"You get me some of that and I'll make sure you get the best stuff."

Ed busied himself trying to adjust the battery then he placed the light on his helmet clasp. "I'll bear that in mind," he said dipping his hand into his pocket and produced a few notes. "Thanks for your help. I'll see what I can do for you next time. No promises."

The door opened and Bismarck entered, letting in warm air and a shaft of brightness that drowned the gloominess of the hut. While Cheek Scars scuttled around the back to get a helmet and a lamp, Bismarck grabbed Ed by the elbow. "No money to change hands in here," he hissed.

Ed narrowed his brows in confusion. "He more or less demanded it with menaces."

Cheek Scars returned and handed the light and battery across to Bismarck and he was rewarded with a surly stare. When they left the hut, Ed was in a mood to argue. "What am I supposed to do Bismarck? It's all very well for you."

"We are trying to stamp out corruption in the underground. It's a safety hazard."

"I daresay, but I want to have equipment that works."

They walked together along the side of the hut and then turned a corner into the full glare of the broiling sun. Lomax 'A' loomed from the middle of a large tarmacked area so high that Ed had to lean back to see the very top. Around the base were upwards of one thousand men, all dressed in the same red overalls that Ed was wearing, shouting and gesticulating good naturedly.

"The next shift," said Bismarck as they walked.

Ed felt the air temperature above the black tarmacadam rising so that sweat broke out on his scalp, and rivulets poured down his back. A double decker cage with enough room on each elevation to transport over a hundred men arrived within the winding house structure. The miners funnelled through a narrow gate and turnstile before heading up a flight of steps made of scaffolding poles. They were stopped at the top by armed guards who allowed them to enter the cage in single file.

Skirting the outside of the crowd, Bismarck and Ed found an alternative entrance guarded by two lads with Kalashnikovs. They were waved through without questions and walked past the queuing miners to join a group of waiting African geologists.

"We'll wait for the upper deck. It can get awfully wet on the lower," said Bismarck. There was some knowing laughter and Ed stepped back.

"Good idea," he said.

When the miners on the lower deck were cheek by jowl, complaining good naturedly to the guards, the cage moved down so that the next phase of the shift could enter the upper cage. Bismarck made his way on with his fellow geologists, followed closely by a few tall white engineers who nodded to Ed and then stood to one side, expressionless. The cage gate slammed shut even though the upper deck was only half full.

In front of the waiting cage was a huge sign warning everybody to be careful because there had been 'no fatality-free shifts, nor injury-free shifts, in the last twenty-four hours'. The miners were too busy jabbering to take any notice, almost as if the sign was a never changing part of the scenery. Probably a management initiative that had been quietly forgotten, Ed decided.

With a ringing of buzzers and a great jolt that made his stomach vibrate, the cage began to fall. Slow at first, then faster, past great, lit open spaces inhabited by men and machinery. A diesel laden wind rose to meet the plummeting cage, it swirled around them before escaping up to the surface.

Leaning against the chain link fence of the cage wall, Ed began to think about the letter he would have to write and his mind started to see Dave Smith with his jutting lip and open mouth sitting next to his special, Anna, in the bar. He knew so little about him and what he did know was not the sort of thing a wife would like to know. His thoughts shifted to blood stains on Dave's sheet and mattress, the clump of blonde hair on the bed frame. He wondered what, if anything, Dave's assailants had found and who had attacked him. One name popped readily into his mind.

But why? Dave was soft, almost half-witted, a man with no hidden depth. Perhaps he'd stolen money from the mine because his seamstresses were bleeding him dry.

He shook his head. The mine was hardly likely to send the boys around, much neater just to give him his cards and wave goodbye. On the other hand, the fact that there was an effort to cover up his killing suggested a more surreptitious motive. Perhaps Dave was party to knowledge about something, had come across information as part of his job which meant he had to be eliminated. Ed struggled to think what sort of information could be measured against a man's life, unless the murderer believed that he could act with impunity. The face of Chiri, and those of his acolytes, swam across his mind again.

Then there was the fact that the air conditioner had been stolen leaving a gap big enough for a man to crawl through. Allen had said that Greg's air conditioner had also been stolen on the night he disappeared. The coincidence was too great to ignore.

For the rest of the descent into The Deeps, Ed found himself day dreaming about snakes in trenches and small ornaments ground into the dirt. Above all, he thought about Bismarck and his admission that he knew about Ed and his relationship to Greg. He hoped that in the next few hours he'd learn more about what Bismarck knew. But he'd have to be careful not to overplay his hand.

A jolt indicated that the cage was slowing down at last. During the half an hour of the journey the atmosphere had become progressively hotter and wetter. In the last few minutes, his fellow geologists had stopped talking and started to check equipment or simply stared, faces blank and apprehensive.

A light appeared below which showed that they were approaching their destination. The cage had slowed so that its progress down was almost imperceptible. There was a shudder, the door to the lower deck was thrown open and upwards of a hundred men walked out and made their way down the tunnel. Then the cage shuddered again and lowered so the geologists and engineers could dismount.

The atmosphere cloyed and stank of diesel fumes and the temperature was such that sweat appeared on Ed's skin spontaneously. He took off his helmet and wiped his soaking hair. For one mad moment he was tempted not to put it back on.

Bismarck waved to him and together they started down the dark tunnel, the lights from their helmets illuminating dense diesel fumes. Ed's throat tightened so that he soon felt short of breath. At first he walked down the middle of the drive so that he stumbled over rails and sleepers. Adjusting his gait, he managed to walk more easily, but eventually he followed Bismarck's lead and moved to the side of the drive which was clearer of hidden obstructions.

For a further ten minutes they met groups of miners coming in the opposite direction, helmet lights building in size until the profile of a man could be detected. They nodded respectfully at Bismarck as they passed, but for the most part ignored Ed.

Stopping periodically Bismarck peered at jagged pieces of disintegrated rock that lay in semi-circular arcs on the floor. These were the remnants of rock bursts, where the wall had bowed into the drive, and then exploded. Ed had not seen this phenomenon before, despite working in many other gold mines; then again, he had never been this deep beneath the earth.

A distant clatter of a diesel engine reminded him of the noise made by Taid's old tractor which Greg had managed to keep working well beyond the time when it should have been scrapped. It had been a smelly old thing and could do very few miles to the gallon, but you couldn't have a farm without a tractor.

As the noise grew, and the ground began to shake, Bismarck pushed him into the side. "We'll wait here," he said. "Not at the corner." Ed flattened himself against the wall and stood on a mound of explosive debris they'd been examining only seconds before.

When the massive engine appeared around the bend it was so large that it barely missed the walls. The fumes and the heat were overwhelming, forcing Ed to turn his head sideways to find unpolluted air. The ground bent under its weight and then rebounded as it trundled away.

After that came a long trail of rock-laden trucks which rattled and swayed alarmingly as they passed.

Sweat poured from Ed's head and dripped into his eyes, but he dared not lift a hand for fear of losing an elbow. And then the train was gone into the darkness leaving only a distant clatter, and the enriched smell of diesel. Gradually peeling himself away from the wall, Ed looked around to see that Bismarck was already walking the bend from which the locomotive had appeared. "You gotta watch those things on the corners," he called over his shoulder. Ed nodded to himself before wiping his brow of excess moisture.

By the time he reached the bend in the drive, Bismarck was approaching a group of drillers gathered around a set of lights. They had canteens of melting ice that sparkled in the torch light as they poured it over their heads or down their throats. Ed felt tempted to grab a canteen and do the same as the others, but he shook his head when one was offered. He liked to know the source of the water he drank.

Bismarck, his face a mask of sweat, inspected the shaft of a drill that was sticking into the wall. He listened to what the operators were saying before turning to Ed and pointing back down the drive. "They need a spare part to get the drill working again. There's one in the drilling cuddy at the end."

Away in the darkness they could hear a high pitched mechanical squeal which modulated up and down. Over there, somebody was shoving a pin into hard, crystalline rock and not succeeding.

"Golf Club's close," Bismarck said, as if in warning.

"I thought he and Forge never left the comfort of their offices."

Bismarck shook his head. "Golf Club works down here every day."

At the bar, Golf Club had seemed to suggest that his job was a lot less cushy than Allen's. "What does he do?" he asked.

"Health and Safety."

Ed found himself laughing, despite the oppressive heat. "Is he the one who maintains the signs about fatality-free shifts?"

Bismarck nodded.

"Does he ever bother to change the number of shifts?"

A quick nod of the head, and then Bismarck marched off down the drive in the direction of the sound. Sensing the tightness in his chest more acutely, Ed wandered after him. He wanted to ask Bismarck about the nickname Golf Club, but when he caught up they had rounded a small curve in the drive and found themselves next to another cuddy in which there was a group of rehydrating miners standing next to an idle drill. In their midst was the broad, squat figure of Golf Club, a nine iron clutched in his hand.

Golf Club turned. "It's Greg's successor, and Allen's new best mate." His voice was dark and unfriendly. He soon walked off into the gloom.

"You've met?" asked Bismarck.

"In the compound bar. Allen nearly broke a bottle across his head."

Bismarck turned to a driller and had a hurried conversation before returning to Ed. He pointed down the drive again and they headed off.

"Why's he carry the golf club?"

Bismarck was unwilling to respond at first, but then he scowled. "He uses it to enforce Health and Safety."

"You mean he hits people with it?"

"Occasionally. And he carries it for protection of course."

"When does he hit people? When he sees them doing something unsafe?"

"Sometimes. But mostly it's to ensure the stope clearers do their jobs." They wandered on together, Ed in some confusion. "Stope clearers?" he asked eventually.

A sigh as Bismarck stopped. "It was the case a few years ago that when the ore was blasted in the stopes, men would rush in to try and get to the free gold. They'd steal it if they could. But then the walls of the stopes would collapse and many would be killed." He walked on, continuing to talk. "They employed Golf Club. He stopped them rushing in. But they still found that the walls were unsafe, so they employed stope clearers. It's their job to go in and look up at the walls and then use levers to bring down unsafe parts. It's a difficult and dangerous job, not one I'd fancy."

Ed was still confused. "So he uses the golf club because…?"

A tut, as if Ed was a silly and recalcitrant pupil. "Sometimes they refuse to enter the stope because it's too dangerous, so he forces them by swinging the golf club."

"Must make him popular," Ed said sarcastically.

"Not amongst the stope clearers."

The sound of drilling stopped, and Bismarck put his finger to his mouth. "Sound travels along these tunnels like nothing else."

They walked on for a few more minutes until the lights of the final drilling cuddy could be seen. By now, Ed was beginning to feel the effects of a prolonged sauna with exercise. On arriving, he decided to grab the iced water then he took off his helmet and poured a good measure over his head. The freezing cold dribbles went down his back and stomach, giving him the delicious feeling of being doused.

Bismarck finished talking and indicated that they needed to go back. "Everything's OK here. They'll send the part along soon. I need to get back to the surface and get to a meeting."

Ed was not going to argue. He put his helmet back on his head and followed Bismarck's retreating back into the darkness.

Thirty minutes later they sat by the cage entrance in companionable silence. The shaft sucked air away from the main tunnels and it acted as a form of evaporative air conditioning on the sweat that covered their bodies. Even so, Ed was still hotter than he liked, and the thought of making conversation was the last thing on his mind.

"Greg often used to talk about you," said Bismarck. Ed, his head down, watching sweat pour from out of his helmet, gradually looked up. "I knew who you were the moment I saw you," he continued. "He described you very well, and he has photographs of you. And then I saw your pendant and it was confirmed."

"The pendant?" replied Ed bringing it up from around his neck.

"Of course. He described it in great detail, and how you came to have it."

Ed looked down at the small piece of jewellery, simply decorated with red gems. "It belonged to my grandfather," he said.

"And ordered to be made by your great grandmother. It was for her dead son, brother of your grandfather."

Ed nodded and then pursed his lips in thought. "Did he say how Uncle Eddy died?"

"He died in the Gresford mining disaster in which many hundreds of other men died as well," said Bismarck, proud of his knowledge.

Ed nodded. "Did you know that the only compensation that came from the mine was half a shift's pay, because the disaster had happened half way through the shift? The family made this pendent with the money; this is the only evidence that Uncle Eddy ever existed."

Bismarck looked at him blankly.

"It's an irony that both Greg and I ended up working in mines, and that Greg worked for one of the biggest mine owners in the world. Taid would have been very upset."

Bismarck looked away. "And why have you decided to work for Lucky Lomax?"

"Part necessity, but also I want to find out about Greg. We were as close as brothers at one time. I feel I owe it to him. If he isn't dead, then I need to get him back. And if he is dead, I need to find out how he died."

"Why?"

"What do you mean, why?"

"Just that," repeated Bismarck. "Why is it necessary to find out why he died?"

"Justice."

Bismarck shook his head. His eyes were completely obscured by reflections on his glasses so his expression was unreadable. "There is no justice in Africa, or if there is, it's arbitrary justice."

Silence.

"Go home," he said.

Ed shook his head. "Even if I can't get justice, I mean to make sure there's nothing else I can do for him."

Bismarck sighed in exasperation.

Just then, a voice. "Whatcha doin' down here?"

Ed recognised the hard Cockney cadence of Golf Club. Despite the revulsion he felt inside, he forced a smile. Golf Club rocked backward and forward on his feet, hands inside the belt that held his light battery.

"Bismarck's giving me a tour." He looked sideways and noticed Bismarck was suddenly interested in something in the opposite direction.

"I notice your Irish mate's not 'ere. Scared I suppose."

"I think he's busy."

A cackle and a curl of the lip. "I don't doubt he is. Fancy a drink at the golf club after work? Makes a difference to that compound you favour."

An instinctive 'no' was stifled on Ed's lips; he was here to investigate Greg's disappearance not to build a social life. On the other hand, the golf club bar would be a source of gossip that might be of interest. "Not sure if I'll have time. I said to Allen I'd meet him for dinner tonight."

Golf Club roared with laughter. "You two pooftas or what?"

It was a cheap shot and brought a small smile to Ed's face. "That's right. Didn't you know?"

An uncertain look came across Golf Club's face, but then his expression cleared. "Whatever. You're still welcome for a drink."

A clank and a buzzer indicated the arrival of the lift and all the men who were sitting around the shaft rose to their feet. Golf Club waited with Bismarck and Ed until the upper cage was lowered, and then they walked on. Bismarck took up a position as far away as possible from Golf Club, and Ed joined him.

Back in the office an hour later, rehydrating with bottled water, Bismarck sat down at his drafting table and leaned back. "Tell me about your relationship with Greg," he said suddenly.

Ed pursed his lips, wary about telling anybody about himself but conscious he needed to gain Bismarck's trust. "Greg was a troublemaker taken on as a farmhand by my grandfather. Taid had a liberal streak a mile-wide running from top to bottom. He saw Greg as a project. He believed he would be able to turn him into a fine upstanding member of the community by offering him work and trust. He was right as well. Greg changed when he was given responsibility and shown what he could achieve with his own hands."

Bismarck leaned back and looked across. "And he tried to marry your sister."

"He did."

"And your mother and father disapproved."

Ed nodded his agreement.

"Why did they not like the arrangement?"

'Why indeed'? thought Ed. He coughed and shuffled uncomfortably wondering whether Bismarck would understand land and ownership in Britain. "Taid had the freehold of his farm, one hundred acres on the Welsh borders. It's poor land, good only for some grazing, cold and wet in winter and dry as a bone in summer, but it's very valuable. The family thought he was marrying my sister so he could get his hands on the land."

Bismarck nodded very quickly and then went back to his drawing; it was clear that Bismarck understood only too well.

"When Taid died, Greg was thrown out by the family and the land was sold. He was destitute and my sister had gone to university by then."

Turning his head away Bismarck implied that the conversation was at an end. Ed was happy to let the talk drop, there was something banging at the back of his head trying its best to attract his attention, something to do with the combination lock on the top of Greg's strong box.

Greg would have chosen numbers that he learned as a child, such as the number of the house where he lived, the number of a locker in school, the phone numbers of friends. These are the numbers you're guaranteed to remember and they would mean nothing to anybody else. The combination lock on the box would need more than four numbers, which meant that Greg might have used a telephone number and Greg only knew two when he was a young man; Taid's farm and Ed's phone number in Liverpool.

"You shared a flat." Bismarck had turned back to him, his dark eyes gazing through the over large lenses.

"We did. Greg needed a straight man, somebody who wouldn't compete with him, who'd be dour and unreadable." He stopped and grinned. "That's what he liked to say anyway."

"He stole your woman," said Bismarck, ignoring Ed's attempt at humour.

"He said that?"

Bismarck nodded.

"I suppose he did. We both shared a flat with another woman, Alice. She was a nurse."

"And Greg won?"

Ed shrugged. That was not quite as he remembered it. Whatever the reason, Alice had chosen Greg in the end. "Me and Greg have known Alice since childhood, she was a relative of one of Taid's neighbours, we were like cousins. She married Greg because I…" he hesitated because 'disappeared' was a loaded word in the current circumstance, "was absent," he said eventually.

For a moment Bismarck stared at him, his expression unfathomable, then he turned back to his desk. "Go back and tell her Greg's dead and that she should now marry you instead."

Several hours later, at around five o'clock, Ed drew up outside a long, low wooden building with a sign, 'Lomax Golf Club'. Telling Frank he wouldn't be long, he opened the door and stepped out. The club house was painted green and had a wide veranda on which many chairs and benches were positioned to look out onto the ninth hole. The fairways were flanked by razor wire, and beyond was the corrugated iron and mud brick of the Lomax township, but otherwise it was like any other small golf course in England.

Walking up the main stairs, he passed through a large door and into a long room with substantial windows. Intensively polished wooden floors stretched for twenty metres to where the solitary figure of Golf Club leaned against a tall mahogany bar and drank a gin and tonic from a pint glass. He was here for the evening and was prepared to bore the living daylights out of anybody who came near him.

"Thought I'd take you up on your offer," Ed said sitting on the stool next door.

Golf Club acknowledged his presence and then eyed him carefully. "You were lying about you and Allen being pooftas, right?"

Ed decided that he was going to quash the rumour before it started, it would get in the way of milking Golf Club for information. "Of course," he said.

Looking suspicious Golf Club flicked a finger at the barman and before long an ice cold beer arrived in front of Ed. "How've you found working at the mine?" asked Golf Club, now settling on his bar stool and leaning against the wall behind him. "I guess it's much bigger than anywhere else you'll have worked."

"I'm not used to working in such an established mine," agreed Ed. "It looks to have been going a long time."

"Started back at the turn of the last century. The locals had mined the gravels for gold but left much of the stuff in the ground untouched. It was only when we arrived that the mine became a serious concern."

"We?" asked Ed.

"The English, of course."

Ed took a drink of beer and nodded his head. "So how come Lucky Lomax owns it now?"

Scoffing, Golf Club took a swig of his gin and tonic. "Couldn't organise a piss up in a brewery, this lot. Nor could they make a profit from one of the richest gold mines in the world. Place went to rack and ruin after independence. You should hear some of the older hands talk. At one stage they ran out of five amp fuses, and because of this they couldn't get the lorries to run, or the diesel locomotives. Lucky Lomax stepped in with an offer to make the place tick again."

"So how much did he pay?"

A shrug. "Market rate at the time, which wasn't very much compared to what it's worth now." He put a finger up and shoved the empty pint glass across the bar to the solitary barman. When the gin and tonic arrived back, filled to the brim, he took a large swig and replaced it on the bar. "World's gone mad here, same as everywhere else."

"What do you mean?"

"Not allowed to call people black or white anymore. So I call everyone green. There's the light green, and then there's the dark green."

"I don't understand."

Golf Club laughed. "Have you not heard of the old London bus joke about the colour blind conductor? He insisted that everybody was green and that the dark green ones went upstairs and the light green ones stayed downstairs."

Ed was silent, uncomfortable.

"Your mate Allen is as dark green as they come. He's Irish after all. That's all this lot are," he nodded at the waiter behind the bar who was as far away as possible, cleaning glasses. "Sun-tanned Irishmen."

Ed finished his drink and rose to leave. "See you around then, Golf Club."

"Give my best to your Irish friend. Don't turn your back on him though, he'll have the shirt off it before you can blink. Like he did with Greg."

Ed halted.

"That's right," Golf Club said.

"What do you mean?"

"I mean just what I say."

"You mean he stole from him?"

Satisfied he'd got Ed's attention, Golf Club took a swig from the massive gin and tonic. "Allen's here because he stole from his previous employers. Lomax decided he needed someone who could catch his own poachers."

"Poachers?"

A tut and a shake of his head. "You must realise by now that there's something odd happening here? You were at the meeting with Forge. All those prospects packed with gold being sold off at rock bottom prices."

Ed nodded his head.

"Allen knows all the tricks and Greg was meant to keep an eye on him. They worked as a team, until Greg disappeared of course."

"Are you saying Allen is responsible for Greg's disappearance?"

Another shrug. "Allen has not been very successful at finding out how come all those prospects packed with gold were sold off. And then Greg disappeared. You draw your own conclusion."

Ed thanked the barman before leaving. It was one of the more sordid conversations Ed had had whilst at the mine. As he walked out he reminded himself that people like Golf Club and Forge who live in bars are apt to make up stories in their cups, they retell the stories so often to each other that it becomes the truth. He visualised Golf Club and Forge talking to one another as they drank, racist jokes becoming more outrageous, conspiracy theories more fantastical.

No doubt there would be a conspiracy theory about Ed before long, that he had been planted by Lomax in order to investigate Greg's disappearance. Stopping, he smiled to himself, perhaps it would be dangerous to dismiss Golf Club's half chewed thoughts; there may be grains of truth in them. Climbing into the pickup he nodded at Frank who revved the engine and turned out onto the road that ran next to the golf course. Nobody was playing.

****

Although Allen had his own residence on the outskirts of town, he liked to socialise with the contractors. "Good company and discourse are worth their weight in gold," he said. "And both are difficult to come by around here. Forge and Golf Club are not what you call Renaissance men, and mining engineers have as much sparkle as a wet weekend in Limerick."

They ordered dinner over beers in the bar and then went and sat in the dining room. Moonlight the waitress was particularly attentive and Allen winked at her several times. "Adzo's sister," he said in an undertone.

Ed smiled. "I met Golf Club today in the Deeps."

"What club did he have, the nine iron or the sand wedge?"

Ed shrugged. "A nine iron I think."

Allen grinned. "Obviously expecting trouble."

"Bismarck is definitely nervous of him."

"I think most of the locals are nervous. It's rumoured that he also carries a gun in case he's cornered."

Over dinner Allen launched into stories of the mine and his time working as an exploration geologist in Africa. Listening intently, Ed recognised that most of the anecdotes were about incidents that had occurred to other people, very few involved Allen. He wondered if the omission was deliberate.

The Manchester Navvies entered shouting for service and rearranging the furniture so they could all sit together. Ed found himself bolting his food as the level of noise in the dining room increased.

"I notice they haven't brought Dave's girls in here to dine with them," said Allen who stared with contempt as they shouted obscenities at Moonlight.

Ed groaned. "I haven't managed to write the letter to Dave's wife yet. I searched his desk drawers the other day while Forge was ill. I wanted to see if I could discover a picture of her or something."

"And?"

"I found a key to his room."

"I'm guessing from the way you've come over all coy that you've found something that's odd."

Ed nodded.

"Intriguing. Please tell," he said, cupping a hand behind his ear.

"Perhaps it's best if I show you. Bring your beer with you."

Sauntering out into the balmy night air with its smell of perfumed orchids they saw Dave's seamstresses sitting in the bar together, waiting.

"Having a well-earned breather until their boyfriends come back," said Allen.

As they wandered across the accommodation complex Ed wondered if he was right to trust Allen. He seemed like a man apart, somebody who had several different life stories from IRA gunman to criminal fraudster. Kojo seemed to trust him.

Arriving on the corridor that led down to Dave Smith's old room Ed reached into his pocket. "I brought the key in case you wanted to have a look."

Allen smirked, "The key to the cockpit."

As the door swung open and they stepped across the threshold they were met with the smell of pine disinfectant and a cold-as-ice atmosphere. The entire room had been cleared of all the debris, even the bedstead and the mattress with its blood stains had been replaced.

"Well?" asked Allen.

"They've cleared the place up." Ed told him what he had discovered when he had first entered the room, of the smell, the evidence of blonde hair smeared on the bedstead, the tear-drop shaped stains on the mattress, the missing air conditioner.

"Looks like somebody cleared up," Allen said looking around the room with interest. "Perhaps we should ask Moonlight the waitress if she knows anything about it." Then he scratched his chin. "On the other hand, perhaps not."

"Why not?"

"Because if we march straight off and start asking questions, whoever killed Dave Smith will be alerted."

"But they probably already know. I was caught in here by one of Dave's seamstresses."

Allen looked grave. "Let's head back."

They had intended to continue their meal, but as they approached the door to the dining room they could hear voices with Manchester accents raised in anger. Somewhere inside the navvies were letting the staff know that they were unhappy with the standard of service, and in particular the lack of butter on bread.

Deciding that the bar was probably a better place to carry on their discussion, they watched as guards arrived from the gate carrying AK 47s. They entered the dining room at a run, rifles lowered and pointing.

"Any luck, they'll wing a few. That'll stop their swagger," said Allen, scratching his chin.

Dave's seamstresses had noticed the guards enter the dining room and it was clear they were thinking the same as Allen. And then Ed realised his feet were taking him across to them; perhaps talking to these women would give him some inspiration for the letter he would have to write to Dave's family. They might have a charming anecdote, or an observation that would go well in a letter and illustrate Dave's warmth and humanity; after all, these were the people who knew him best.

As he approached, he looked over at Allen standing at the bar, ordering beers. It would not take long to talk with the girls and he would understand what Ed was attempting to do.

At first the girls were too busy discussing something, presumably the fracas in the dining room involving their boyfriends. As he hovered, uncertain what to say, the sister of Dave's special turned to look at him.

"Anna's sister," he said. It sounded rude to call her that, but he did not know her real name.

The discussion instantly stopped and six sets of eyes looked up at him. His heart sank as he realised he had made a mistake; they would not be in the least bit interested in talking about a dead punter, especially to somebody as suspect as a white contractor.

Perhaps if he was able to split Anna's sister away from the others, he might stand a bit of a chance. "D'you have a moment?" he said pointing to an empty space off to the side. A chorus of jeers went around the seamstresses as Anna's sister rose from the table. She acknowledged the coarse remarks with a smile and followed him.

Ed looked anxiously to the dining room door. "Any sign of Anna yet?"

A shake of the head, and a bite of the lip.

"I haven't found out anything yet either." He paused. "Thanks for not saying anything."

A shrug of her shoulders.

"I have to write a letter to Dave's widow." This was a stupid idea he realised, why did he think that Dave's wife would want to know anything about Dave's life in Africa. Looking apprehensively at the door, his voice took on a note of pleading. "Anything which you think I should say?"

"He had a wife?"

It was clearly as much of a shock to Anna's sister as it had been for Ed. "And a child," he added.

Biting her lip, she too looked at the dining room door and then she shook her head. "I have nothing a wife might want to know." The dining room door opened, and raucous voices emanated into the night; it seemed the

Manchester Navvies were giving the Kalashnikov-toting guards some fight.

"Anything you can give me about him. Anything at all, I'd be very grateful." The woman thought for a moment, and then nodded. "Also, I can't keep calling you Anna's sister."

"Clarissa."

Parting quickly, Ed went the long way round and emerged from behind Allen and tapped him on the shoulder. Allen threw him a speculative look. "I'm guessing that wasn't a social chit chat?"

"I wanted to know if she could tell us anything about her sister, Anna."

"Well?"

"Nothing. But I've asked her to think on it."

They watched as the Manchester Navvies arrived at the seamstresses' table and made themselves at home. They had a particularly wild look about them, after their confrontation in the dining room.

A MASSACRE

The next morning both men toured the open pits with Bismarck to check the geological mapping. Part way through their inspection, mine militia asked them to go back to their office while the area was swept of stray Galamsey. Not wanting to spend time with Forge, they had considered going back to the compound, but there was a risk of meeting the Manchester Navvies. So Allen had suggested a hill overlooking the open cast workings. At the summit they would be able to see beyond the sprawling conurbation of Lomax, to jungle that stretched for many miles into the far distance. And there was even a chance that they might see the ocean.

They leaned against the side of the vehicle and took in the vista without speaking. At this height there was a stiff breeze which operated like an evaporative air conditioner, erasing memories of the ferocious heat and humidity of the open pits. Despite this, Ed felt nauseous, and he had the beginnings of a monster headache.

Last night, the transformation of Dave's room had given both of them an uneasy feeling. They'd decided to spend time writing the letter to Dave's wife and child in the bar, heads together whispering quietly. After the Manchester Navvies emerged from the dining room, fresh from the confrontation with the lads with Kalashnikovs, they'd moved straight to the seamstresses in the corner of the bar and started drinking like it was their last night at the mine.

Soon their aggression turned to hilarity so that the air was filled with foulmouthed banter. On looking up, Ed had noticed the fattest and coarsest of them making his way across the bar to them. Sitting himself down without invitation, he attempted to read their half-composed letter.

"Heard about your mate," he said.

"Who from?" asked Allen.

"The girls."

Allen again. "Are you the one who shouts at Moonlight if you haven't been given enough butter on your bread?"

"So?"

Allen switched surprisingly quickly from his Irish brogue into a perfect Manchester accent. "I don't know where those sores came from, my love. I kept screaming for more butter to put on them but the bastards refused to bring any."

The infantile comment achieved its desired effect and a fight broke out in which Allen flattened the man with a couple of well-aimed punches. A brutal free-for-all followed, brought to an end by the lads with Kalashnikovs and three barmen armed with baseball bats. Groaning inwardly, Ed's mind turned to Allen's wild-eyed look as he fought men who were much bigger than him. He now sported a black eye, while Ed had escaped unmarked. Allen had enjoyed it, and was used to it.

This morning at breakfast the serving staff had been a lot more attentive than usual; particularly 'Born by Moonlight', the waitress who endured the brunt of the Navvies coarseness.

"You're a stuffed shirt," said Allen unbidden.

"What d'you mean?"

Allen smiled. "It's because of the likes of you that those bastards are so horrid. You treat them like they're a smell under your nose and ignore them. That's how come they walk 'round the place like they own it."

Ed's head pumped with a dull, aching pain, moving and adjusting his position was like shifting a wheelbarrow full of dirt and hard core. "There are so many people like that in Britain," he said finally. "I'm sure Ireland's full of them as well. In fact, I'm absolutely certain of it."

"Yeah, but they don't parade 'round the place like they own it."

"Your problem is that you're a snob."

"Hey, I don't mind being called a snob, particularly about those fatties. Snobbery's a form of self-defence. I detest them because of their ignorance and prejudice. They could be well-spoken, expensively-educated, ignorant and prejudiced. For me, snobbery's a way of coping, not accepting the race to the bottom."

The pounding in Ed's forehead reached a crescendo so he paused for a few seconds waiting for the intensity to diminish. "I wouldn't disagree," he gasped.

Below them, a man burst from the flanking jungle, ran down an access ramp and sprinted across the flat red-brown earth of the pit floor. More figures headed down access ramps and ran along mining terraces. Something unscheduled was beginning to unfold.

"What's going on there then d'you reckon?" he asked.

More men appeared out of the jungle at the head of

the ramp. "Galamsey," Allen said with some concern. He made a choking sound before he burst out laughing. "Look at them go," he shouted. "Wonder where the lads with Kalashnikovs are? They're probably skulking around at the other end of the mine in their scout car."

Streaking across the pit floor to where there was freshly-blasted rock, the Galamsey began to fill large sacking bags with rock and then stacked them onto crude, wheeled stretchers. More men and stretchers arrived so that soon the pit floor was a mass of humanity swarming like ants intent on devouring a carcass.

"Look at that," said Allen in an excited, strangled sort of voice, pointing to an approaching column of dust. "This, I gotta see."

As the scout cars approached Ed's heart filled with foreboding. They would be carrying heavily armed mine militia, not lads with Kalashnikovs. "I wonder if they know there are hundreds of Galamsey in the pit?" he pondered.

"They're about to find out," squeaked Allen, finding it increasingly difficult to contain his anticipation. "It'll be like the Keystone Cops."

"I'm not sure we should really be seeing this." Thump, thump went his head, his vision was starting to swim before his eyes. It was like the whole of the scene was shimmering in the intense convective breeze.

"I'm not about to leave now," replied Allen with something bordering on scorn. "We've the best seats in the house up here and the show's about to truly begin."

It crossed Ed's mind to tell Allen that he was voyeuristic as well as mad, when suddenly it was too late. The sound of semi-automatic gunfire drifted up to them on the strong thermals that swept the hill top.

"Where did they appear from?" asked Allen, pointing

to a small blue scout car that had parked on the main road into the pit.

The gunfire had probably been aimed up in the air, as a warning to disperse, Ed thought. The action had worked, and the Galamsey had begun to move quickly to another exit, away from the scout car. They moved en masse, like an oily liquid, leaving droplets in their wake.

Allen grabbed Ed's arm and squeezed. "Those bastards shot into the crowd," he gasped in astonishment. "Those are bodies on the ground."

It was true. The droplets of oil must be bodies, left by their comrades in the panic to escape. Starting to make its way up a separate ramp out of the open pit, the oily mass looked as though it was defying gravity. But then the momentum in the flow started to slow and eventually stopped its forward movement as another blue scout car arrived at the head of the ramp, and yet more gunfire could be heard. The oily mass rolled backwards down the ramp, as if obeying the inevitable law of nature that fluids must flow down-hill. More small droplets appeared on the ramp, showing that the mine militia had, yet again, directed fire straight into the heart of the crowd.

This was no Keystone Cops short, it was a full-blooded horror film. To the echoing sound of gunfire the oily fluid crossed the floor of the pit to the third and final exit, dropping more of its mass on the way. On reaching the third exit, the Galamsey managed to get out and up into the skirting forest.

Silence followed their disappearance, except for the sound of the cordite-laden wind blowing through the sparse vegetation of the hill top. Nausea rising in his throat and feeling the thumping pain in his head return in full measure, Ed forced himself to do a quick count. "I see fifteen bodies, what about you?"

"Fifteen at least," said Allen in a whisper.

More scout cars joined those on the ramp; none were bothering to drive into the open pit. Movement on the pit floor confirmed that not all the bodies were corpses.

"Where are you going?" asked Allen as Ed started to climb into their truck.

"I'm going down there to try and help those fellas."

Allen grabbed his arm and pulled. "No you're not, you'll stay here, I have the keys to the pickup and you're not going to do any such fat-headed thing. We're going to stand here until those scout cars leave, and then we're going to go back to the office and pretend nothing happened."

His head thumping and feeling hot and giddy, Ed had a surge of certainty that cut through the fog of confusion. "No way; I'm goin' to tell those people exactly what I think of them. Give me the keys."

Allen pushed him away. "Think for a minute, if we start the engine, they'll hear and know there are witnesses. We'll be in the firing line as well."

"I don't care, I'm going down there to tell them I've seen everything and I'm going to shout from the rooftops that they're murderers." He leant against the van and felt his stomach, he could hear it churning and turning over, he would be sick very soon.

"Very clever," said Allen, angry. "You'll have us both killed."

Almost crying, Ed started to shout. "I don't care, I'm going to shout at them that they're murderers."

Lifting his hands to his mouth he made a cup shape, as if he was about to yell down into the pit. Allen jumped on him, pushed him to the floor and stuck his elbow in his mouth.

Ed felt too ill to struggle, and Allen must have realised

that if he kept his elbow blocking his air passages, he was likely to suffocate. Very gradually he released his grip and removed his elbow. Panting for breath, Ed started to weep like a little child, his whole body wracked with pain and cramps.

Raising himself from the ground, Allen brushed down his clothes. "We'll wait till the scout cars go, and then we'll start the engine. They may have heard you already, but if anybody asks we were prospecting on that hilltop over there." He pointed across to a hill some five or so kilometres away. "We heard shots, but thought it was target practice."

"Coward."

"That's right, I'm a coward. But I'll also knock your block off if you even hint to anybody what we've just seen. Do I make myself clear?" There was a mad glint in Allen's eye. "If we keep discipline and keep our stories consistent, we might just get out of this alive. You go shooting your mouth off about being a witness to a massacre then it'll be a bullet in the back of the head." Softening his voice, he began to relax his shoulders and his balled fists. "After all, a bullet in the back of a white contractor's head could always be put down to revenge by the Galamsey. You don't want to be the final victim of the massacre."

"The scout cars seem to be leaving," he mused, looking down into the pit. "That was quick. I thought that they might want to do something with the bodies. It looks like they've left the injured to die." He turned back to Ed, who was still writhing in agony on the floor. "None of this is our business. You do your job, and then get out of this stinking shit-hole at the earliest possible convenience. Once you're out and away you can shout from the rooftops, but not before."

Sensing that Ed was ill, Allen lifted him by the shoulders and helped him into the pickup, then he put the key into the ignition to release the steering, and let off the handbrake. The truck reversed under gravity down the track, eventually coming to rest on a flat section where Allen started the motor.

"I think we're far away enough for them not to have heard that," he said before turning the vehicle and heading down.

Adrenalin and panic began to subside in Ed's chest leaving a mind full of the sight of the massacre, the gunshots and moans of the dead. The smell of cordite hung around his nostrils, he felt sick, really sick. With hot flushes coming thick and fast and a jaw feeling wrenched from its socket, he knew he must be going into shock. Allen was looking at him sideways, concern on his face.

"IRA bastard," he said.

Allen's reply was lost as he sank into unconsciousness. A vision of Alice swam into his mind; they were together in their old flat in Liverpool. She'd just returned from the hospital, she was in a nurse's uniform. Surfacing from the vision he realised Allen had stopped the car and was shaking him. Shivering with cold and sweat he began to think that maybe he was dying and he said as much when Allen asked how he was feeling.

"No you're not," came a voice. "Just a spot of malaria."

Slipping out of consciousness again, Alice reappeared; she held him to keep him warm. There was a smell of rotting damp coming from the window frames in their bedroom. So many experiences they had shared; such a waste. He should have fought Greg harder to keep her, told him that she wasn't his to marry.

He was on a patch of Welsh hillside watching leaves

cascade in orange waves towards him. They were blown on a strong frigid breeze that rushed over and through him, then dashed to intersect Taid's beautiful old stone-built farmhouse. Pin-pricks of moisture collided with his face, a prelude to something more substantial. Maybe snow, given the temperature and the wind direction. He was tempted to head indoors and put a match to the stack of coal and wood in the Rayburn, but not just yet.

When he woke, he saw they were travelling through town. Allen was driving, his face a mask of concern as his eyes flicked the road. Looking around, he saw the familiar sight of ramshackle houses with narrow streets reaching back into a maze of walkways and run-throughs. Small children played in the arsenic yellow dust. He felt a fresh wave of intense tiredness overcome him, his head banging, he fell unconscious again.

HOSPITAL VISITS

Waking in a dark and hot room he had no conception of how long he'd been unconscious, but the headache and fever had gone and he was hungry. Vague shadows played tricks with his eyes so he shut them and listened. An air conditioner was close at hand and far off he could detect the rattle of a generator, the refrain of the tropics. Sniffing the air, he found an unwashed body that had sweated copiously and repeatedly.

He had vague memories of a raging fever in which he was alternately broiled, or plunged into an iced bath. It wasn't hard to determine where he had picked up the malarial parasite. On his short stay in Accra he had used the net that was already hanging from the ceiling, and in the morning, in the light of the sun, he had spotted several rips in the fabric.

A nurse entered with a syringe on a tray and told him to roll onto his stomach. "You have a beautiful bottom," she said, looking down at him.

"Thanks."

After injecting him she left, promising food. He

prayed that the syringe had not been reused. "What time is it?" he called after her.

"Nearly eleven o'clock. They will soon start blasting."

Through the wool that clogged his brain he couldn't think what she meant. 'Blasting'? He called after her. But she had bustled off and was no longer within ear shot.

Looking around the room he saw an old wardrobe opposite the bed, and beside him a chair and a side table. The walls were painted standard green, like hospitals the world over. Out of the window, through the gauze of mosquito net he could see the side of the building next door, and a bit of cloudy sky, but nothing else. This was going to be bad; no books, no view and nothing to observe.

The ground began to rumble, and there was a muffled crash. Loud bangs on the corrugated iron of the roof made him look up in fright. As if on cue, the nurse returned with a sandwich shaking her head and looking annoyed. "They need to be more careful. One day they'll hit this hospital with more than pebbles and we will have casualties."

"How big are the pebbles?" he asked.

"About the size of golf balls."

The nurse left him alone and he turned to the food which was one of the compound dining room sandwiches. He chewed slowly and thoughtfully listening to a far off rhythmic percussion that impacted on his mind like a distant memory; it was the sound of a drum. He wondered if it had been going all the time and it was only now that he had noticed it. Thump, thump, it began to grow in volume, as if coming nearer. The beat became faster. Thumpa, thumpa. And then many other different drums joined in. Thumpa tee tum, thumpa tee tum. He could feel the noise as vibrations through the bed; it was like an angry beast on the edge of waking up.

The drums continued for several hours, sometimes a crescendo, and at other times with a single loud drum banging out a sophisticated rhythm. When he got out of bed, his feet felt the building vibrate like a sounding board, as if the entire fabric of the building had joined the drummers outside and was banging out its own rhythm. And then the drumming stopped, and the world held its breath, waiting. No movement in the hospital and no voices raised outside.

In an information vacuum, the imagination will join the dots. Ed's mind spun, remembering the massacre in the open pits, Allen's attack, the elbow in the mouth. Perhaps Allen had been right to be so violent in restraining him. He hadn't known that Ed was suffering from a bout of malaria. On the other hand, it felt like he had been trying to exert some kind of physical superiority, like a boy in the playground.

A knock on the door and Allen's head poked into the room, his face a mask of cheerful amusement. "How're you doin' today, old son? The nurse said you recovered well overnight so I thought I'd pay my regards."

"Thank you. I'm not bad."

"Great."

A long silence, broken by the hum of the knackered old air conditioner. "I'll report back to Kojo that you're on the mend then," Allen said eventually. He made to go.

"Any word on the massacre?" asked Ed.

"Nothing's been directly mentioned.

"I keep hearing the angry drums in the jungle; surely there'll be reprisals!"

Allen sat down in the only seat in the room and then leaned in close so he could whisper, "I've never seen the district so tense. Best place is in hospital until it all calms down. There's tribal loyalties and old grudges being weighed up. There's people who're just plain scared, and there's others wondering what advantage they can accrue from exacerbating the situation." He looked away quickly, the events on the hilltop like an unspoken barrier between them. "Who's Alice?" he asked casually.

"Why?"

"You burbled away a lot about her."

Ed hesitated wondering whether he should reveal more of himself to this potentially dangerous man. But the angry drums, the massacre they had witnessed together, the strangeness of Forge and Chiri, the murder of Dave… he needed a friend. If he made the first move, might Allen tell him something of himself as well? Something that would make him feel more trustworthy? It was worth a try.

"We used to live together in a little flat in Liverpool in a poorer part of town. It was damp and cold. I had it as a student, after coming out of the army." Allen had gone motionless making Ed feel self-conscious. He was unused to speaking in this intimate way, and he was nervous of giving too much away.

"The flats were built around a central courtyard with an oak tree. Our flat was on the 3rd floor so you could walk out onto a communal balcony, into the tree canopy. Birds sat in the tree and sang; pain in the arse in spring what with the dawn chorus." Allen's outline was disguised by the mosquito net, but Ed could tell that he was listening. "What about you, Allen? Why have you come to the arse end of nowhere to find a living? Was it some girl?"

Allen didn't respond, the silence pressed so Ed offered some more. "She eventually decided she'd had enough. Not easy having a geologist as a partner. I was always away, and when the cat's away..." Or was it simply that Greg had been more keen to land his fish than Ed? "I found separation terrible," he continued. "The closest I can come to express the feeling is bereavement. She isn't there, she's gone. She may as well have been killed, fallen under a bus or been shot, because you're unable to talk to her, make a joke with her, find out what she's done in the day, what she's feeling or thinking. It's a solid grey barrier, like a prison wall, only it goes on for infinity."

He saw Allen shrug his shoulders through the gauze netting, but the gloominess in the room made it impossible to read his expression. "Is that it? Is that all you can do, shrug your shoulders?" He leant back, exhausted by the monologue. "People are basically the same and have the same emotional responses. It's just that some people are brutalised to a greater or lesser extent by their experience or the culture that surrounds them. But people feel the loss of another person very keenly. I put myself in the position of those people out there in the jungle and I would be turning this place into a bloody slaughterhouse. There's a clearly defined cause and an obvious enemy."

"Listen," said Allen, urgently. "Don't go shooting your mouth off about a bloody revolution or defined enemies. It won't be the Galamsey who'll shoot you in the head." An angry retort made its way to Ed's lips, but Allen decided to continue. "Bernie's in town. Got a sniff that something must have happened."

"Bernie?"

"A reporter," Allen said impatiently.

Silence.

"I had Chiri come into my office yesterday while you were out cold. Never seen him in there before; sitting in my seat, at my desk if you please."

"And?"

"He wanted to know if I'd seen or heard anything. Gunshots and the like. I told him we were together on a hillside several kilometres away. You fell ill. We heard gunshots but thought it was target practice."

He stood to go. "I'd suggest you take a line through me. Keep our story consistent so we can both be alive by the time everything calms down." At the door he paused. "Lucky you got a private room. Miriam must like you. When I had malaria, I got a bed on the public ward amongst all the hawkers and the beggars." The door shut behind him.

Ed dozed after Allen left. When he woke, it was hot and dark, night comes quick in the tropics. His air conditioner hummed faintly in the background but there was another noise whispering to him, it pulsed with a frequency that was not mechanical; the drums had started again and the bed was vibrating as if it was attached to a buzzer. The rhythm was insistent, a comforting sound, no doubt, for those who were mourning their dead; it made Ed feel ill-at-ease.

He fought for control of his mind, but every time he forced one memory down, another popped back in its place. Relax, lie back, don't think. Relax, lie back, don't think. Relax, lie back, don't think.

It was no good, the image of Greg arose, grin on his face and slightly mocking expression. Ever since they'd been boys they'd shared everything, or at least Ed had shared everything. Was it this that made Alice think he hadn't cared for her? After returning home the last time he'd had some kind of depression, it was the first time he had experienced its wings enfold him. The gears of his mind had started to slip out of control. He felt the same sensation now.

The drumming increased in intensity and his pillow buzzed more insistently. Turning onto his back to keep cool, he decided there would be no chance of getting back to sleep in this thick humidity, not with a resentful animal awake in the nearby forest and thoughts racing through his head like a runaway train. He had made a mistake to think he could return to Africa with his mind still in pieces.

He sniffed the air.

There was a heavy scent of chilli and roast meat. Opening his eyes slightly he realised somebody was in the chair next to his bed. The deeper shade in the darkness shifted slightly and leaned forward. Ed remained quiet and still, adrenalin pumping, hair on his head standing on end. Thump, thump thump. His heart kept beat with the drums.

The silence emanating from the figure deafened and blinded him to all other sensations. An enormous flash of lightening illuminated the room revealing several men, arranged around the walls, like cats in an ally. All had their eyes on him.

Before darkness reasserted itself he saw that the man in the chair was large with cheek scars. Then the room was plunged back into night, leaving an impression of its silent occupants on the back of his retina. A clash of thunder broke about the hospital, the walls shook and the iron roof rattled. The drums increased their intensity sending vibrations through the walls and atmosphere that drowned all thought.

Still the men remained silent, watching. He thought he should say something and then another flash of lightening revealed Chiri out of his chair looming over him, his face close to the gauze of the mosquito net, forehead and cheeks covered in beads of perspiration. The outline of the window glinted off his dead, opaque eyes.

The room plunged back into darkness, a clap of thunder followed, louder than the last, like the opening of an artillery barrage. Chiri's outline was now firmly fixed on his retina. He opened his mouth to speak, but found that he choked initially on his own breath before squeezing out a hoarse whisper. "What d'you want?"

Thump, thump, thump. The smell of hot chili grew stronger, and this time he detected the sweet smell of alcohol. "We would like to know what you know."

"About what?"

Thumpa, thumpa, thumpa.

"Galamsey."

Ed opened and closed his mouth, remembered the warning of Allen. "Galamsey?"

Thumpa tee tum, thumpa tee tum, thumpa tee tum.

"You were on the hill overlooking the mine. You may have seen or heard something." His voice was supernatural, like that of an evil spirit calling the dead.

"Not me. I've been ill."

Thumpa, thumpa, thumpa

"You were there, with Allen. We know you were there." The voice was becoming more material and less like a distant memory.

Ed's throat tightened in terror. His words came unsteadily, panic betrayed his voice. "I saw nothing."

The first drops of rain pinged on the corrugated roof. Slow at first, building to a timpani, overtaking the drums that still vibrated through the building.

"I expect journalists will come and ask questions. You don't want the same fate as Greg Boston. Or Dave Smith." The dark shape shifted and moved away, the smell of chilli reduced. "Don't leave the mine, the road to Accra is full of murderous bandits."

What should he say? Make some reassuring sound to tell Chiri that he had no intention of leaving? Instead he lay in bed trembling with fright, unwilling to say anything in case Chiri should misinterpret his meaning. Seconds passed. Flash.

The door was open, and nobody in the room.

The heavens opened and the tropical rain storm started in earnest. Flashes of lightening and rolls of thunder continued to reverberate across the forest and the hospital for the next hour, stopping the drums and blotting out further thought.

Rising from his bed, he shut the door, propped the chair against it and placed a glass on the chair. He shook with fright, but the heat of the night had gone and he was no longer perspiring. Climbing back into bed he lay under the net, listening to the sound of the storm, and any movement in the corridor outside.

In his feverish mind, he was back in his womb-like kitchen with a bashed old Rayburn belching heat while a storm blasted the windows and levelled trees outside. He grabbed at the image like a drowning man. On a large wooden chair sat Greg. Then more images flooded his mind, this time there was blood and body parts with an accompanying soundtrack of screaming. He felt small gears in his mind start to slip and he sought sanctuary in the kitchen, but it was empty now, and cold, the chairs and tables musty and damp from lack of use.

Another horror came to his mind born from his months lost in the jungle. He was being forced out of a small corrugated iron house into the ferocious heat of an afternoon by a gang of men with machetes. One of them leant across and swung his knife so it impacted on the man next to Ed.

Falling from the bed and hitting his head against the

floor he awoke from his nightmare trance. Picking himself up, rubbing an elbow, he checked the booby-trapped door before climbing back into bed.

The drums started soon after breakfast; they sounded a long way off, as if the players had been forced further away from the mine. He was sick of the mosquito gauze and threw it off to give him some more air then he leaned into his pillow and sunk back into his own mind.

Chiri's words came back to him…

"Are you decent?" came a husky, American, female voice from the corridor outside. The door opened a fraction and a piercing blue eye appeared followed by a tall, blond-haired woman in her thirties. She sidled into the room, hand on her hip, bag swinging rhythmically on her shoulder. Her face was heavily made up, and she had a knowing look, as if she was appraising him. It said she knew everything there was to know about men, and Ed in particular.

"James said to call," she said. "And here I am."

"You what?" Ed felt his own Liverpool accent grind against the chocolate smooth American, and found he didn't care very much.

"I'm Bernie," she said, flashing a knowing smile. "I'm a journalist."

Ed felt himself tense. "Bernie?"

"Short for Bernice." Turning, she shut the door before walking towards him, hips swaying in well-fitting khaki shorts. Sitting down in the seat only recently vacated by Chiri she produced a hip flask and two small glasses from her shoulder bag. As she poured a small measure in each and handed him one he realised he could do with a drink, particularly after last night. "Cheers," she said, and held hers up. Glass clashed on glass, and there was a moment while both swigged.

"So you're Greg's replacement. Ever heard of the term, Dead Man's Shoes?"

Lowering his glass slowly he glanced at her; not the first time he'd heard the statement. It made him feel uncomfortable, almost like she thought he was some kind of circling vulture. "What d'you mean?"

Bernie gave a bright smile, full of polished teeth that glowed against her beautiful, tanned skin. "Greg's dead, right? And you're the next man in line."

He nodded, unsure.

"O' course the company hushed everything, but rumours leak out."

"Rumours?"

"Didn't they tell you?"

"No, they told me he disappeared."

She laughed into her glass. "It was such a daft lie that everybody got interested." She pursed her lips. "Details are very sketchy, but it looks like he got on the wrong side of whoever runs this town. O' course nobody's too sure who that is. Some suggestion is that it's this Herman union leader, but that's codswallop in my opinion. He's too loud and stupid."

Another smile, and a sip from her cup. "This mine interests me. There's a massive gap between what is said and what is done. You must know that Lomax Mine has the worst safety record of anywhere in this part of the world. That interests me. There's some kind of secret union with a front man who nobody trusts. That interests me. There's investment decisions that seem crazy and suicidal, like selling off prime exploration prospects at rock bottom prices. That interests me." She began to swill her glass reflectively. In the light from the lamp next to the table she looked older than Ed had first supposed. He touched his own thinning hair, and then his rough, unshaven chin that showed grey hairs.

"I want to find out the reasons, and the true extent of the dangerousness of the place," she said.

"An unsafe gold mine is hardly big news."

"Nevertheless," she insisted, "I'd like to know."

"Is the mine aware that you're talking to me?"

A smile and a shrug of her beautiful shoulders.

He did his best to respond. "If anything comes up, I'll let you know."

For a few moments she was quiet, then, sniffing her drink, she looked around the room. "A full dose of malaria, and the jungle drums are beating," she said almost to herself.

"I don't think the two are linked. I hope not."

"Why're the drums going?" she asked.

"Must be angry I suppose."

Bernie crossed her beautiful legs and leaned across. Her blouse fell open. "Now why would they be angry d'you suppose?" Her whole body indicated that she was interested in him and him alone.

"You'll have to ask Chiri, or James Allen. I've been ill in hospital."

She looked searchingly at him. She was not convinced. "So," she said eventually, "what's your first impressions? Have you worked out who's hiding and who's running away yet?"

He shrugged.

"Miriam visits me when she comes to Accra. Doesn't get the bus of course, comes on the Hercules that transports the gold to the bank." She leaned back in her chair, her blouse closing up. She undid her legs. "She's a traditional old bird, a bit old school for me, but she has some interesting theories about people in this mine. James Allen for instance…"

The eleven o'clock blast erupted and shook the hospital worse than before. Bernie looked up at the ceiling and grabbed the handles of her seat as the inevitable shower of rocks fell on the roof. "What's that?" she said.

"Blasting," said Ed like an old hand. A thought suddenly occurred to him. "Perhaps there is a way you can help me."

"Oh?" she leant forward again.

"One of the geological team dropped dead the other day. I've been ordered to write to his widow."

"Who?"

"Dave Smith."

She smiled knowingly. "I'm guessing he wasn't alone when he passed on?"

"Indeed."

"And you'd like to know the sort of thing a grieving widow might want to hear?"

A nod of the head.

"Well I'm no expert, never having been married or bereaved. I don't suppose she'd like to know about all his girlfriends. Does no good for a gal's ego. You could embellish his death a little and suggest that he died with her name on his lips. What's her name?"

He shrugged. "Louise, I think."

"Best not to guess," she mused. "No good saying he died whispering Louise when her name is Emily. I'd check that out. Don't lie too much either. She's bound to know what he's like, so no use pretending he lived the simple life of a monk, consumed nothing but bread and turnips and went to bed at seven o'clock sharp." She clicked her tongue for a few moments. "Has Forge got anything to say?"

"Very little. He has nothing nice to say about anybody,

least of all David Smith."

"He has form. His last assistant walked out after three months. He thought Forge a sociopath, intent on hurting and destroying. It's an insight into Dave's behaviour. Loveless marriage, sociopathic boss, deeply inadequate personality." She screwed up her face in dissatisfaction and handed across her card. "Give me a call if you've something on your mind."

Ed placed it carelessly on his table, expecting her to stand up and walk out. Instead she turned and produced the hip flask again, like a rabbit from a hat. Her look had shifted from business-like to soft and dewy. He shrank back slightly.

"How's a man from Wales end up in a place like this?" her tone was conversational, and her body tilted forward, as if desperate to hear anything he could provide.

"I was assigned the job by my contracting company, John Williams Consulting Ltd," he said. "There's nothing particularly exciting or interesting. John Williams charges ten percent commission on anything I earn. He has the contacts and I have the expertise."

"But I heard you'd resigned from this type of thing. What makes a man like you decide to change his mind?"

Irritated by her knowledge, it was on the tip of his tongue to demand her sources, but then he decided to shrug. "Got bored," he said. "I needed to earn some money."

"A midlife crisis," she said knowingly. "Africa as the equivalent of a sports car with hydrofoils."

Ed smiled and laughed a little, which made her bend in closer. "I'm guessing there's a breakdown of a relationship, and you're showing her you don't need her. Or you're trying to forget, like joining the French Foreign Legion." She looked satisfied that she had guessed correctly and then sat back. "You'll find you're not the only one running away around here. They're either trying to get rich, trying to run away, or trying to hide. You'll have to guess for yourself which is which."

She looked away. "My dad worked Ghana Airways as a pilot. I was born and raised in Ghana. I can't pretend it's an easy life. But there ain't much competition to be foreign correspondent for big western news agencies." She sat back expectantly, like she'd made a bid by offering something of herself.

"I guess it's a dangerous place for a woman, particularly a white woman," he said.

She thought for a few moments. "Perhaps up country, away from Accra. But I feel safe in the capital, and of course I always take precautions. Besides, I'm part Ghanaian, although you wouldn't know. My grandmother had a fling with a British soldier from Hartlepool."

"I never would have guessed," he said. "You come across as full American."

She shrugged. "I've taken my African name. Bernice Armanour. I tend to use Bernie.

"Is it lawless elsewhere, then?" he asked.

"Not since Jerry Rawlins. Many thank him for cleaning the place up. Of course there was a price to pay; he wasn't too choice in his methods of eliminating opponents. Many have a poor opinion of him."

"And what's your opinion?"

"That's the point. I can have an opinion, and I can still write an opinion. Many can't in Africa." She finished her drink. "Lovely meeting you, Ed. Remember to keep in touch. Careful about email, though, you never know who's reading it. Letters can be opened, texts can be read. If you have something of real importance best to see one another face-to-face or fax it." She turned to go, but then a thought occurred to her. "If you're back in town, call me. We can do dinner and things."

THE COMBINATION LOCK

"Doctor says you can leave today," said the nurse who'd been his only companion since waking from his fever two long days ago.

"What day is it?"

"Saturday," she said. "Mr Kojo's organising a lift back to the compound for you, then you can have all day tomorrow restin'. The car'll be along in half an hour." She smiled at him for the first time. "And no carryin' on with those girls up there."

Ed's attempted smile slid off his face.

When the nurse left the room he sat up, threw off his sheets and dressed before making his way out of the door and down the corridor, past the public ward and out into a large yard. He had no memory of arriving and so he was taken by surprise to see a large number of open air showers and dressing stations. This was a hospital that could treat large numbers of people very quickly.

In a shaded spot around the corner from the emergency dressing stations there was a beautiful garden full of orchids which had a seat in the shade of a tall tree.

Pushing the sight of dead and dying men to the back of his mind he sat down and took stock of his situation. Gone were the feverish thoughts of a few nights ago when he thought his mind was unravelling. Instead, there was a series of controlled visions which he managed to summon and disperse at will. He was in a reflective mood.

Gold mining had been a difficult career to follow, especially after the army where life had been so regular and ordered. It was the deceit and the lying he found most difficult, and the men who would cut another's throat for an ounce of metal.

This mine provided much needed foreign reserves for the government, but none of that wealth came near the people who lived and worked here. They survived off the smell of an oily rag on the basis of a promissory note which was never honoured. The profit from the mine went to Lucky Lomax and his fellow shareholders who lived in beautiful mansions in Surrey with crystal basins and gold taps. People 'round here were sadly mistaken if Lomax would willingly part with a penny more than was absolutely necessary. Herman the Helmet and his union were absolutely right to fight him.

A gecko appeared from the long grass and stared up at him, his mouth wide open, eyes bulging, a bit like Dave Smith. Several more appeared and scuttled around on the pavement, stopping occasionally to stare, two feet in the air and two feet on the ground. They stimulated his thoughts in the direction of how he was going to write the letter to Dave's wife.

Chiri's warning on the night of his visit was tantamount to a confession that he had killed Greg, as well as Dave. For the first time Ed began to accept the probability of Greg's death. Greg, and Dave may have discovered something Chiri wanted hidden. But how come Forge had escaped Chiri's wrath? There could only be one explanation.

The sound of a gurgling diesel engine made him turn and he espied a brand new pickup making its way along the beautifully maintained tarmacked road. It was coming from the geological section and was heading very slowly in his direction. He stood up and waited, expecting Frank to poke his head out of the window. Instead, he saw Kojo's beaming smile. "Ed, lovely to see you well enough again," he said. "Frank's not available at the moment so I said I would be delighted to take you home."

He leaned across and threw open the passenger door and Ed climbed in beside him, into the most frigid air he had yet experienced in Africa. Kojo laughed at his expression. "I thought you Obrunis loved it like the Arctic," he said.

"We do, but only in the Arctic."

Kojo started his laugh again and did a U-turn so that he was now heading for the main gates of the mine. The guard waved them through and they were soon travelling along the dirt track that was the main artery through Lomax.

Looking out of the window at the now-familiar scene of corrugated iron, standing pools of stagnant water and mud, he wondered whether the mine had ever decided to do anything for the town that was the source of its labour. He turned to Kojo and looked at the smiling, beaming face, opened his mouth, and then shut it again.

Kojo looked at him. "What?" he asked.

Shaking his head, he dismissed what he was about to say. But then he thought of a way that he might frame a question that would not seem like an implicit criticism. "Isn't it very inefficient for the mine to have this road in such a state?"

For the first time Kojo looked serious. "Indeed," he said. "Mr Lomax has tried hard to upgrade the roads through this town, but the money has always been diverted by the local government."

The mine, it appeared, was as helpless as the common citizen against the corruption that was the curse of West Africa. Surely a mine the size of Lomax would be able to demand that the work was carried out. There would be strings attached.

Kojo was a company man used to promoting the company narrative; there was little to be gained by arguing with him. And as for the rest of them, they were white contractors and mining engineers who ensured that their own families lived in places where the water and electricity worked.

"How are you getting on with Allen?" Kojo asked suddenly.

It was a leading question and took him surprise. "Fine…"

"Only I know he isn't everybody's cup of tea."

"What do you mean?"

"There are those who are willing to think very badly of him, but he's really a first class guy. He's employed by Lucky Lomax to oversee exploration strategy. He is my eyes and ears, specially selected by the Mine Manager himself."

"Oh?"

A beaming smile and a nod of the head. "He has enormous experience from all round the planet. He has been Exploration Manager and has even run his own exploration companies. Lucky Lomax bought his company. I believe he had promising prospects further along the coast. Part of the deal was that he would bring his expertise to Lomax for a few years."

'Interesting', thought Ed; yet another story about Allen. He was a terrorist, convicted fraudster and successful gold mining entrepreneur. Could he be all three?

"I have keys for you," said Kojo holding up his hand. "Bismarck's and Forge's office. The Mine Manager over-ruled Forge's objection." He laughed uproariously again.

"It's my winning personality," said Ed, taking the keys and putting them in his pocket.

"The Mine Manager wants to have you over for Sunday dinner tomorrow. He says he'll send a car for you to the compound."

"Tell him to send the car to Geological Services. I need to catch up on some work, and it'll be good to get it done without Forge looking over my shoulder."

A large beaming smile again. "I have a login for you, and an email address. I put it on your desk. Sorry it's taken so long, but the authorisation has just come back from the Mine Manager."

They had arrived at the compound. "Thanks for everything," said Ed. "Can you arrange a car for me tomorrow morning to go to the mine?"

Another beaming smile and a nod, then Kojo turned the wheel and made a U-turn. Ed watched him disappear then walked through the gate, past the guards.

Back in his room, he had a swift trickle shower and lay on his bed, enjoying the feel of the efficient air conditioning. His mind was still whirring with the sights and sounds of what he had experienced over the last few days. He decided he needed a whisky.

When he went to the rucksack in his cupboard, hunting for the single malt, his hand fell on something hard and square. He hurriedly pulled it out and saw

Greg's strong box. The conversation with Bismarck came back to him where he had speculated that the combination might be a number that Greg had used routinely when he was young. He shut his eyes to help him conjure the number of his grandfather's farm. It had begun with 017, of that he was sure, but the trouble was that he could remember very little else. His grandfather had been notorious for never answering the phone. He only really used it when he needed to summon a vet, or get the doctor out for his wife, Ed's grandmother.

What was Ed's home phone number? This was much easier 7245565. He dialled in the numbers and tugged at the box lid, but nothing happened. He sank on the bed, disappointed. That was pretty much his only shot, unless he could remember Taid's number.

Reaching for the single malt he lay down and speculated about whether he was thinking about this in the correct way. How many numbers were required for the lock? He had put in seven, but what if eight were required?

Greg did not live in Liverpool. He would have needed to use the city code, 0151 to ring Carys at home. He tried again, 01517245. Nothing again.

17245565; nothing.

Disappointed, again. It must have been Taid's number, or a number about which he had no idea. He would have to creep up on his grandfather's number and then quickly write it down at the time of remembrance. It would most likely come to him in a dream.

Eyes tight shut he thought back to the old telephone that would sit on the electricity meter cupboard on the hallway of their house in Garston. He could see the pale yellow colour and the classic dialling wheel with the home number written on a piece of paper in the centre. It was a

Bakelite classic. Every home in Britain had one. A wave of nostalgia washed over him as he saw his sister in the hall. She was standing in a bathrobe, hair in a towel, laughing at something Greg was saying.

He sat up, sloshing his whisky, his eyes wide open. There was something he'd forgotten, something very important. At one stage, telephone codes were shorter by a single digit. At some point they had decided that they were running out of numbers, and so a 1 had been added in front of the 5. Taid had never bothered adding in the 1 on the address book pinned to his wall. The number Greg would have seen, every day of his life, on Taid's wall, would not have been 0151, it would have been 051. Greg had often pointed it out to Ed and laughed. 'It changed ten years ago, but the old man refuses to allow me to modify it. Says there's no need, it'll spoil the look of the display.'

He scrabbled around on the floor for the strong box and then placed it on his knee. 05172455. There was a click. It was a much louder click than previously. He pulled at the wheel, and the lid miraculously came away.

Stunned with his success he sat on the bed blinking down at the contents, unable to rationalise what he was seeing. It was as if everything was out of focus for a few moments. But then the two images from his eyes slid together to give a perfect stereographic vision of the box contents.

A few sheets of folded paper.

He tentatively put in his hand and held them up as if they were jewels. Opening them out he stared at Greg's beautiful copper plate, heart thumping. Blinking slightly, forcing down the feeling of elation, he bent to read. But instead of the words being easily recognisable, they looked to be just a jumble of letters. At first he thought of a foreign language, like Twi, but Greg knew only English. He tried looking at the form of each word, to see if it was pronounceable, perhaps he could find a way of translating by making out the sounds. But the syllables and consonants were mixed randomly, in one case a single word was made entirely of the letter C.

Shaking the papers to see if there was anything hidden inside, a smaller piece fell out and landed on the bed. It looked to be a fax confirmation saying when the message had been sent and when it had been received; only a few days before Greg disappeared. More significantly, it had the number to which it had been sent. The country code was missing but he thought he could recognise the city code for Accra.

Looking inside the box again he discovered a green USB stick, exactly like he had retrieved from Dave Smith's desk. Closing his hand around it he shut his eyes in frustration. Nothing in this box made any sense. It must have already been forced open and the most important documents removed.

Disappointed, he rolled onto his side and gazed at the air conditioner, listening to its noisy purr. He had hoped that what was in the box would make sense straight away, that somehow Greg had managed to scribble a note saying exactly what had happened to him. The incomprehensible mumbo jumbo on the paper was like an admonition, as if Greg was jabbing a finger and telling him that he'd have to try harder. Looking down at the memory stick he realised that the chase was not yet over. He would be able to read its contents tomorrow when he got into the office.

The next morning he found that the compound had returned spare shirts and trousers for him to wear. Gratefully, he shoved his old and smelly attire into the washing bag before showering, dressing and walking out into the early morning, broiling sun. The staff were clearing up after the Saturday night festivities and by the look of things there had been quite a considerable party. Frank was waiting in the car park, fast asleep with the engine running. Rapping hard on the window, he was rewarded with a dirty look and a sullen acknowledgement.

Only children were out in the streets; he wondered whether the adults were at church or nursing a collective hangover. The guards at Lomax 'A' looked bored as they waved the pickup through, no need to stop and ask for identification on a lazy Sunday.

Nothing moved inside the mine, except a few white engineers who were playing golf on the small nine pin course. Each man had a boy to carry their golf clubs. As they passed, he saw Paul Forge was one of the players, his caddy so small he was barely able to carry the bag of clubs.

Anger rose in Ed, at the stupidity of Forge engaging a boy who was several inches smaller than the bag of clubs he was meant to be carrying; it was symptomatic of a sociopathic personality. Next to Forge was Golf Club, swinging a nine iron in the same way as he did in the underground, narrowly missing both his own and Forge's caddy.

The feeling of resentment didn't leave Ed until he had reached the office and realised that if Forge was out on the golf course then he was not here. Dipping a hand into his pocket, he felt the two USB sticks which had belonged to Greg and Dave. He wanted to investigate their contents before the Mine Manager's driver came and picked him up for Sunday lunch.

Climbing the steps to the office, his stomach knotted with anticipation, he realised it would be a miracle if his plan worked. He stopped to look through the window, half expecting to see Forge sitting at his desk, somehow magically teleported from the golf course. But the light was off, and the computer on Forge's desk was most definitely powered down. "Perfect," he mumbled to himself feeling inside his bag for the key marked 'Forge's office' which Kojo had given him the previous day.

To his amazement the key slid home and turned. Waves of cold air met him as he walked inside. His hand slid into his pocket and retrieved the two USB sticks. Part two of the operation required that he log into Forge's computer so he could read their contents. A single sheet of paper lying on his desk turned out to be the login details left by Kojo the previous day. Blessing Kojo for his efficiency, Ed sat in Forge's seat and switched on the computer.

While waiting for it to complete its boot sequence, he looked around the room. Sitting in Forge's seat felt almost like committing sacrilege against a local deity. From here he could see out of the walkway window, down the stairs to the car park. You could see everybody coming through the main gates and entering Geology Services.

The computer beeped that it was ready for him to enter his login details. Looking down at the piece of paper he carefully entered the combination of numbers and letters. After a few moments a message appeared, encouraging him to change his password. Then suddenly the screen changed colour and a window materialised welcoming him to the Lomax Gold Mine network.

Before anything could go wrong, he quickly leant forward and plunged Dave Smith's memory stick into the slot, the auto-run software kicked in and two spreadsheet icons appeared. He opened them both and discovered that at the top of each was a title: Rusty Lion prospect. Staring in confusion he saw that both displayed gold mineralisation values from the same drill hole. Disappointed, he realised that there was nothing unusual here, at least nothing that he could see immediately. At any minute Forge might decide to abandon his golf match and swing by his office, so he pressed the print button on both and was gratified to hear the sound of a laser-jet printer chattering beneath the desk.

With the memory stick from Greg's strong box slipped into the slot, Dave's two spreadsheets were replaced with a view of a series of icons labelled WAV. Feeling his eyebrows narrow, he double clicked on the first file, which Greg had helpfully called 'aaaaa'. Immediately, a blue screen popped up and the sound of a man's voice, clear and strong, came across the speakers. The voice spoke Twi, it was excited, almost angry, and there were some other voices in the background who would occasionally agree with what was being said. As he listened, he began to recognise the voice was that of Bismarck. At first he was uncertain because he had never heard Bismarck speak in anything other than a hushed voice. As the recording continued, Bismarck's voice became more strident, even angry.

Pressing the stop button on the blue screen, he retrieved both USB sticks and put them back in his pocket and shut down the computer. Then he leant down and grabbed the print-outs from the printer under the desk before standing up. Glancing out of the window, he saw that a brand new pickup had arrived in the car park and a man in green with yellow trim was walking up the steps. The time had arrived for his first meeting with the Mine Manager.

The Mine Manager's big villa on the top of the hill was one of the most visible buildings in the district; it looked down on the mine and surrounding town like the residence of some local chief of the tribe. This impression was enhanced because the Mine Manager was all but invisible to everybody except a few senior engineers. By strictly rationing his appearances, he was able to develop a mystique for his post which was similar to a high functionary in the church. Few dare challenge the authority of a Bishop, until they meet him and realise that he's human after all. An invitation to dinner was therefore a rare privilege, only awarded to a few very lucky individuals.

When Ed emerged onto the Mine Manager's hilltop, it felt like he'd travelled into an entirely new world, like he had reached some plain where only gods dwell. No sight or smell of a shanty town reached this exalted height; the lawns were immaculate and the flower beds had monumental African art which were designed to impress rather than divert.

On stepping out of the pickup he saw a helicopter parked on a circular piece of tarmac. For a moment he wondered if this was at the disposal of the Mine Manager, or whether another had been invited to the meeting.

He turned his head to face into a stiff and refreshing breeze that emanated from the south. Putting his hand up to shield his eyes from the glare of the sun he saw, far off and almost translucent, white flecks of ocean waves breaking across skerries. He had forgotten that Lomax township was so close to the coast.

A sudden surge of emotion brought a memory of travelling with Taid in his old Land Rover over the Cambrian Mountains where they had glimpsed the grey, cold waters of Cardigan Bay. The sea never failed to stir his spirit, even under a furnace-like sky in Africa. It was a physical barrier and conduit, uniting and dividing humanity at one and the same time.

At last he turned and looked up at the colonial hall with its vast verandas and black painted iron work. He stared at the windows to see if anybody was watching him, then he followed the driver inside.

The polished and waxed floors of the reception area creaked under the pressure of his boots as if protesting at the presence of such a lowly contractor amidst the fine porcelain, period pictures, animal skins and statuesque African art. The driver knocked on a large wooden door leading off to the right and then turned the polished brass handle. Ed was ushered into a beautiful, high ceilinged room with a Persian carpet and polished period furniture that would not have been out of place in a grand English country home.

Two men sat in large leather armchairs, both dressed in the green of the mine. One was small and bald with a creased face like a deflated football. Heavy brows overhung his eyes as if designed as a permanent sun-shade. His age was difficult to guess, but Ed thought mid-sixties.

The other man was much younger, whispy-thin and blonde. He radiated superiority in the way that some cars emit fumes. It was in the languorous way he picked imagined fluff from his silk, paisley neckerchief, or the unhurried manner in which he rose to shake Ed by the hand, like it was a tedious duty.

The older man beckoned Ed to come further into the room. "Wonderful to see you up on your feet. Of course I've been having twice daily updates on your condition from dear old Kojo." His accent would not have been out of place reading the BBC news. "You've met Jeremy before I gather," he said indicating the much younger man.

Ed nodded and then attempted one of his sliding smiles. "We met in London."

"My name's Dan by the way. Please call me Mine Manager. It helps to keep everything tidy if we obey the niceties of hierarchy." He moved to a crystal decanter perched on top of an elegant sideboard at the edge of the room and poured three sherries which he handed around.

"Cheers," he said and tilted his head back.

Jeremy took a small sip before wrinkling his nose and putting the glass down on a table within easy reach of his languid and elegant arm.

"I suppose Mr Lomax wants a report?" Ed said

"Please have a seat, Ed," said the Mine Manager. "You prefer Ed to Edryd I presume?" Ed found a vacant leather armchair and sat stiffly, sherry glass in hand trying to think what to say.

"Well?" asked the Mine Manager. "What d'you think?"

Ed shrugged. It was a gesture that brought Jeremy out of his seat. He looked angry and nervous. "Can I remind you that Mr Lomax is paying a lot of money. So far as I can see all you've managed to pick up is a bout of malaria."

There was something in the way that Jeremy loomed over him which Ed found faintly funny. He was trying to copy his master, a man with a reputation for having a towering temper and who endlessly bullied his staff. If Jeremy went home empty-handed then he was liable for the full Lomax treatment. Ed tried to smile reassuringly.

Jeremy threw himself forward, his beautiful St Tropez tan darkening, his fists clenching and unclenching like he was getting ready to leap. Gazing at him calmly, Ed took another sip of his sherry.

"Gentlemen, gentlemen," interrupted the Mine Manager. "This is hardly a way to conduct a debriefing."

Breathing hard through his nostrils, Jeremy continued to lean over him. "I want to remind Mr Evans that he needs to get results. Mr Lomax is not forgiving of failure, and if he returns without the required information then…" Arm raised, Jeremy tried to think what was going to be his threat. He'd probably rehearsed this moment and memorised the words he was going to say, but had then fluffed his lines.

"Then what?" Ed asked.

Recovering himself, Jeremy hissed, "You'd better come up with something useful or else not return back to your rotten little farmhouse, because Mr Lomax will be waiting."

"Perhaps I should recommend that you replace me," said Ed staring hard into Jeremy's deep blue eyes. Ten years he'd spent in the army with the likes of Jeremy, and in all that time he had believed that in some way he was part of something noble.

Jeremy retreated, his job as Lomax-proxy complete.

"I've made some progress, but there've been problems," Ed told the Mine Manager.

"Oh?"

"First thing is that the mine is so full of factions it's difficult to determine whether the obstructiveness is habit or because they have something to hide."

Nodding his head sagely as if he recognised what Ed was saying, the Mine Manager pushed for details. "But none of Greg's stuff was touched in his office. I made sure that clear instructions were given on that score, and we managed to secure all his belongings. You went through all of those before you came here."

"I don't think the stuff in the office has been

touched," said Ed, not wanting to talk about what he'd found in Greg's secure box until he understood its full meaning. "There's also the death of Dave Smith," he added

"Over-exertion, surely?" Jeremy again. "Nothing to do with our current problem. Couldn't keep his hand out of the sweet jar."

Ed turned his eyes on Jeremy, who gazed back down his nose. "Have you been keeping a watch on his room from Lomax Towers?" Jeremy shook his head and took another sniff of his sherry. "Pity," said Ed, "because then we'd at least know who was responsible for bashing his brains out and slicing him up."

"You mean he was murdered?" asked the Mine Manager in open amazement.

Ed nodded, somewhat discomforted by the reaction he was getting. "I'd sort of hoped that it was you who arranged to keep the crime scene intact so it could be examined."

"Not at all."

"Any idea yet about who was responsible for Greg's disappearance?" said Jeremy.

"Not a clue," Ed lied. He was not yet going to outline his suspicions about Chiri until he had unpicked the strands of loyalty in the mine.

"What about the fraud?" asked the Mine Manager. "Any further on that?"

Ed narrowed his eyebrows, in a characteristic gesture of confusion. "Are you sure it's fraud and not simple incompetence? Your Exploration Manager is not the best..."

Jeremy exploded again. "You don't think Mr Lomax relied on the word of that dickhead? We had the best consultants look at the data."

There was a ringing silence. "In that case can I suggest you look at who owns Tremendous Resources of London, because they've been the best placed company."

"Idiot," screamed Jeremy. "Don't you think we've done that?"

Ed leaned forward out of his seat and put his sherry glass down, but before he could rise, the dinner gong sounded somewhere in the house. "Excellent," shouted the Mine Manager. "I do believe it's roast beef and Yorkshire pudding. I do enjoy having visitors so I can push the boat out. Chef has brought up some of the better Bordeaux from the cellar as well." They moved through to a beautiful dining room and sat down at a large, polished table where they were served with dinner.

In a hushed voice the Mine Manager started the conversation again. "Can I remind you gentlemen that walls have ears and I need you to keep your voices down. We can assume that anything overheard from this house will find its way into the ears of any rogue element."

A clang as Jeremy threw his knife and fork down onto his plate. "You need to change your staff if that's the case."

The Mine Manager smiled at him. "I can see that you're a real operator in your own world, Jeremy, but leave me to operate in mine. Africa's not the City of London. I think you'll find that Mr Lomax appreciates the conditions under which Ed and I have to work."
Silence.

"So we'll just have to keep our voices low."

Silence.

He turned back to Ed. "So I can assume that we are no further forward finding out about the fraud in the mine?"

Ed shook his head. "Nor to finding out why Greg

disappeared and if he's still alive."

"Greg disappeared because he was getting close to finding out about the fraud," said the Mine Manager.

"Was Dave Smith employed directly by Mr Lomax as well, like me?" asked Ed.

"Do me a favour, will you," said Jeremy in a loud voice.

The Mine Manager quelled him with a look. "Voice down. This is not one of your awful London Clubs. We can hear you perfectly well." Then to Ed, "He certainly wasn't employed directly by Mr Lomax, as far as I know. He came through an agency used by Chiri. I rather think that Chiri feels threatened by people who are more intelligent. Witness his treatment of Bismarck over the years, and his bitter opposition to my appointment of Kojo."

"And what about James Allen?" asked Ed. "What's his history. I've heard several different stories about him."

Both men stirred and exchanged glances. Eventually the Mine Manager turned back to Ed. "He's been employed by Mr Lomax on my recommendation. Kojo has a big future in this company and James is here to mentor and watch over him and keep an eye on Chiri."

Silence while they ate, except for the echoing clash of knife on china. Ed had calmed down sufficiently to appreciate his surroundings. Beautiful, polished floors, tastefully painted walls and ceiling to floor length curtains. "And what about Bismarck?" he asked. "Does he have a future in the company?"

The Mine Manager finished chewing his mouthful and then he brought his wine to his lips. "I'm afraid to say Bismarck paid the price for allowing Kojo to be promoted over the head of Chiri. He will go no further in this mine unless, or until, Chiri leaves. And that will never happen, so I am led to believe by those in power in Accra."

Jeremy pushed his plate away with much of the meal untouched. "Shall we get to the point of this meeting? I've got to fly back to Accra so I can catch my flight back to London."

The Mine Manager touched his lips with his serviette. "Delicious, don't you think Ed?" he asked indicating the food.

"Very nice," Ed agreed.

"So difficult to get really top notch beef in such a hot climate. Must be something to do with the warmth that prevents the beast eating well and putting on meat." He paused for a few moments. "We've had a contact from the union. They want to have a meeting where they will set out their demands. Jeremy has said he would never agree to meet them or discuss terms. I feel that this is wrongheaded, personally, that we should have some form of dialogue, even if unofficially..."

"Fortunately, that's not your decision," said Jeremy.

The Mine Manager ignored the interruption. "If there's one thing I've learnt from a life time working in Africa it's that posturing very rarely works well. In my estimation it is a mistake to ignore the hand of peace. It is tantamount to declaring war. Far better to jaw, jaw than war, war."

"They'll have to withdraw their threat of joining with the Galamsey," interjected Jeremy.

The Mine Manager stopped, exasperated, and then turned his head. "Perhaps if we'd agreed to talk seriously earlier they might not have been forced to these desperate measures. After all that unpleasantness a few days ago in the open pits, it's unsurprising they've made common cause." Turning to Ed he said, "They want you as the go-between."

Silence.

"Me? Why me?"

The Mine Manager shook his head and then opened his mouth, but Jeremy jumped in first. "Precisely what Mr Lomax wants to know. Why you?"

"But I've just arrived," said Ed. "How can the union possibly know anything about who I am?"

"I rather think," said the Mine Manager, "that you are the replacement for Greg. You see, Greg was the unofficial go-between before Jeremy discovered I was talking with the union."

Silence.

"And I needn't warn you that you should be very careful. We are beset by a sea of enemies, and our worst enemies are those we least suspect."

"And what does Lucky Lomax think of this policy of no negotiation?" asked Ed.

"He has complete trust in my ability to get the job done," Jeremy replied with a sneer.

On his way back to the compound, the Mine Manager's warnings of enemies rang in Ed's ears. He let himself into his room and sat on the bed thinking about his rapidly narrowing options. Grabbing the single malt from the cupboard he poured himself a stiff measure then lay down, exhausted from the aftermath of the malaria and depressed by the situation in which he found himself.

'Should have taken John William's advice and told Lomax where to stick his money', he thought. On the other hand, if he got out of this alive, and he was careful, he might never have to see another gold mine for as long as he lived. He could sit up on his cold Welsh hillside and take the odd job for pocket money to relieve the boredom.

Perhaps he could persuade Alice to come and live with him. He shook his head and laughed at the thought of Alice in a drafty old farmhouse. It would never happen. He propped himself up and pulled the pieces of paper he had printed off earlier that day towards him. Losing himself in figures would allow him to forget about Chiri, the union boss he would soon have to meet, and Alice with her auburn hair and freckles, gentle smile and soft body.

Later on that day, Ed sat in the bar on his own, waiting for Allen to appear. He'd positioned himself away from all the Faces and far enough from the Manchester Navvies so he couldn't hear their foul language. Darkness had brought its cooling balm and there was little to do but drink beer and pretend to be deeply engrossed in a novel in the expectation that people would get the message and stay away. But he was out of luck.

A Manchester Navvy with the residue of a once-prominent black eye, sidled over. He was bald and had a gut that poked between jeans and white t-shirt. "Where's your Irish friend?" he asked, his fleshy face distorted into a scowl.

"He'll be along soon." Ed replied reluctantly.

"I thought he might not want to show his face here again."

"On the contrary, I think he enjoys a good work out."

The man scowled and looked around. "Tell him we don't need his sort around here," he said before walking back to his table. He could see them all discussing what had just been said; there was dark looks in his direction, but then they soon lost interest and returned their attention to the seamstresses.

A tap on his shoulder and a familiar Irish voice, "Consorting with the enemy? Or just catching up with your fellow countrymen?" The twinkling eyes of James Allen looked down on him. He was dressed in khaki, not green. Ed wondered momentarily why he refused to wear the mine uniform; he thought about asking him, but then decided against.

"I'm from Liverpool and they're from Manchester."

"And you're more Welsh than English?"

Ed shrugged. "I suppose so. I've never felt myself to be part of any tribe."

Levering himself down into a seat, Allen placed two bottles of beer on the table. "I know what you mean, I've tended to avoid my own countrymen as much as possible."

After a moment's silence, while they both swigged back some beer, Ed gave a conspiratorial flash of his eyebrows and looked around to see if they were being observed by anybody. Then, taking papers from his top shirt pocket he spread them out on the table. "Have a look at that and tell me what you think."

Allen pulled the papers towards him.

"I don't understand," he said eventually, "what are these meant to be?"

"They're the results that the mine will publish to potential investors, I assume," replied Ed. "For Rusty Lion." He waited for Allen to scan down the list.

"They seem a bit on the low side," Allan said carefully.

"On the low side?" replied Ed, incredulous. "We visited that prospect together, remember? The ground was stuffed with gold mineralisation."

A shake of the head. "There was mineralisation, but not necessarily gold mineralisation. I've been round here long enough to know that everything that gleams is not necessarily golden."

"The figures show only trace amounts of gold,"

insisted Ed. "With all the stuff we were seeing in the drilling and in the trenches there has to be something beyond background."

Nodding his agreement, Allen looked up at Ed with something like resentment in his eyes. "How come you got to see this? I've only received this by email today."

"I found them on a memory stick in Dave Smith's desk."

Anger flared across Allen's face. "How come Dave Smith saw them before I did?"

Good point.

Handing the paper back to Ed, Allen took another swig of his beer before giving his opinion. "It's strange. I've been waiting for these results to arrive and I've been pestering Kojo for them. And now I find everybody's seen them before me, including ol' mosquito trap."

"What did Kojo say was the reason for the delay?" asked Ed.

The question hung in the air for a while before Allen answered. "He said Forge had not yet received the results and he was chasing them."

"Where's the lab based?"

"London, I think."

Ed produced a second piece of paper. "This should interest you," he said.

"What's this?"

"It's the contents of the second file on the memory stick I found in Dave's desk."

Allen picked up the print-out and gave it a cursory glance. "It's more results from Rusty Lion," he said with a dismissive flick of his head.

"Keep looking," said Ed

A resigned look on his face, he picked up the print-out again and began looking down the list. Then he stopped, eyes widening in astonishment.

"It's the same drill hole but with some differences," Ed said, glad that Allen had spotted the same thing he had.

"Is this a joke?" Allen asked sharply. The twinkle in the eye had gone, replaced with a piercing, almost angry look.

"Don't shoot the messenger," Ed said holding up his hands. "I'm just showing you what I've found."

Looking down at the sheet of paper again, he studied the figures more closely. "These are bonanza grades," he commented. He checked the drilling serial numbers. "These are from exactly the same drill holes as the other sheet." The angry look had gone, to be replaced by a confused and mystified expression. He was calculating and working out the possibilities.

"Which set of figures do you believe?" Ed asked.

A piercing stare. "Good point. Which do you believe?"

"I'm not the local expert, you are," replied Ed. "But based on what I've seen I'd say the figures you're holding are the correct ones."

"In which case…" started Allen.

"In which case somebody's being modifying the assay results," said Ed leaning across and tapping his finger on the table for emphasis. "Shouldn't we go straight to the top and tell the Mine Manager what's going on?" he asked.

Allen sniffed. "You know how this place works. The manager may be white, but he won't go against Chiri with all his contacts in the local tribe. Let's face it, honest men will look at the reported grades and decide not to invest. I assume Chiri's motive for modifying the data is either to buy these prospects himself or to sell the information to a third party, or a bit of both? I wonder if we dug a little into Chiri's business dealings we'd find a link between him and a company like this Tremendous Resources of London? They seem to be the lucky recipient of all the prospects that this mine is flogging off."

"Forge must have some role as well," said Ed. "He has the opportunity and the access."

"Perhaps," said Allen. "But Chiri's the man who receives the data first. He puts it in a spreadsheet to check if there's any null data, and then he puts it into a secure database. Forge has no access until it's in a database. He does a check, and then releases the password."

"So how come Dave Smith had results on his memory stick?"

Allen shook his head. "He must have been able to hack into the computer system."

"Do you suppose Dave modified the data?"

A shrug.

"Or did he happen upon this data?"

Allen looked at him quizzically.

"When Forge was out at a meeting I mean," insisted Ed

"Forge is meticulous when it comes to security. Dave'd have had to know the password," said Allen

"Even so…"

"I know you despise Forge, just like me, but Forge wouldn't have the imagination for such a thing, and nor would Dave Smith."

"And neither would Chiri," said Ed with passion.

"On the contrary," replied Allen. "Chiri's as cunning as a shithouse rat, and has the arrogance to think that he has the right to do whatever he likes."

"I'll talk with Kojo in the morning…" began Ed.

Allen shook his head. "I'm not sure we should get that involved with this. After all, it's up to the mine to establish that Chiri's making a monkey out of them. It's not for us to get involved." He leaned across the table and fixed Ed earnestly in the eye. "I tell you, if we go to the mine management it might land us in more trouble. Chiri would go on the war path with his acolytes and we would be lucky to escape from here. In fact," he lowered his voice and leant closer to Ed, "the fact that Chiri is in the pocket of a small-time exploration company will not have gone un-noticed in the City of London. Tremendous Resources have an astronomical price. No doubt Chiri has a major shareholding, or a profit share or something." He leaned back a little and became slightly less intense.

"So how do we proceed with this?"

"Forget that you ever discovered it."

Ed shifted in his seat uncomfortably. The sight and smell of Dave's room came back to him. Could this be the reason why Dave had died? Had he found out about the fraud and threatened to tell? But how had he found out?

"Another beer?"

Ed nodded, his mind elsewhere. Allen rose and went into the crowd of Faces at the bar and then returned a few minutes later, grimacing. "One of your fellow countrymen just collared me and told me I wasn't welcome around here."

"Which one?"

"The fat, ugly one."

"Doesn't narrow it down much," said Ed accepting the beer. "The really, really fat, ugly one was over here before you arrived telling me the same thing."

"Bald? Face like a slapped arse?"

"That's him."

Allen looked at the bar. "I can see he's out for trouble tonight. Perhaps I'll finish and go. Don't want the reputation of a brawler. I really came to ask how you got on with the Mine Manager today. What did he want?"

"Wanted to know how I was after the malaria."

"Lomax's helicopter took off in the afternoon."

"Lomax wasn't there, it was a man named Jeremy. Know him?"

Allen's face grew dark. "Met him once or twice before. I think he oversees Lomax's African operations. About as much clue about Africa as Slapped Arse over there." He indicated with his thumb while taking a drink from his bottle. "What did he want?"

Ed shrugged. "Coincidence I think. He just happened to be visiting." He was getting uncomfortable with Allen's sudden interest. "Chiri visited me in hospital. Scared the wits out of me."

"What did he want?"

"Told me he knew we were on the hill overlooking the open pit. Says if I try and leave the mine he'll kill me."

MEETING HERMAN HELMET

Next day, two men sporting flowery shirts and wrap-around glasses turned up at Ed's door and demanded that he come with them to see Herman the Helmet. They escorted him to the car park, one in front and the other behind, and then told him to get into the passenger seat of a large white pickup. Gulping down his apprehension, Ed climbed inside and asked tremulously where they were going. "To a meeting," the larger of the two had replied before slamming the door.

They passed the main mine gates with its blue scout cars and high watch towers and turned left to travel along the main town thoroughfare. Except during his arrival on the regular mine service bus Ed had never been along this road. Initially it was clogged with a sea of humanity vying for control with taxis, lorries and road-side stalls, but with distance the congestion lifted and the pickup was able to increase speed. Gazing to his left and right, Ed noticed narrow alleyways which he guessed must lead into the labyrinthine passages that formed the connective tissue of the town. Inside, children played football and caused choking billows of dust to rise in the air. Groups of men gathered at their entrances to gossip, heads swinging absent-mindedly as the pickup went past.

Sitting back in his seat, he reflected that the union was hardly likely to harm its chosen arbitrator, and the Mine Manager had told him to be prepared for such a visit. Shutting his mind to Bernie's suggestion that Herman the Helmet might have been involved in Greg's disappearance, he returned to his conversation with Allen in the bar last night. Surely, as the man with oversight of exploration, he had a duty to report wrongdoing, and yet Allen had been content to sit on his hands and even urged Ed to do the same.

Perhaps he should have pursued Jeremy more closely about who owned Tremendous Resources. He had been ready to shout it at him before the Mine Manager had intervened.

They were approaching the outskirts of the town near an area with hills devoid of vegetation like massive spoil heaps. The Faces in the bar said they were natural, denuded of vegetation because they were down-wind of the arsenic residue vented into the atmosphere from the processing plant. The dust that choked the narrow streets in this part of the town was heavily contaminated.

The driver swung the wheel and turned into a side street that was dissected by channels filled with white water. The road dropped steeply, emerging into an area of open space with sparse trees and patchy grass. Approximately a hundred metres away, a block of dwellings was arranged in a rough circle. As the pickup approached, Ed was able to see that only people on foot could enter the conurbation, one at a time, through narrow alleyways. It looked defensive and secretive, as if the people who lived inside expected to be besieged and felt safer living in a form of splendid isolation.

The driver got out and signalled to Ed that he should do the same before putting out a hand, palm up, in the universal signal to halt. "Wait here," he said, then followed his partner into the housing complex. Looking around him Ed noticed no children, despite a set of primitive goalposts and tyre swings hanging from every tree. The eerie silence combined with the dust devils chasing each other across the parched grassland gave Ed the feeling he was in some kind of Wild West movie, only tumbleweed was needed to make the scene complete. He was probably the first European since Greg to have visited this place. The thought gave him no comfort.

A small boy of six or seven years old looked at him from one of the alleyways. He was dressed in a pair of blue shorts and had very short hair; resentment was fixed in his face, even when Ed attempted a friendly and encouraging smile. They stared at each other for several seconds, Ed's eyes watering. It was as if the boy was taking in Ed's shape and features for future reference. Slowly, the boy raised his fingers in the shape of a gun and fired, then ducked his head back behind the corner and was gone.

A loud bang from the clash of metal rang out and drifted across the open space. Heart thumping, he heard barked orders spoken in the local language and five men appeared from a small entrance way. Four were dressed in jeans and t-shirts, noticeably bulky around the shoulders, early thirties or possibly younger with hair cut short. They had blank, automotan-like stares which focussed on something in the middle distance. The fifth man wore a red, silk dressing gown that reached all the way down to the ground where it brushed against open-toed leather sandals. His head was broad and rounded at the top, like a helmet.

Herman was in his forties, rotund, with messianic eyes that bulged out of his skull. A large cigar poked from his mouth, its lighted point directed at Ed, billows of smoke streaking away to join the dust devils on their excursions around the local area. As he walked forward, the dressing gown flapped open to reveal jeans and a t-shirt like those of his four companions. Holding out his hand, Herman smiled like he was greeting one of his admirers.

"Welcome, Mr Evans. I am glad you could come."

He chewed the cigar and then changed its position to the right side of his mouth, and then to the left. He had a deep voice and spoke like he was used to people listening. Ed took his hand warily and they stood together, clasped like two chiefs meeting in no-man's land. "I wish to tell you our demands and then my man will take you back to your residence." Ed nodded his head to indicate that he was listening, then reached into his pocket and produced a notebook and pencil.

"First, pay to be raised by twenty percent. Second, two weeks' holiday pay for everybody. Third, every miner should have insurance so that if they are killed or injured their family will have a pension." He reached into the pocket of his silk dressing gown and produced a folded piece of paper which he handed across. "All of our demands are written on here. I think you'll agree that our demands are reasonable and will bring my members' terms and conditions closer to those enjoyed by workers in your own country, Mr Evans."

Ed took the paper, doubt written across his face. A bright smile broke out across Herman Helmet's face at the look, as if he recognised what was going across Ed's mind. "You doubt whether we will be successful," he said.

A shrug of the shoulders. "Mr Lomax's representative has told the Mine Manager that there should be no negotiations, under any circumstances. That is what I have been instructed to tell you."

Herman casually shifted the cigar to the other side of his mouth and took a long puff before blowing out a concentrated billow in Ed's direction. "You can tell your Mine Manager that we will have to bring his boss to the negotiating table. We have the power and the ability." He adjusted his smile to make it look less pleasant and more menacing. "We will hit Mr Lomax where it hurts, in the pocket. We have the ability to bring his mine to a complete stand still. And now," he announced, "my driver will take you back to your accommodation."

"What will you do?"

Herman looked at him very keenly. "You'll see," he said.

"But..."

"My driver will take you back. Then you will tell the Mine Manager our demands, and also tell him what might happen if there is a refusal to negotiate. He needs to call the pre-arranged number if he wishes to meet and avoid our demonstration of strength." Turning on his heel he walked away, followed closely by the four men in jeans and T-shirts. As he disappeared through the gap between the ramshackle houses Ed heard mumbling, and then laughing and a fiercely-barked order.

The driver, complete with wrap-around dark glasses, reappeared a few seconds later and gestured to Ed that he should get back into the pickup. And then they were off up the hill.

Travelling back, his mind a jumble of confused thoughts, he kept hearing Helmet's threat, and seeing the boy with the pretend gun. It was this latter memory that stuck the most, not until that point had he felt his vulnerability. It reminded him that Greg must have visited there, maybe experienced exactly the same scene. And now he was probably buried in a shallow grave somewhere out in the jungle that surrounded the mine.

Shutting his eyes, he tried to dispel the claustrophobia of being caught between Chiri, Lucky Lomax and the union. He remembered the strange recording of Bismarck on the USB stick in Greg's strong box. What on earth had Bismarck been saying with such vociferation, and why had Greg faxed gobbledygook to a number in Accra? He made a mental note to check the fax number against the one on Bernie's business card.

But most of all he saw the massacre in the open pits. The waiting scout cars suggested an element of premeditation; they had been waiting, guns at the ready, keeping an eye on what was happening. That's why Chiri knew Ed and Allen had been on the hill overlooking the pit.

Chiri may have even killed Dave Smith himself, would have enjoyed doing it. Only Chiri had the means to order the militia to cover his tracks; the Exploration department and the Mine Militia stood shoulder to shoulder. He tried to think how Chiri could have known Dave had evidence of fraud at Rusty Lion. Perhaps Dave had tried to blackmail him, or maybe he had told Anna, his special seamstress, who had blurted it out to her friends. That would explain why Anna was nowhere to be found.

What part if any did Forge play? Here was a man with a seat that looked out over the entrance to the mine and saw all the comings and goings. He was friendly with the so-called Health and Safety Officer, Golf Club. Both of them were very close, thick as thieves, and no doubt exchanged information on a regular basis. Golf Club had been dispatched to the compound bar on the evening after Dave Smith's death to gather more information and report back to Forge. He had gone out of his way to talk with Allen when he saw him sitting with Ed in a quiet corner.

Did these two unholy goblins have a secret pact with Chiri? To keep him informed of what was being discussed and debated amongst the ex-pats who notionally had control of the mine? Or were they scared of Chiri? Perhaps that's how the relationship worked, through fear, and Dave Smith had paid the price, as a demonstration of Chiri's power.

Pressing his finger and thumb into his eyes, he realised that whichever way he looked he saw enemies; the whole place was a network of unspoken alliances that existed beneath the surface. And like bulldogs fighting under a carpet there was no way of knowing who was winning and who was losing.

The only one who swam above everything keeping his hands clean was James Allen. But how could a man in such a position possibly be clean? It was impossible. Returning to Miriam's warning that Allen was not as he seemed, he dismissed the idea that he was involved in the IRA. But nevertheless, there was quite a bit he'd like to know about James Allen, such as how come he was here in this mine?

Finally, there was James Allen's employer, Lucky Lomax, the man who stayed out of the fray, guarded in his mansion in Surrey, sailing the oceans in his yacht, and meddling in the internal affairs of foreign countries. It was all very well for him to declare that there should be no negotiations but he did not have to live with the consequences. Or was the no negotiation edict something that Jeremy had decided unilaterally?

Turning into the gates of the compound, the pickup stopped for Ed to get out before the driver reversed and sped away, enveloping the guards in a cloud of dust. After watching him go, Ed walked into the compound office, his mind a whorl of thoughts and half-digested ideas, and asked to make a phone call to the Mine Manager.

Two hours later he was once again standing in the beautiful hill-top garden looking out to the sea and its white-capped waves. He could feel the temperature up here was several degrees lower than down below. Picking up a scent of manure that he knew came off the flower beds, he remembered that he had ordered a load of horse manure and compost before he left Wales and he had forked it into the undernourished, thin earth that had been his grandfather's allotment. The sight and smell made him feel homesick.

Turning to the villa he noticed the Mine Manager was waiting for him on the doorstep, his hands behind his back bouncing up and down on the balls of his feet. He walked inside when Ed approached, leaving the door to the sitting room open so that it was obvious where the meeting was to take place.

On entering, Ed found the Mine Manager at the whisky decanter pouring two large measures into beautiful crystal glasses. He motioned to Ed to sit in a chair. "Well," he asked. "What news?" The Mine Manager's hand shook as he exchanged Ed's drink for Lucky Lomax's demands. Taking the sheet of paper to a clutterless desk that looked out across the lawn towards the sea, he asked, "Did Herman say anything else?"

"He said that unless you call the number saying that there would be negotiations then the union would flex its muscle."

The Mine Manager visibly deflated and shrank before

moving his hands up to rub bloodshot eyes. Taking the drink from the desk he moved across the room and collapsed down into one of the leather armchairs. "That's it then," he said. "We shall have to wait and see what happens." A thought occurred to him and he went to open a desk drawer. He looked down for a number of seconds, gazing intently, weighing, then he strode towards Ed, a revolver clutched in his right hand. Relieved that it was not pointed at him, Ed gazed up in some alarm at the Mine Manager's tired eyes.

"I hear you're a military man," said the Mine Manager, a thoughtful look on his face. "You'll know how to use this. It's loaded. A westerner won't last long in the local lock up and it could be a while before I can get you out. I'd only use it in extremis." He sat down again and lifted his whisky to his lips.

The gun sat comfortably in Ed's palm. He'd promised himself that he would never use one of these again, would never get himself into a situation where using one was a strong possibility. He put the gun in his lap and nodded his thanks. After all, it might be necessary.

"Jeremy told me something of your history. He said it took a little while to persuade you to take this job."

It was as much a question as a statement and an answer was expected. "I've just bought my grandfather's old farm."

"In the hills west of Oswestry?"

"That's right."

"Why did you decide to take this job?"

"Money mostly, and of course I knew Greg, and I felt I needed to know what had happened to him."

The Mine Manager nodded his head again. "So what have you found out?" he asked.

"I'm pretty certain he's dead, but that's all. I have no

evidence." He paused, unsure if he dared voice some of his half-digested thoughts.

"Tell me your hunches then."

Silence while Ed took a moment to compose himself. He sniffed his whisky before taking a sip. "There's so much that's unseen that it's difficult to be sure what's going on."

The Mine Manager smiled. "It seems like that a lot of the time."

Ed took another swig of his whisky before making his mind up. "Chiri has influence in this mine, way beyond his actual position. Would that be fair?"

The Mine Manager nodded his head.

"In fact, he's a law unto himself. He's out of control."

The Mine Manager stood and turned to look out of the window, his back to Ed, he rocked backwards and forwards on the balls of his feet again. "Anything else?" he asked.

There was little more to say. "Dave Smith was killed by him, I'm pretty sure. I think Greg was probably killed by him. I'm wondering if I'll be next. Particularly as he suspects I was witness to his massacre of the Galamsey."

He saw the Mine Manager stir and partially look around. "You're right. But I've been suspicious for a while that he may not be that autonomous."

It took a while for the meaning of his words to sink into Ed's tired and stressed mind. "I don't understand."

A sigh and a sip of whisky. "I'd have thought my meaning was clear. That Chiri's taking orders from somebody else. And it doesn't take much to imagine who. I'm a mining engineer, not a politician or a Mafioso. For two years I've been completely out of my depth, ever since Jeremy became the chief of Lomax's African operations."

Ed waited, wanting him to expand on this theme, but the Mine Manager merely shook his head sadly. "I've lived in Africa all my life. My father was in the colonial service, in charge of sanitation." He laughed to himself before looking away. "I've grown up in the culture and I love this country. I've tried hard to do the right thing. I've been accused of having too much of a paternalistic attitude by many of my colleagues. To tell you the truth I despise my own kind with their casual racism and their effortless superiority." He fell quiet, lost in his own thoughts, concentrating his gaze on a spot that was a metre above Ed's head.

"And?" asked Ed. "What's your point?"

The Mine Manager looked back, confused. He recovered himself with a shake. "My point is …" he said, "my point is that…there are very few people who have this country's best interests at heart. The last thing that's needed is the likes of Jeremy, and Chiri. And yet these are the men who are sponsored." His speech over, he subsided into his chair. "Why should I care? I'll be retired in few months and it'll be somebody else's problem."

Silence.

"What about James Allen, does he care?"

At the name, the Mine Manager stirred and then sniffed. "I grant you he's always occurred to me as decent. But he was employed by Lomax. I wanted somebody to make sure Kojo was protected and suddenly James Allen appeared. Of course I dug around."

What was it with this Mine Manager? He was frustratingly vague and shiftless. Ed could feel the anger rising. "And?" he said with more force than was necessary.

The Mine Manager jumped in his seat and looked around, startled. "And…he's worked in many other of

Lomax's operations. In fact, I heard that he left under a bit of cloud from his last job. There was a dispute with some rival gold exploration company. There was a fire and a few deaths. It was a Canadian company and the authorities over there are keen to question him. He's here under Lomax protection."

"You mean he's under suspicion of murder?"

"Something like that, yes. But as long as he stays here and protects Lomax interests, he's fine." The Mine Manager looked up suddenly. "Some are here to get rich, some are running away, and some are hiding. I'd also add that some are here because they have few alternatives. James Allen is definitely in the latter category, although I daresay part of him is wanting to get rich, and another part is running away." The Mine Manager took another swig of his whisky and then fixed him with a meaningful stare. "Which are you?"

"I don't understand what you mean," said Ed, shifting uncomfortably in his chair.

"I mean that you are the only person I've heard about who came to Africa expecting to find justice," he said echoing Bismarck's comment. "Forgive me, I don't believe it. I suspect that you're here for other reasons. Lomax generally has a hold over people whom he employs. He likes the stick and carrot approach, more stick than carrot."

The grey face and the tired blue eyes made Ed think of a dog waiting to be put out of its misery. "Well it looks like I'm unique. I've come to find out what happened to a friend and to help him if I can. I know that he's probably dead. I want to find out why so I can tell his widow."

THE LOCOMOTIVE

The next day Ed arrived in the office late. Forge glared at him and then shook his head before returning to sheets of figures laid out on his desk. Ed thought about asking after his health in an effort to demonstrate how more normal people behaved. But then again, why bother?
Sighing, he slumped down in his seat, pulling Greg's notebook towards him. So far, the day had failed to deliver on its early morning promise when Bismarck had sent a message to the compound to say that a seam of pure gold had been found in the Lomax Deeps and would he like to see it. The thought of a vein filled with pure gold no longer excited Ed, but on the hand it would be an excellent opportunity for Bismarck to introduce him to some of the other geologists who had worked with Greg.

But after an hour watching the night shift arrive and the morning shift leave, he was told that Bismarck was caught in a meeting and he should wait in Forge's office. Frustrated and hot he had returned to his pickup only to find Frank missing.

Forcing down the image of his chauffeur lying asleep on canvas sacks in the quartermaster's stores – it had taken a full hour to find him – he concentrated on the copious descriptions of drill core mineral assemblage in Greg's book. These had been cross referenced with chemical analyses and each section ended with a short interpretation. Ed was impressed with how meticulously the data had been gathered; it said a lot about Greg's methodical mind, but revealed next to nothing about why he might have disappeared.

A feeling of frustration rumbled up from his chest and he began to flick through the pages randomly. Strange, given the rigour with which Greg kept records of his observations of drill core that he left no mention of his other activities, such as secretly recording Bismarck declaiming angrily in his own tongue.

Rubbing his chin between forefinger and thumb, he didn't immediately notice Bismarck's face appear at the walkway window. It turned out that the meeting had been a complete waste of time and as a consequence Bismarck was in a bad mood. Rejecting any attempt at prolonged conversation he behaved as if taking Ed underground was very inconvenient.

When they arrived at the quartermaster's stores Cheek Scars received little more than a scowl and a curl of the lip. "We'll take the explosives cage," he said, heading out of the stores and towards the winding tower.

"Explosives?" asked Ed nervously.

"Ammonium Nitrate. But don't worry it needs a huge dose of energy to set it off. Perfectly safe."

The explosives cage turned out to be a tiny metal box where no more than four men could stand abreast. On the floor were ten large sacks laid one on top of the other. One of the middle sacks had a rip from which small white pellets leaked. Bismarck climbed aboard and squatted down, encouraging Ed to follow with a wave of his hand and the first beaming smile of the morning.

A tang of rust and diesel met Ed's nostrils as he joined Bismarck. He had been in explosives cages before, if never one so hot and cramped. A sense of foreboding gripped him, but he tried hard to force a smile. As he sat down on the sacks and crossed his legs, feeling his helmet scraping the ceiling, he offered up a small prayer for the safety of his soul. His younger self scoffed at his trepidation.

The cage door was thrown shut so that the only light came from tiny slits level with Ed's eyes. For a moment he watched curtains of dust drift in and out of the narrow beams of illumination. Then he looked out at the world beyond his tin coffin. He saw a sign, 'Welcome to Lomax 'A' shaft, depth 2.5km. Deepest gold mine in Ghana'.

He could hear a clamour of African voices and toe-capped boots clanging on metal as miners entered the main cage next to them. The voices were relaxed and cheerful, full of camaraderie. Ed wondered why Bismarck had chosen the explosives cage when the main cage was heading off at the same time. But before he had time to ask a claxon sounded; there was a clash and a bang and the boisterous, happy voices disappeared.

"Us next," murmured Bismarck. "Once we've delivered the explosives it'll be a one way trip to the Deeps. The main cage will be transferring a locomotive between levels for the next few hours."

With a jolt of complaining struts and wire hawser the explosives cage set off. Very soon the metallic clanking gave way to the roar of hot wind laden with the unmistakable smell of oil and diesel heading up from the depths of the shaft.

The cage picked up speed and the bright lights at each level whizzed faster. Then, just as they got started, Ed felt a sharp tug around his midriff as the elevator started to slow. It was the drop off for the first consignments of explosives.

The gate was thrown open and Bismarck jumped out, dragged two sacks and then signalled that he was ready to get to the next level. At the next drop off several minutes later they caught up with the main cage and its small consignment of men. They were involved in a tricky manoeuvre to get a large diesel locomotive onto the cage's lower deck. The upper deck still had ten men, all of whom were looking down at the locomotive with concerned eyes.

A number of miners milled around close to the shaft and watched as the engine driver crept the locomotive's front wheels towards the cage floor. There was much gesticulation from several people nearby and shouting from a man who looked to be in charge of the operation. Ed took the chance to look around and noticed that he was standing next to a mining engineer who was a head taller than anybody else. He had an impassive face, arms folded and a look of blank disinterest in his intensely-blue eyes.

The locomotive looked impossibly big for the cage, and even if it could fit on the lower deck. Ed wondered whether the hawsers that lifted and lowered the cage were strong enough. Sure enough, as the driver inched the front wheels onto the cage floor, the massive steel cables stretched under its huge weight. The nose of the locomotive started to tilt downwards and simultaneously the noise level amongst those present lifted dramatically. Frantic waving of arms was followed by pushing and shoving to get away from the danger area. The downward progression of the engine nose continued until the locomotive was tilted at forty-five degrees down the shaft, rocking precariously around a pivot. Then, as if a cork had been popped from a bottle, diesel exploded from the tank. A fountain of foaming liquid soaked the ten miners in the upper deck of the cage before hitting the ceiling and raining down across the crowd. Ed looked around, trying to find a position where he could take shelter and saw that the tall mining engineer, arms still folded, had moved a metre to his left. A few dark spots of teardrop diesel spotted his overalls, otherwise he was untouched.

Voices of complaint and admonition echoed around the brightly lit chamber. Many ran back up the drive into darkness, away from the flammable spout; Ed followed the mining engineer and managed to get to a position where he was out of the main line of fire. Gradually the diesel spout subsided as the wheel house at the surface pulled the cage floor back to the horizontal. Gallons must have been ejected across the drive, and Ed thought of the stack of explosives they were carrying. This was not a safe place to hang around.

He waved to Bismarck who nodded. They both jumped back into the explosives cage and signalled that they needed to be taken to the next destination. The cage shuddered and then started to move, gathering speed before shuddering again and stopping. Bismarck turned to Ed, his eyes glimmering with concern in the dim light from his head torch.

"Were just above the next level," he said. "Look."

Ed looked down and saw the bright strip lighting that was ever present at each level. Then, through the echoing shaft they heard the horrible noise of panicked men. A low moan grew into a crescendo where individual shouts and screams could be heard. Above the terrified voices there was the screeching of metal scraping together.

Looking up, he saw there were sparks and flames; the panicked shouts had become outright screams of terror that Ed knew would stay with him for as long as he lived. They were coming from the men who were stuck in the top deck of the cage, unable to move, soaked in diesel, and now.... Ed's mind could not deal with the dreadful thought.

Something truly awful had happened, and whatever had caused it might be heading their way. They waited, hanging free in the shaft listening to the shouts and screams of the terribly burned and dying, knowing that directly above them was a locomotive full of diesel fuel.

A jolt beneath their feet made Ed start with fear, but then the cage began to move again. To Ed's relief, it came to a shuddering halt at the nearest level. They jumped out and joined others at the shaft gate, craning their heads to find out what was happening.

The screaming was at an end now and there was an ominous silence. Men were turning to look at one another, the horror that was in Ed's mind reflected in their faces. After a further few seconds the fuel in the locomotive tanks ignited and the explosion rocked the ground on which they stood and echoed down the long drives that led away from the shaft. Everybody looked up again, this time in fear that the ceiling would collapse.

A sound of rending metal drew the assembled men's attention back to the main shaft. The blasted and flaming main cage had somehow detached itself and it was approaching them, slowly at first and then faster, until all were gifted the view of the locomotive, rent apart by the force of the explosion and wrapped in an inferno. The top deck of the cage passed, its walls wreathed in flames, masking the vague forms of the twisted limbs within. The rending metal of the falling cage changed note in a dreadful demonstration of the Doppler effect, and then it was gone, like a shooting star falling to earth.

A new sound of rending metal brought their attention to the failsafe system which had detached itself from the main cage and was falling, scraping the sides of the shaft. It hit the explosives' cage with an enormous clash. The explosives' cage swung wildly and its supporting metal hawsers creaked but then the heavy metal of the failsafe freed itself and began to follow the main cage down the shaft, its trailing cables whipping against the sides. It looked like the explosives' cage would survive, but at the last moment a stray piece of metal caught on its base causing the floor to peel away like the lid of a sardine tin. All the remaining sacks of explosives fell out and headed down the shaft after the flaming diesel engine and the cremated remains of the miners.

Ears straining to hear whether, by some miracle, the cage had stopped, Ed heard nothing but the rushing, diesel wind and his own panicked breath coming in short terrified bursts. After what seemed like an eternity, a bright, fast-spreading flame appeared far below, then a massive flash followed by an explosion of noise that echoed at ear drum bursting intensity. A huge fireball rose, driven by the strong up-draft.

Realising that if they didn't move quickly they would be engulfed in flame, Ed and many of the other miners retreated from the edge and he threw himself to the ground. Looking around, Ed saw that Bismarck was still gazing down the shaft. "What the hell are you doing?" he shouted, but Bismarck was transfixed, unable to register that he was in mortal danger and that nobody else had remained at the edge of the shaft.

Without thought of the consequences, Ed jumped to his feet and grabbed Bismarck by the back of his overalls and threw him to the floor. The demon fire swept past forcing air ahead of it and pushed Ed off his feet so he landed on top of Bismarck. The inferno lasted for a full five or ten seconds during which he sensed that his plastic hat was being partially melted, moulding itself to his head. It was like being doused by extremely hot candle wax. Then, just as the metal studs on his overalls burned hot against his skin, the fire was gone.

Slowly, he pushed himself up, felt the intense heat around his head and threw off his helmet. Overcome by curiosity, he crawled to the edge of the shaft and looked down into the depths where he saw nothing but darkness.

A new pain appeared, this time on his back, and there was the unmistakable smell of diesel fire. His overalls were alight and being fanned by the tremendous up-draft. He noticed that Bismarck's overalls were also on fire so he shouted, partly in pain and also to warn Bismarck of the danger. Bismarck started to roll backwards and forwards, and Ed followed his lead, careful not to go over into the shaft.

Running feet indicated their predicament had been noticed and soon they were both doused in water and some kind of foam substance. Panting on the floor, Ed felt a burning sensation give way to a dull ache. After several minutes, he was gently shoved and pulled and told to lie on the benches which were usually the preserve of miners waiting for the arrival of the cage at the end of the shift. In a haze of pain and exhaustion, he shut out the sound of the screaming voices and the vision of the twisted, flaming limbs that appeared to beckon to him as the cage sped past on its way down into the depths.

People were beginning to shout at Bismarck,

demanding something. Bismarck was pushing his glasses up his nose and speaking to them. It looked as if he was making a speech, issuing orders, making plans. Like a General commanding an army.

Or was that just Ed's imagination?

Ed was beginning to recover himself. The pain from the melted helmet and the singed clothing had been superficial and was at a level that was easily manageable. He would feel sore for a few days, but he had experienced worse in the army. He wanted to observe the scene, understand why the twenty or so miners on the level had all turned to one man.

But just as he sat up, the crowd dispersed and sprinted off up the drive. Bismarck walked over to where he lay. "Can you walk?" he asked.

Ed nodded. "I'm fine. I think I must have had a lungful of smoke or diesel fumes or something."

"We'll have to walk the mile or so to the smaller shaft at the north end. Hopefully the ceiling has not caved in anywhere. If we stay here there's a chance of a carbon monoxide build up."

The walk north through the dust that had been liberated by the shaking from the explosion was noxious. Holding a piece of cloth to his mouth, Ed occasionally saw miners heading towards them, their lights shining like stars in the night sky. Several times Bismarck barked orders to people who were walking in the wrong direction.

This place, which was normally a hive of activity, of shouting and blasting machinery, was eerily quiet. His nerves had felt smeared out so thin that at any point they might just evaporate, but the silence of the walk allowed him to gather his thoughts together about what had just happened. And all the time as he walked through the darkness and the silence, his mind kept thinking back to the conversation with Herman the Helmet. There, in the blazing hot daylight of an African morning, Helmet had declared that if no message had been received then there would be a show of strength. Was this the threatened blow to hit Lomax where it hurts? Surely they would not consign their own people to a bonfire in order to prove a point, would they? Unless it had all gone terribly wrong and had got out of hand.

Hours later, after he had managed to get onto an overcrowded cage to the surface, and then been taken home by Frank, he listened to the rhythmic hum of the air conditioner in his room. He could hear no other noise, nothing came through the small windows of his room, and there was no sound in the corridor outside. It was as if the place was dead.

There had been scenes of panic at Lomax 'B' shaft when the cage had arrived at their level. Yet again, Bismarck had talked the panicking men into calmness. He had marshalled their energy by asking them to go and help their brothers. Like the captain of a sinking ship, Bismarck was one of the last men to emerge onto the surface. He had been transformed from a geologist who sat in his office, fussing with his glasses, polishing them and pushing them up his nose, into a man who acted and sounded like the one on the recording in Greg's strong box.

Step forward the real Bismarck.

It was not hard to determine why Bismarck chose to cultivate the persona of a meek and mild academic. He was a survivor, and to survive in a world that contained Chiri he needed to dissemble his real nature.

Such were Ed's thoughts in the hours after he arrived back from the mine, as he drifted in and out of a restless sleep. Time was meaningless, and so was work. He needed to hide in his room until such time as he could build the courage to re-emerge into a world he had come to fear. Under his pillow he felt the reassuring hardness of the Mine Manager's gun. From now on he would keep the weapon close.

A knock on his door made his heart beat faster. The noise was soft, but had come out of complete silence. He decided to ignore it and listened intently for any indication that whoever was outside was making more radical plans for entry. He reached under his pillow and checked the gun magazine to ensure there was a full load.

The knocking came again, and this time it was accompanied by a female voice. "It's me, Bernie. I know you're in there."

He fell back into the pillows and cursed; his brain was too exhausted with sights and sounds to cope with the subtle innuendo of a journalist's questions. "Okay," he said, rising from the bed.

Pocketing the gun, he walked to the door and looked through the spyhole. She was on her own, the knowing smile fixed firmly on her face, so he opened the door and then looked up and down the corridor before moving out of the way to allow her to enter.

"Wow," she said. "I don't usually make it my business to enter strange men's rooms. Not after just one meeting." She smiled coquettishly and then sat in the soft upholstery chair that was in the corner of the room. "I'm afraid you'll have to supply the drinks this time, Forge has managed to consume the entire content of my flask. You gotta sup with the devil if you want the real story."

Ed walked to his cupboard and reached inside; there was barely a third of his bottle left. He poured out two stiff measures and handed one across to Bernie. "You wouldn't be trying to get me drunk would you?" she asked.

He returned to his bed and lay down. "What did Forge say?"

Bernie took a swig and then placed her glass down on a nearby chest of drawers. "Word is that it was no accident. Word is that you came back the other day with dire warnings that the union was planning retribution. That they'd joined forces with the Galamsey and were planning to attack the mine."

Ed felt his heart sink. "It was an accident, pure and simple. If Forge ever went underground he'd be able to tell you what it's like."

"You tell me what it's like then," she said. "Women aren't allowed underground so I don't have the opportunity to observe for myself."

The vision of the mine Health and Safety officer and his golf club came to mind and he shook his head, he didn't want to trivialise the events he had witnessed. "It was a terrible accident, caused by a cavalier attitude towards equipment and flammable liquid." He described events as he had witnessed them, the transfer of the massive diesel locomotive, the spray of liquid, the explosion and the plunge of the cage followed by the deadly consignment of explosives. "It was an accident waiting to happen."

Bernie took hold of her drink and swirled around the dregs in her glass. "They've arrested the driver of the train and everybody who was on the level assisting."

"Who have?"

"The mine militia. They're waiting for the official police to arrive from Accra. Many of the men are known to be union sympathisers, or actual card-carrying members."

Ed snorted. "I'd be a member of a union if I could." He reached instinctively to his neck and felt for the reassuring touch of Uncle Eddy's pendent. "Unions are a good thing when mines are run by the likes of Lomax and his cronies. The union didn't cause the accident, it was Lomax and his henchmen. Have you managed to speak to the Mine Manager?" he asked.

Bernie shook her head. "He's been relieved of his duties and shipped off to Accra. Jeremy's taken overall charge with the Chief Engineer running the mine day-to-day."

Ed sat up. "Jeremy's in charge? You mean he's going to take up residence at the hill-top hacienda?"

"Not likely. He'll be dropping in from time to time by helicopter."

Ed put his head in his hands. "Bad to worse," he said to himself.

"Why are you still here, Ed? I thought you mid-life crisis boys were only here for the fun."

Ed stood up and crossed to the remnants of the whisky bottle "I'm trapped," he said eventually and poured some liquid into his own glass and the rest into Bernie's. "Chiri'll get me going, and then Lomax and Jeremy'll have me coming."

Bernie looked at him carefully. "My journalist nose is twitching. I feel the story."

Ed walked back to his bed and sat down again. He suddenly thought that maybe he should not reveal all just yet. His survival instinct, long dormant from lack of use, was beginning to kick in. He needed to keep this woman on his side by providing her with information, but not about himself.

"I've been investigating Greg's disappearance," he announced. "I've emptied his desk and discovered a few useful bits." He rose from the bed again and rummaged in a cupboard until he found Greg's strong box. "I found a series of sheets with encoded writing in here." He paused and wondered whether he should also mention the recording of Bismarck. But then he decided he owed Bismarck some loyalty, whatever he was saying on that recording might get him into trouble.

On the other hand, Dave Smith's drilling data was interesting. He would be breaking all sorts of taboos if he showed this to a journalist before anybody senior in the mine. If Chiri became aware that Ed was in possession of such data then his life would not be worth an ounce of gold. "I also searched Dave's desk and found a memory stick with data which I think he must have pinched from somewhere."

Bernie looked at him over her glass. "Interesting," she said.

He spun the lock on the top of the box and opened the lid. "I have no idea what the encoded message means. I know that he faxed the papers to a number in Accra, to your number, in fact."

Bernie smiled. "Yes, he sent me a very strange message a couple of days before he died. Did you look at my card? Faxes are much less likely to get intercepted than an email or text. It doesn't hang around on servers."

He removed the folded sheets from inside the box. "You must know what it all says then," he said.

But Bernie shook her head. "Not a chance. He forgot, accidentally on purpose, to leave a reference to the cipher. I have no way of finding out what it says."

"Seems a bit cloak and dagger for Greg."

"It wasn't him who suggested encoding, it was me."

"And what sort of things was he communicating?" he asked.

Bernie shrugged her shoulders. "This was the first and last attempt to send a message."

"And?"

She shook her head and took a sip of her whisky. "No use asking me, I haven't a clue."

"But surely…"

"Look, I'm as frustrated as you about it but until I have the cipher, there's nothing I can do."

Ed rubbed his hair. "What might this cipher look like? Perhaps I could search around for it."

"My original instruction was to use a section from a book. But he failed to tell me which book and which section he was using."

Ed continued stroking his hair, but then a thought occurred to him. He looked up, barely able to believe what she had just said. "Like a Gideon bible?"

"That's right. I gave him a copy in case he wanted to send anything to me, and I gave him instructions on how to use it."

"I have the copy. It was in his desk drawers."

Bernie shook her head. "No good. I'd have to know the exact section; chapter and verse."

"But this bible is marked," he said. "It has certain chunks outlined in pen or pencil."

"I outlined a section for him," she said, "but he didn't use it to encipher."

Ed was on his feet and marching to the cupboard. He found the two bibles and handed them across. "Strange you should also give Dave a book," he said.

"I know. He was such spare part, but he kept coming to me with scurrilous stories so I thought it best to give him a bible as well."

"What sort of stories?"

"Oh, the usual tittle tattle about who was stabbing

who in the back. Very little of any substance, but useful background. He managed to get Forge's password. Don't ask me how he did it."

"And?"

She smiled. "Name of trilobite followed by a 01." With this comment, she buried her head into the bibles and began flicking the pages. It didn't take long for her to let out an exclamation. "I only outlined quotes from Matthew, but there's one here from Romans. This must be it, the cipher, unless of course he used this quote for something different."

"Such as?"

"Another message?"

"How long till you decipher it?"

She shrugged. "Should have the substance by tomorrow."

Tucking the message and the bibles away in her bag she turned to him. "And what was this about Dave Smith? More tittle tattle?" She'd leaned towards him, like he was something fascinating. The attention made him feel edgy.

"He had some data on a pen stick. Looks like somebody's been modifying exploration data."

"And you say Dave discovered this?"

Ed nodded. "Seems incredible to me as well. Perhaps he had hidden depths."

"And why," she asked, now with her chin perched on top of her up-turned hand, "why would the mine wish to fiddle their data?"

Ed hesitated. It sounded amazing, even to him. "I'm not sure it's the mine per se. I think it could be somebody in the mine. My guess is Paul Forge, but James Allen says I'm mistaken."

Bernie weighed what he said. "And who does our Irish

man of mystery believe did it?"

"He's convinced it's Chiri."

Silence.

"Why would Chiri fiddle?"

"James reckons he has a profit share with the company who's been benefiting."

Bernie finished her whisky and made to stand up. "Thanks for the tip. When I get back I'll investigate. Anything else you wish to confess?"

Ed made to open his mouth. There were huge amounts more he wanted to tell. But that would wait. He felt invigorated, like he was beginning to make progress. Bernie would have to report back to him about what Greg had put in his fax before he gave anything more.

DEATH-BED CONFESSION

At breakfast the next morning there was no sign of Bernie. Moreover, reception denied that any woman had officially stayed the previous night. Mystified, Ed made his way to the front of the compound and found Frank waiting, engine running and music blasting from the stereo. "Just us this morning?" Ed asked casually as he climbed into the passenger seat. There was a nod of the head before the engine was gunned and the pickup reversed in a cloud of dust and exhaust fumes. They zoomed out of the gate, past guards who looked alert and nervous.

They journeyed to work via the Lomax 'A' shaft gates which were deserted except for lads with Kalashnikovs. Most of the miners, and particularly those that went to work at the shaft, had been laid off until further notice. They flew past the winding house and along the road that skirted the deserted nine-hole golf course and then screeched to a halt in the Geological Services' car park.

Ed stepped out onto the immaculate tarmac and once again looked at the long set of steps that led up to the offices. No doubt Forge was already in his office, slugging back his coffee and looking through his figures, sucking any joy from the atmosphere. He trudged up the steps, each tread feeling heavier than the last. Where had Bernie stayed and why had she not been in touch?

Tramp, tramp, tramp.

The sweat was beginning to roll down his back already. He would be trapped in the office all day with Forge; he almost stopped and turned back, but where would he go? He couldn't hide in his room forever. Eventually, he made it to the top of the steps and along the walkway to Forge's office window.

He had expected to see the object of his loathing sitting at his desk, face illuminated by the light from his computer screen, coffee cup in hand, surrounded by gleaming trilobites. But instead, the room was completely empty. The computer hadn't even been turned on. When he entered the room, the atmosphere was cold because the air conditioning in this office was never switched off, or turned down.

"Paul?" he called, expecting a voice from beneath his desk. Silence. He crossed the room, boots squeaking on the floor boards. Forge's desk was exactly as it had been; crammed with trilobites. There was nothing unusual.

He walked up to the book shelves and selected a volume labelled Lomax 'A', the Deeps 1. He plucked it from the shelf then walked back to his seat before leafing through. He kept glancing up, expecting to see Forge's face appear at the window, puce with outrage. Was he at a meeting? It was so unusual to find him absent at this time of the day.

Footsteps on the walkway made him look up, but it was a bunch of geologists on their way to offices further along. The noise of their boots changed note as they passed reminding him of the Doppler shift he'd experienced yesterday as the cage plunged past the level on which he stood. His stomach gave a great jolt as he remembered the screams of the dying and the smell of diesel with the undertone of scorched flesh. Another pair of boots came tramping along the walkway, but this time there was no change of note because the owner, whoever it was, had stopped.

The door opened to reveal James Allen. He beckoned to Ed, who immediately stood and walked out of the office. "How're you doing?" he asked.

"A bit sore in the back and the head," Ed replied. "But it's minor. At least I'm still alive."

"What happened? I hear there was a fire and an engine exploded or something."

"Load of fuel sprayed out of a diesel engine then caught light."

"Diesel sprayed?"

For the next few minutes Ed explained what had happened. The manoeuvre with the engine on the cage brought a shake of the head, and then the explosion and subsequent dive of the cage down to the depths brought a sucking of breath.

"Don't suppose you saw old Golf Club?"

Ed shook his head. "Why?"

"There's a rumour that he died as well. His body was found with his head staved in. Looks like somebody got to him with his own nine iron."

"What?"

"That's right. Couldn't have happened to a nicer fella."

Ed looked back into the office. "Forge isn't here, not to be wondered at."

Was this the show of force by the union? The explosion in the shaft and the death of the ten men was clearly an accident, but Golf Club being beaten to death with his own club was more the sort of thing that would have pleased the miners and sent a strong message to the management. They entered the office and Allen made himself at home in Forge's chair. "You've been out of circulation. I thought of calling in last night and asking how you were."

"I've been a bit shattered to be honest," replied Ed. "It took such a long time to emerge from the reserve shaft."

A nod and a wink. "I hear Bernice came 'round and stayed for an hour or more."

"She was trying to sniff out a story," said Ed, rolling his eyes at Allen's innuendo. "She wanted to know what had happened in the shaft."

There was something in the way that Allen looked at him which made Ed jumpy. "I didn't tell her anything about seeing the massacre, or about Dave being murdered."

"So what did you discuss then?"

"We had a chat about how things were going, and that's it."

"So what did you talk about for all that time? You were with her for an hour. That's a lot of small talk."

"I gave her the sheet of paper with the drilling data."

Allen's face drained slightly. "You what?" he said very quietly. His voice was calm, but Ed could tell that he was near to shouting. "Have you a death wish? I told you that was not healthy information."

"She said she'd treat it in confidence."

A blank, disbelieving look this time. "She's a journalist. She deals in information. It'll get out."

"So?"

"So, it's only a small number of people with access to

that sort of data." He hid his face in his hands. "You really shouldn't have done that."

Ed stuck out his chin defiantly. "I trust her," he said.

An eye poked out between Allen's fingers. His hands slipped up his forehead and combed through his hair. "You trust her?" he said.

"As much as I trust anybody."

A sigh, then Allen sat back in Forge's chair and twiddled his fingers. "I understand you and Greg's wife were more than friends at one time? Greg was very free with information when he'd had a few beers at the compound bar. You were the other man in the relationship according to him. The one Alice always wished she'd married."

Ed kept a blank face. He wondered how long Allen had known and why he was bringing this up now? Presumably Bismarck had told him, thought Ed. Despite himself, he was curious about what else Greg had confided about his relationship with Alice.

"Greg was deeply upset. He said he'd lost a friend and gained a loveless marriage, which was presumably why he was always disappearing off to Accra and Bernice's."

Ed gaped. "Greg was having an affair with Bernie?"

"And I bet he told her a lot of things," said Allen nodding. "I'm sure Bernie can be very persuasive. My point is, she's dangerous cargo and when Greg disappeared…" A pair of boots thumped along the walkway outside and Allen broke off what he was about to say and looked around as the door burst open. It was Kojo, breathing hard.

"Forge is down at the hospital. He's been attacked."

They made their way down together, Kojo in a state of considerable excitement. "He's asking for John Stone," he said over and over, as if in disbelief.

"John Stone?" asked Ed through the side of his mouth.

"Golf Club," said Allen.

When they reached the hospital, Allen took Kojo aside and told him to calm down. "Go back to your office. Call your wife. Get Bismarck. We'll go in and see what we can do. He's probably still unconscious so there's no need for you to be there." Kojo nodded his head and walked briskly away, glad to be relieved of at least one responsibility. Allen watched him disappear back up the road. "His wife and Bismarck are siblings," he said as if in explanation. "Very close family."

They headed into the gloomy interior of the hospital and were directed to the room Ed had inhabited until only a few days ago. He'd hoped never again to see its green walls, or hear the strange gurgle of the air conditioner. This time, however, the knowledge that he could leave when he wished made the fixtures in the room far less claustrophobic.

Forge was lying on his back, his features masked by swathes of mosquito net. Despite the gloominess it was clear that both Forge's eyes were bruised shut and his arms and legs were splinted. Bandages around his head and body were red and blood dripped from the bed like prime steak in a butcher's shop.

Nausea rose in Ed's throat at the sight and then he heard a voice out of the shadows that made him jump with fright; it with a peculiarly nasal London accent asking Forge to wake up. Looking around, Ed wondered how Golf Club had managed to return from the dead, but very quickly he realised that it was Allen.

A grunt from the bed indicated that Forge was conscious.

"Wot 'appened me ol' son," said Allen.

A burst of coughing, and then a gurgle, indicated that Forge was getting ready to speak. "I swear I never mentioned your name."

"Good lad," replied Allen without pausing.

Another outburst of coughing and Forge's breathing became noisy and erratic, as if he was trying to imitate the room's dying air conditioner. "Should I get the nurse?" Allen asked. A vigorous shake of the head, and then more coughing.

"It's like we thought. They've been suspicious ever since Dave tried to sell information to Chiri."

The cogs in Allen's mind seemed to whirr, trying to frame a question that would not be suspicious. "Oh?" he asked, putting the slightest intonation on the end, trying to invite confidence.

But Forge was not going to explain what he meant. "Take the keys," he said.

For a moment, Allen was at a loss. "The keys?"

An arm lifted from the bed, but then dropped back to the covers. A grunt of pain emanated from somewhere in the mosquito net. Ed realised Forge was trying to point somewhere. There was a bunch of keys, a handkerchief and a wallet on Forge's bedside table. Forge began to cough again; Ed took the opportunity to move closer to Allen. "Table," Ed whispered urgently, pointing.

The sound of keys clinking alerted Forge that his instruction had been understood. "Main filing cabinet with my will."

"What's that then?" asked Allen

Something akin to annoyance escaped from Forge. It was a hoarse cough and a spit. "Don't pretend you can't remember. You promised."

"Don't worry. You know me, a promise is a promise."

Beneath the mosquito net shroud there was an

exhalation of breath, like a long sigh of pleasure and relief. "Good lad. Take care o' yourself. Dave didn't talk, and neither did I. You and the others got time."

"Oo did this?" asked Allen.

No response.

"Don't go to sleep on me now." Allen raised his hand, as if to push the sleeping figure. There were so many questions needing to be asked. Forge's breathing was shallow and regular; it was as if he had suddenly fallen asleep. "Forge?" asked Allen. A rattley breath came from the bed, and then silence. "I'll get the doctor."

They both charged into the corridor. No nurses and doctors. "Outside," said Allen in a hushed whisper. They ran down the echoing passage until they reached a room where nurses sat drinking their mid-morning cup. Ed began to slow down, but Allen pushed him past and out through the doors into strong sunlight. "The nurses…" Ed began.

"He knows," said Allen. "I asked the wrong question. He knows it wasn't Golf Club. We send in a nurse he can get a message to whoever else. We need to get into his flat. Find that will."

Forge lived in a villa along the mine road, close to where it took off up the hill towards the Mine Manager's. This was where Allen headed at a brisk walk, all the time looking through Forge's set of keys, picking each one and then letting it go. "One to get in through the front door and one to get into his flat. There'll be a porter on the door. We can blag our way in."

After a few minutes' brisk walk, both of them were dripping in sweat so that when they arrived at the villa they looked wild and disarranged. Allen glanced at Ed then started to flatten his own hair. He used a handkerchief to mop his brow, and then handed it across to Ed and suggested he do the same. "Cool as you like," he said.

Through the glass door of the villa they spotted a man in green uniform sitting at a desk. He was on his mobile phone talking animatedly. It occurred to Ed to wonder if Forge had already sent a message out. He reminded himself that Forge was dying in a hospital bed and unlikely to be able to clearly express a wish, even if a doctor was available to hear.

Allen knocked on the door and gestured for it to be opened. The man stood and made his way across, no suspicion on his face. The door swung open and Allen barged through.

The inside of the villa was an exact replica of the Chief Engineer's. A dark corridor led to a shiny and bright room, wood panelling was everywhere, and the atmosphere was cold and dry as a bone. To the side was a wide, wooden staircase with pictures on the wall and African stools on the floor. "Forge needs a few things," said Allen. He stopped and licked his lips. "Did you hear about Golf Club?"

The man nodded his head. "I'll need some piece of paper saying you have permission."

"Forge just gave us permission," Allen shot back.

"Mr Chiri's given me strict instructions. Nobody's to enter Golf Club's or Mr Forge's." He stuck his chin out and closed his eyes. "I'm to inform him immediately."

Allen turned on his heel and ran up the creaking staircase. The porter's eyes flew open in surprise and he looked as if he was going to set off in pursuit until Ed barged him away and followed Allen himself. On the second floor he found Allen fiddling with keys. "You find the right key," he said handing over the bunch. "I'll pick Golf Club's lock. Find Forge's will and whatever it is that he wants to give to Golf Club. Mr Chiri'll be here soon. Better be out quick."

There were many keys, and all of them looked similar so it took some time to eventually determine which fitted the lock. Then he pushed open the door and gazed inside at a dimly-lit small rectangular room with ensuite facilities. It was warm and fetid, and the curtains were closed so that only the bare shape of the room was visible. A sour smell reached his nostrils, like sweaty feet in festering socks; it reminded him of Dave's room.

There was no easily accessible light switch at the door so he took a tentative step into the gloomy interior and found that his feet started to slip beneath him. Steadying himself against the wall he tested the floor with the sole of his boot. Finding a sticky, glutinous fluid that spread an unknown distance he took another step and crunched rock underfoot. Was it rock? Or was it glass? Standing still he fought the urge to run from the room. Then he reminded himself that he needed to get to Forge's filing cabinet and that he needed light.

Taking a deep breath, he crunched into the room, senses heightened so that each step sounded like a gunshot. On reaching the window he threw open the curtains and turned quickly. The glutinous patch near the door was a pool of blood that spread into the centre of the room. There were many bloody footprints, all of them made by boots of standard mine issue.

Fossil trilobites lay in pieces on the floor, their compound eyes winking at him through thousands of tiny hexagonal crystals as if they were watching his every move. The only place free of blood and rock debris was a small, single bed wedged in a corner

Opposite, guarding the door that opened into a bathroom, was a filing cabinet, standard grey and chest high. He marched across to it, trying not to think of the value of the specimens he was crunching underfoot. Presuming that the correct key for the filing cabinet was small he started flicking through the large bunch until he had isolated a few that looked likely. He wondered why the porter was not at his elbow pushing him out of the room; presumably too busy talking with Mr Chiri on the phone. He ignored his anxiety and checked through the large wedge of keys to make sure he hadn't missed any. Why the hell did Forge carry so many keys?

The choice was now narrowed down to three, which he tried each in turn. The third one went home and he heard the satisfactory click which meant the cabinet was now open. The top drawer glided towards him and he stared in disbelief; it was full of trilobites; the man was obsessed.

Flinging open a second drawer he was rewarded with a series of neatly labelled folders sticking out of the racking. Picking up one labelled 'Will', he opened it and found a piece of paper and a trilobite about the same size as his fist. Slamming the door shut, he turned and surveyed the room. Forge had been beaten to a pulp and no doubt had been forced to watch as Chiri and his acolytes had systematically smashed the bulk of his fossil collection to pieces. Ed's geologist mind was appalled.

The pieces were mostly grey or black, except for one patch by the bed which had a rusty red hue. Deciding that he didn't care, he rushed across to the door and looked up and down the corridor. The loud banging from Golf Club's room indicated that Allen was not being very discrete. No sign of Chiri yet, so he re-entered Forge's room and made his way carefully across to the bed, mindful that he was leaving his own footprints in the blood to join those of Forge's assailants.

As expected, he found that the small rusty red fossil was the one he had given to Greg all those years ago; Taid's trilobite. What was it doing here? The last time he had seen it was in Bismarck's room.

Like all the others on the floor it had been broken apart. When he picked it up by the thoracic section the head hung down, swinging freely on a thin wire. He gazed, unable to comprehend what this meant. Then he stuffed the specimen in his pocket and walked out, carefully shutting and locking the door. Entering Golf Club's room, he found books and papers flung across the room, ornaments smashed and clothes covering the floor.

"What the hell are you doing?" he asked.

"Like this when I arrived," said Allen. "Somebody's been here looking for something, probably Chiri. He pointed to blood stains on the rug by the bed. "I bet they brought Forge in here. What's his room like?"

"A bloody, trilobite graveyard."

"Whatever they wanted was in here as well. Forge must've been lying when he said he never mentioned Golf Club's name." He stopped rooting around in the chaos and was frozen to the spot. "Which begs the question, who betrayed him? And what was there to betray?"

"What d'you mean?"

"Why has Chiri gone to the trouble of nearly killing Forge and actually killing Golf Club?"

"There's no evidence that Chiri killed Golf Club. I'd have said it was more likely to have been the miners' union."

"Nevertheless," said Allen. "Chiri's favourite in my mind. What did you find in Forge's?"

"A will and a trilobite," he said bringing out both so Allen could see. They stared at one another in confusion.

"Trilobites and keys are what Forge does best," Allen mused. He looked around the room. "Wish I knew what Chiri was after, and whether he found it."

He was struck with an idea and strode to the far end of the room where he picked up a bin full of beer mats. A smile and a wink. "We need a smoke screen."

He marched to the door and then out of the room and down the corridor. "There's nothing more we can do here. We'll find out some more when Chiri catches up with us. I'd rather that was somewhere else."

On the way out, Allen dead-eyed the porter who had charged around from behind his desk. "Tell Mr Chiri we couldn't find what Forge wanted."

"What have you got?"

"Some old beer mats. I thought they would look good in my house. Golf Club was always offering to swap me some. I got some rare Guinness ones he liked."

They marched out into the steaming sunshine before the porter could try and prevent them. "We'll head back to Forge's office," said Allen. "Good to be around witnesses."

It took ten minutes to reach the office, by which time both men were pouring with sweat again. They climbed the stairs in silence and entered the habitual coolness of Forge's office. After a while Allen rose and went next door to have a word with Bismarck but returned saying that he was absent. "Apparently he hasn't been in work since the accident in the underground."

Not surprising, thought Ed. Bismarck had a wife and family and no doubt needed to stay with them for recuperation. The thought made Ed feel very lonely. There would be nobody to mourn for him if he had died, or give him comfort from an unforgiving world.

The coolness of the room was starting to make his

thoughts less febrile and panicked. He picked up Forge's folder and took out the will and the trilobite, Allen appeared at his shoulder. "Where does he want his money to go? A home for destitute fossils?"

Ed handed the will across to him then he turned the trilobite over in his fingers before placing it in the palm of his hand. There was nothing extraordinary about it, beyond the amazing compound eyes which protruded in three dimensions from the head carapace. 'Dave had not talked, and neither had Forge,' despite Chiri's beatings, and destruction of the beloved trilobite collection. "Will he live d'you think?" he asked Allen

Silence, then a shake of the head. "Unless they can get him to a proper hospital, I would have thought his chances weren't good. Did you notice the blood on his bandages and the bed spread?" He stood up and passed the paper back to Ed. "This looks all very legitimate to me. He's left the bulk of his money to his sister and her family. There's nothing suspicious here, except for the last statement where he left a trilobite specimen to Golf Club." He held out his hand for the fossil.

For some reason, Ed found difficulty handing the trilobite across. He hesitated, looked at Allen's outstretched hand, and then very reluctantly gave him the fossil. He was surprised at his own reaction; Forge's fossil had very little intrinsic value. On the other hand, it had a very significant meaning for Forge and Golf Club.

To distract him from grabbing the fossil off Allen forthwith, he fished in his pocket and produced Taid's trilobite. The wire that attached the two parts together hadn't snapped in his pocket. He noticed that it fitted into a tiny metal cylinder embedded in the base of the specimen. Taking it to the window he picked up a hand lens from Forge's desk on the way. On closer examination he could see that a hole had been gouged from the rock to house the device, and then been filled with a cement of exactly the same colour.

"What's that?" came a voice from the other side of the room. Allen had finished playing with Forge's trilobite and had placed it on the desk.

"Have a look," said Ed.

Allen took the hand lens and peered closely. "What d'you think?"

"Bugging device?"

A nod. "The question is, whose bugging device?"

The thought had occurred to Ed. "Greg leant this fossil to Forge, and then to Bismarck. I saw it on Bismarck's shelves the other day, but Forge must have retrieved it for some reason, and then taken it back to his room."

"So Greg was spying on Forge and Bismarck?"

A shrug, "Could have been."

But there was no doubt in Ed's mind. The recording of Bismarck declaiming angrily in his native tongue was sufficient evidence. There might be other conversations involving Forge and Golf Club somewhere, perhaps there was one which would shed some light on the significance of the trilobite in Forge's will. And for what purpose had Greg been recording these conversations? He rubbed his brow in a sign that the situation might be getting to him. "I wonder where Chiri has got to. I would have expected him to arrive by now."

Allen opened the door. "I'll go and check on Kojo. See how he's getting on."

As Allen stepped out of the office, Ed darted to the trilobite specimen and threw it into an inner pocket of his bag. Greg's metal box back in his room suggested itself as a better storage area, or should he dig a hole? But what if he needed it in a hurry?

Forge's fossil gave him some control; it was a bargaining chip. And if he was to get out of this in one piece he would have to have something with which he could negotiate. Sitting down, he waited for Allen to return. He fretted about why Chiri had suddenly decided to go on the war path. Then he remembered Bernie and her promise to decode Greg's fax. If she hadn't stayed at the compound last night, where had she stayed?

A sudden knock on the door shook him from his reverie. It was Frank, his driver. "Mr Kojo and Mr Allen have gone to the Exploration Offices on an urgent errand. I'm to take you back to the compound when you are ready." He hovered at the door, rocking slightly. It was clear that Frank expected Ed to be ready to leave straightaway, nothing else would have forced him to make such a long and erudite speech.

"Okay," Ed said, picking up his bag with the trilobite. Perhaps Bernie would be waiting back at the compound, deciphered fax in hand, the reason for Greg's death obvious for everybody to see.

MORE TRILOBITES

Back in his room at the compound, Ed sat on his bed and licked his lips. He needed a drink again. For a second he thought of going to the bar, but instead he lay down on the bed, closed his eyes and thought about what Allen had said about Greg and Bernie having an affair. He was not shocked by the revelation, after all Bernie was hardly forbidden fruit. Come to that, neither was Alice.

He took out the trilobite and turned it around in his hand, the eyes of the long-dead animal followed him. What sights had those eyes seen when the animal had swum or crawled in the early Cambrian seas? The light passing through its crystalline eyes would have revealed a world that was completely different, one in which there was a single-minded determination to cling on to life at whatever cost. There would have been no humans to weave a web of deceit and cunning.

Nothing for it, he needed a drink, if only to wash away the bad taste in his mouth. He marched to the door and walked down to the end of the corridor where he could see quite a few revellers through the glass doors that led to the outside. Stepping out into the warm night he instinctively turned his head to make sure nobody lurked close by. A deeper shade behind the building shrank back with a hissing that made Ed step away, thinking of snakes. The shape moved forward and the hissing sound came louder before a sudden burst of laughter from the crowd in the bar caused the figure to shrink back again before reappearing, beckoning insistently.

Holding his ground, Ed refused to be tempted to follow the shadow into the night beyond where the lights from the bar penetrated. There was an exasperated sigh and a woman dressed in black and yellow with a large bag slung over her shoulder moved into the dim light. Her eyes were nearly shut from bruising and her nose was out of centre. "I have a present," she lisped through swollen lips and broken teeth. "For David's wife and child."

For several moments Ed was mystified. Then the truth stole up on him that this was Clarissa, Anna's sister. She shrank back when she noticed Ed's look of disgust at her appearance. "He gave it to Anna and he said it was valuable. I will give it to you for 200 US dollars," she said from the shadows.

"Oh?" asked Ed, recovering himself. "What gives you the impression I have that sort of money?"

"All you Obruni's are loaded."

"I'd have to see it first," he said.

She nodded, dipped her hand into a shoulder bag and produced a small, dark object that Ed found difficult to recognise in the gloom. He tried to move closer, to make out exactly what it was, but she shrank back again. A pickup arrived in the car park, its lights on full beam, she fell further back into the darkness behind the accommodation block. But Ed had seen that she was holding a trilobite, its polished thoracic sections had gleamed in the light of the headlamps.

The lights dimmed, the door slammed shut and there was silence again. "Are you still there?" he called into the darkness.

"Yes." Her voice was trembling and tiny.

"Dave gave this to Anna?"

"Yes."

"Why?"

Silence for the gloom. Then, "He wanted her to keep it safe. He said it was worth a lot of money."

"And you want to sell it?" he said, fighting to keep his voice calm.

"Two hundred dollars," she repeated.

There were two one hundred dollar notes in the folder that his agent, John Williams, had given him. He wondered if she had been into his room already and seen it, or maybe one of the staff who cleaned had investigated more thoroughly than was strictly necessary. "Wait there. I'll be back in a few minutes."

Returning several seconds later he whispered into the darkness. "Got it." A hand stretched out and made a grab for the money but Ed held on tightly. "Where's the goods?"

"Tcha," from the shadows and another hand appeared, this one clutching the trilobite. Stretching out he took the trilobite, simultaneously letting go of the money. A sigh of relief came from the shadows and a rustle of hemp as the money was deposited in the bag.

"Who beat you up?" asked Ed.

Silence.

"I'm going home to Nigeria." A whisper of cloth, and the shadow was gone.

For a moment Ed stared at the spot where the form of Clarissa had stood and then a loud and raucous cheer came from the bar. One of the Manchester Navvies had fallen over in a drunken stupor and was rolling around trying to get to his feet while his friends laughed.

Back in his room he got both the trilobites out and placed them side by side on the top of the bed. They looked up at him, black and shiny in the small light from the bedside lamp. Both were virtually identical, except Dave's was slightly curled.

"Now why did Dave give you away?" he murmured.

Forge had been beaten to within an inch of his life and not said a thing about his trilobite to the attackers. To Ed this suggested that it had a worth way beyond its intrinsic value. On the base of each specimen there were serial numbers painted. Taking out a hand lens he gave each of the trilobites a careful examination but found no evidence of wires or other blemishes that might indicate that they had been modified in some way.

Replacing them on the bed, he sat down and put his head in his hands. They must have some significance. He went through the possibilities in his head. Were they some kind of key? Perhaps if he was to deliver each trilobite to the correct person, it would illicit money. A soft knock at the door reminded him about his arrangement to meet Allen in the bar. Staring through the spy hole he was reassured to see the familiar sandy hair and he quickly opened the door and beckoned him through.

"I've just been caught by Clarissa." He indicated the bed with the two trilobites. "She sold me Dave's trilobite."

A moment's silence followed as Allen looked down at the two virtually identical fossil specimens. For once, Allen was dumbfounded. "Why bother buying one? You could take one of Forge's, he'll never notice, even if he does manage to pull through and he's able to walk and talk again."

"Dave told Anna that this trilobite was very valuable; that it would be worth a lot of money."

Allen looked sceptical. "He's right, you might get fifty dollars for it at a fossil store. That's a lot of money for a seamstress."

Ed let out a snort of frustration. "This must be a counterpart fossil to Forge's."

"You think?" asked Allen sceptically.

"I do, and I'm willing to bet that Golf Club had one as well."

Allen shrugged his shoulders in a dismissive fashion. "Coming for a drink?" he asked.

"Yes," Ed said with a sigh. "But let's avoid those Manchester Navvies. You may enjoy having them around, but I don't, especially after what they did to poor Clarissa."

They walked to the bar as Ed described Clarissa's facial injuries. Allen looked suitably disgusted and chose a position out of the direct line of sight of the navvies before ordering Ed to go to the bar and buy the beers.

When he returned, Allen decided to tell him all his news. "I didn't come back this afternoon because Kojo called me away to help him. The Exploration Office out in the jungle was attacked by Galamsey. The mine management are in a tail spin. First the mine disaster, the death of Golf Club, the unexplained accident to Forge, and now this. They believe the miners' union and the Galamsey have joined forces and are plotting to destroy the viability of the mine."

"Explains why Chiri didn't arrive this afternoon," said Ed.

"Precisely. And notice that no finger of suspicion has

been pointed at him? Nobody has suggested that it might be Chiri who attacked Forge and killed Golf Club."

"What's your point?" asked Ed.

Allen tut tutted bad temperedly. "The mine management are scared of him. They dare not accuse him of anything. They know it was he who organised the massacre in the pits and kicked off the current unrest."

"Have you worked out why Chiri went for Forge last night?" asked Ed taking a sip from his beer.

"Isn't it obvious? It's about these exploration prospects sold off to Tremendous Resources of London." He made a croak sound like a supressed laugh.

Ed's mind travelled back to the meeting that had occurred out in the exploration offices where Allen had outlined the sale of four prospects. The company that bought them, Tremendous Resources of London, had gone on to find major gold deposits. At the time, it had struck Ed as extremely odd. Chiri might be incompetent, but Kojo wasn't, nor was Bismarck. All three couldn't have been hoodwinked unless the chemical data had been systematically altered.

"So what is Chiri up to then?"

"I haven't quite worked that one out yet. But what we haven't considered is that he might be entirely innocent of any fraud, in which case he's been made to look very foolish, suffered a huge loss of face, and maybe he's exacting revenge. You heard what Forge said this afternoon, just like I did."

"You mean that part about Dave not talking and neither did he?"

Allen slammed his beer bottled down on the table in annoyance. "So who told Chiri that it was Forge who had been fiddling the figures? Who knows about Rusty Lion except you and me?" A thin seam of disquiet hit Ed in the chest as he realised what Allen was trying to intimate. "What else did you tell her?" Allen asked.

"Nothing else," Ed said automatically, and then hesitated.

It was enough for Allen to pounce. "What?" he demanded.

"I found a coded note in Greg's handwriting." He briefly explained the circumstances under which he had found the note, and how Bernie said she would be able to decipher it. "She said she'd see me this morning and tell me all about it."

Allen shook his head. "I think we've just found Chiri's source of information."

"Bernice?"

"She probably deciphered it and then went to Chiri and asked for his comment. Greg probably fed her an awful lot of information before he disappeared. You need to be careful what you say around her. The likes of Chiri are clever enough to listen to her questions and not to answer them."

He swigged back his beer and stood up, looking across at the Manchester Navvies. They were too busy carousing to have noticed his presence. "Which one d'you reckon smashed Clarissa?"

"The big fat one you clobbered the other night."

Nodding, he turned on his heel and headed across the lawn to his pickup. Ed returned to the accommodation block; it had been a long day and he suddenly felt very tired. He needed time to think through what he'd learned and to interpret the transformation of Allen. That afternoon he'd become like a blood hound, leading the chase for clues; what was his game? It was not simple curiosity that caused him to burst forth in a strong nasal London accent; he had been as hungry as Ed to find out what had happened to Forge. And then he had dashed across to Forge's rooms, telling the porter to go to hell and charging up the stairs.

The more he thought about it, the stranger Allen's behaviour seemed. He had shown little interest in Forge or Golf Club before, except to go out of his way to annoy them. So could his interest be a determination to pursue some personal vendetta? Could he have been brought in by Lomax as an investigator, in the same way as Greg? Perhaps Allen was given the task of looking at the exploration side while Greg looked at the mining side. After all, Allen had arrived soon after the sales of the prospects, when Lomax would have suspected that something had gone wrong.

He arrived back in his room and walked up to his bed; the trilobites looked back at him, tight lipped and staring, their secret intact. Allen was of the opinion that Dave's trilobite was of no real significance but was this Allen's attempt to throw him off the scent? In which case why?

The bashed face of Clarissa swam before his eyes; the trilobite in her hands. He saw the drunken figure of one of her tormentors, his shaved head and his large gut sticking out of his t-shirt. These trilobites held the key, he was sure. And if he was right then there would be no end of people trying to get their hands on them. He needed to put them somewhere he could get to quickly, and yet would be out of sight and in a place nobody would guess; they may yet prove his salvation. If Allen and Chiri turned nasty, he could at least negotiate with them.

He picked them up and put them in his bag. He would sleep with them tonight and then take them to work. There might be some cupboard or drawer he could find which would not be an obvious hiding place. A knock on the door caused him to stop; he took the revolver out of his bag and put it in his pocket then looked through the tiny spyhole. It was Bernie, dressed in her usual fashionable safari suit. Perhaps now he would get some answers. He opened the door and she sauntered in, bag slung over her shoulder.

"I've b'in trying to find you alone," she said. "I heard from Kojo you b'in a busy boy, visitin' the sick an' stuff." She sat down in the comfortable chair and pulled out a small bottle of whisky. "Beakers?" she asked looking across at the small table next to Ed where sat two small glasses. He gave them to her and she poured two large measures and then sat back. "Well, we were right about the cipher. It revealed the message."

"And?"

"Turns out to have been a transcript of a discussion between Forge and Golf Club about money. Appears that they've b'in naughty boys. They b'in enriching themselves at the expense of the mine. Looks like Dave Smith got angry about his cut. Thought he was due a much bigger slice of the pie. Threatened to tell Chiri if he didn't get equal shares. It looks like Greg was also after a slice."

"Have you got the transcript?" asked Ed.

Bernie reached into her bag and produced a series of sheets of paper. "It's a mess, but I think I captured the essence." The translation covered less than two pages, even with a large amount of crossings out. The original message had covered three sides.

"Is this it?" he asked.

"I had to cut out all the padding. I reckon he must have added in extra letters to mislead." She took a swig of her whisky and then started to refill.

He read down the page. "What does it mean by getting the union involved?" he asked.

Bernie shrugged. "Just that, I suppose. They must

have contacts in the union who they could call upon."

"So does that mean the union was involved in Greg's disappearance?" he asked.

"Looks like it. And the union was complicit in the scam."

Ed stood up and started to pace around the room. "This does not make sense. Why would Greg copy down a transcript of a conversation that incriminated himself and then fax it off to the local news agency." He turned towards Bernie.

"He demanded $10,000 for providing the cipher key, and another $10,000 for the actual recording of the conversation. I don't have that sort of money so I asked my bosses. While I was waiting for a reply, he disappeared."

Silence.

"Why didn't you say this before?"

A shrug of the shoulders and another swig of whisky. "I guess I didn't know whether I could trust you. And you never asked. It's highly unlikely that Forge would have a direct link to Herman Helmet; there must be an intermediary. We need to find out who it is and exactly how the union's involved."

"And why do we need to do that?" Ed asked. "What possible benefit would it be to me?"

"I can be very generous. There would be money and fame for the people who uncovered such a fraud. It could be the start of something for both of us."

"Is that all you can offer? Famous for a day and a few thousand quid?"

"I'm sure I could offer a supplement." She walked across the room and sat next to him on the bed. Her hand shot out and tried to take his, but he shied away. He stood up and walked to the nearest wall. "D'you not find me attractive?" she said, head on one side and a pout on her face.

"You were having an affair with Greg," he said. "Allen told me."

For a moment she looked puzzled. "Why should that matter," she asked. "He never showed you much respect."

"What d'you mean?"

"Didn't he go out of the way to prize Alice away from you? Split you apart? That's what he told me."

The knowledge that Bernie had grasped some part of his hesitation alarmed him. But he was keen to disabuse her of a misconception. "It has nothing to do with honour. Greg is missing, and I have still to understand why."

"Then we want the same thing," she insisted. "Greg's disappearance is bound up with this fraud. Solve one and you solve the other. Our interests coincide exactly."

He shook his head. "I doubt it. The moment I discovered anything of interest you'd hang me out to dry, just like you did to Greg and Dave Smith. They both had the Gideon bible code books and they were both in secret communication with you. Dave's dead, and in all likelihood so is Greg."

"That's pure coincidence," she said, looking offended. "I'm a journalist. I would never betray my sources."

"Oh?" he replied, feeling anger rise in his chest. "Then how come Forge was attacked the very day I gave you evidence that pointed to his guilt?"

"That's nonsense…"

"Who did you tell?" he said in a raised voice.

"I didn't tell anyone," she insisted.

"When you deciphered Greg's fax you went straight to Chiri, who then headed across to Forge and knocked seven bells out of him. You are the only person who could have known of Forge's complicity; the only person to have deciphered Greg's transcript, to have seen the Rusty Lion drilling."

"You're wrong."

"Then tell me how it could have happened," he shouted.

Bernie looked frightened and on the edge of tears. "I don't know what you're talking about. I've spent the day deciphering the fax. Sure, I went to talk with Chiri, but that was later in the day. I went to ask him if the rumours of him attacking Forge were true. He denied any part in the assault."

The lie brought Ed up abruptly. Had she not heard that Chiri had been trapped in the exploration compound all afternoon? She must have been elsewhere. Anybody who had been circulating freely, sniffing out a story, would have picked up information about the raid by the Galamsey. It was all over town. So where had she been?

"You're making me all flustered with your anger. It wasn't today, it was yesterday I talked with Chiri," she corrected. "I've been shut up in my room all day deciphering this fax. I haven't been able to get out and about."

"Where are you staying?" asked Ed. "I asked the compound staff if there were any female guests last night and they were adamant there were none."

She bridled with indignation. "I certainly do not stay here. I stay with friends on the outskirts of town. My editor's sister if you must know."

Suddenly, Ed stopped his anger. It was now clear to him that Bernie had something to do with Greg's disappearance. She was too well connected and too knowledgeable about the mine and its personnel. She was lying through her teeth. Wherever she stayed last night he was sure it had nothing to do with her editor.

He was tired all of a sudden. The last thing he wanted was to play footsie with Bernie; she was way out of his league, and she knew it. He pinched himself either side of his nose bridge in a sign of resignation. "Who do you think is this intermediary?" he asked in a much calmer voice.

Perhaps it was his quieter voice, or his much less aggressive body language, but Bernie decided that she had won in some way. She decided to push home her advantage. "Greg may have had a recording. He appears to have made secret recordings of quite a few people without them knowing."

A smile came to Ed's lips as he contemplated what she was saying. He guessed that this piece of information about a recording came from the bit of the fax that Bernie was not showing him; the part she had declared as padding. "You're right," he said, trying to play along. "I managed to find quite a few recordings on spare memory sticks. He kept them in the same place as the fax, in the strong box." He indicated the open strong box with his finger, just inside the wardrobe. She rose and went and peered inside. "But they aren't there anymore," he said. "I took them into the office and put them in my top drawer."

A sigh of frustration came from Bernie's mouth. "You really should be me more careful about security. Just leaving things like that about could get you into a lot of trouble."

"Come and see me tomorrow in the office," he said. "Bring your laptop, we can play them and see if there's anything of interest."

She went and picked up her bag and then swigged

back the rest of her whisky. "I'll get there in the morning. In the meantime, try to think of any other bits and pieces you've picked up that could help stitch together what's going on."

As Ed watched her leave he reflected that Bernie wasn't exactly as she wished to appear. She was very selective about what she told him, and never volunteered information unless Ed forced it from her. This was no basis for a business relationship.

CHIRI ON THE WAR-PATH

The next morning, as Ed walked up the steps to the office, and along the walkway, his thoughts were pre-occupied with Bernie. He wondered whether he should have been less forthright in voicing his suspicions, perhaps he should have played along for a while.
Shaking his head, he strode into Forge's office and stopped dead; five men sat in chairs, or else leaned against the wall, each had their head turned to stare at him, like cats staring at a mouse. Chiri took pride of place at Forge's desk, leaning back in the chair holding a trilobite in his hand.

There was a nod at an acolyte and the door to the office was pushed shut. The encircling men glowered, their expressions unreadable.

Moistening his lips, he attempted to detach himself from his thumping heart. There were no unoccupied seats; he thought he might perch on Dave's desk, but then decided that this would look suspiciously relaxed. "Surprised to see you lot," he said, trying to sound chummy. "Last I heard you were besieged in your headquarters."

Chiri acknowledged the question with a nod of his head. "Very annoying. But now the road is clear again."

"These Galamsey are becoming more than an inconvenience..."

But Chiri shook his head irritably. "You visited Forge."

The words had the consistency of hot lead; Ed felt sweat roll down his back, his mind started to whirr. "Sure," he said with a reassuring smile.

"Kojo said you were there with Allen when you visited."

Without meaning to, Ed looked around the room at all the hungry faces. "That's right."

"Why did Forge want to see you?"

A shrug of the shoulders. "I'm not sure he did, we went along to see if we could do anything for him."

"Nevertheless," said Chiri, "You talked with him, what did he say?"

Ed gaped. "He told us where to find his will, it was important for him; he gave us the keys to his room and told us to make sure his will was executed." Fear was making him gambol and say more than he needed, he cursed himself.

"Really?" said Chiri, his right eyebrow raised. "Why would he trust you?"

"I don't suppose he has many friends, he's probably desperate now that Golf Club's dead."

A look of cunning came into Chiri's normally un-animated face. "But he doesn't know Golf Club's dead."

"It's true," replied Ed. "He was asking for Golf Club to come and see him, but he seemed just as pleased to see us."

"So what was his desperation to see Golf Club all

about?"

"Was he desperate to see Golf Club? I didn't hear that."

A sound of air escaping a football came from Chiri's lips. "Don't be stupid, the staff in the hospital told me he was calling out for Golf Club to visit him, and then you and Allen arrived. What did he say to you?"

"Just about his will, that we were to make sure it was executed."

"Where is the will?"

"Allen has it."

Chiri looked up at one of his acolytes and nodded, the acolyte levered himself away from the wall and walked languidly to the door. Ed watched him go, pleased to have something different on which to focus; it meant he was not forced to look into Chiri's dead eyes.

"You visited Forge's room," said Chiri. "What did you make of it?"

The door closed, and Ed's route out evaporated; he turned back to Chiri and nodded, then narrowed his eyes. This was a trap for the unwary. "Looked to me like he was attacked as he slept, there was a lot of blood."

"Unfortunately there were no witnesses," said Chiri. "Who can say what really happened?"

"Nobody," agreed Ed. "But it didn't look as if he'd just fallen out of bed."

I'm told you also saw Dave's room too before the management got 'round to clearing up." Ed was unsure whether this was a rhetorical question. He decided the least said the better.

"You see the sort of people with whom we are dealing?" continued Chiri. "But you should not worry about yourself; I have given Mr Lomax my personal assurance that you will be protected. He was very disappointed when your friend Greg disappeared. He gave me quite a telling off." Turning to his four remaining acolytes he made a laughing noise to which they responded and soon the room was filled with chortling. It was not a happy sound.

"I don't suppose you have any idea what happened to Greg?" he asked eventually.

"None, as yet," replied Ed. "At first sight I would say he was murdered by the same people who killed Dave."

The smile disappeared as suddenly as it had appeared, and the deadly sound of laughing ceased. Chiri looked angry. "Dave had discovered a crime and was about to report it to me. You should look for the criminals who are doing their best to make me look like a fool. Dave was trying to sell us information about the conspiracy."

The acolyte returned, stepped smartly past Ed and murmured something to Chiri, who stood and walked across to Greg's old desk. Pulling open the top drawer he retrieved a slip of paper before walking back to his seat and flattening it out with the palm of his hand.

Ed looked around nervously and noticed with some relief that the acolytes were all looking at the floor or at the ceiling, or at Chiri, none had their gaze fixed on him.

"Do you have the fossil? The one mentioned in this will?" asked Chiri eventually.

A firm shake of the head. "There were a load of smashed trilobites on the floor of Forge's room, perhaps it was one of them." Looking around at the display of beautiful fossil trilobites on the shelves he stepped smartly to one of them. It had a trident projecting from between its beautiful compound eyes. "Could be any of these strange looking blighters, or maybe one of these plainer looking specimens," he said carefully.

"Where is Bismarck?" asked Chiri. The change in

direction caught Ed slightly off guard. His confusion must have shown in his face because Chiri smiled. "You have not seen Bismarck since the fire in the mine?" he asked.

"No. We were the last to get to the surface. He was very tired."

"Nobody has seen him since the incident," interrupted Chiri. "He has disappeared." A menacing silence drifted across the desk, the acolytes arranged around the walls stiffened and became noticeably more watchful.

"Have you looked for him at home?" asked Ed helpfully.

A nod of the head and a sniff. "His wife claims she has no idea of his whereabouts."

"I don't understand; why would he have disappeared? Has he done something wrong?"

"We were hoping you might be able to tell us."

This was a strange new game, like pin the tail on the donkey and see if Chiri thinks it fits. "There might be any number of reasons why Bismarck has disappeared; perhaps he's fallen out with his wife and gone back to live with his mother, or maybe he's gone fishing without telling her."

"You haven't heard anything?" Chiri's voice had gone quiet and Ed became more aware of his surroundings, of how closely he was being examined by the acolytes.

"He doesn't keep me informed of his social calendar."

"You are friendly with him, I know."

"Sure, he showed me around the mine. He was a lot more welcoming than others, much more talkative."

"In your talks with him, has he mentioned anything to you, about other activities he gets up to?"

"What's all this about," Ed said angrily. "What is he supposed to have done?"

Chiri bent his head forward so it was inches away from Ed's, his voice went softer, more menacing and Ed smelt chilli mixed with roasted meat. "If you have any information about his whereabouts, you better tell me. If I find you've been holding out on me and protecting an enemy of this mine I will forget all about my promise to Mr Lomax." He sat back in his chair, satisfied that he had made himself clear.

Ed squirmed, fighting against his instincts to run away from the biggest bully in the playground. "What has he done?" he asked.

Chiri was not inclined to answer; instead he stood from his chair and walked from the room, followed in strict order by his men. Ed watched them disappear along the walkway and down the stairs into the car park. Each maintained exactly the same position, some close together and others a significant distance behind. They pushed through the queue of Galamsey outside the gate and disappeared up the road towards engineering.

Reflecting that Bismarck was very wise to keep clear for the time being, Ed sat down in his seat and pondered the rows upon rows of trilobites on the shelves opposite. It would be unwise to under-estimate Chiri now that he had seen Forge's will and was aware that trilobites were significant. He needed to off-load the trilobites before Chiri returned and searched the office.

Forge's desk was packed with trilobites, but they all had intricate filigree patterns on their carapace which were very different from the ones he needed to hide. On the other hand, the trilobites marking the Lomax 'A' drilling volumes were simple, very similar in their overall form.

Footsteps echoed along the walkway outside so he backed away from the shelves and pretended to look interested in the trilobites on Forge's desk. Allen burst into the room. "Has he gone yet?"

"A few minutes ago."

"Where's the trilobite?"

Ed hesitated, and Allen came into the room shutting the door. "If he's read the will, he must know about the trilobite. What did you say?"

"That it was probably one of the trilobites I found smashed on Forge's floor."

"So he doesn't yet know we have it?"

"No."

Allen sagged with relief and then sat down in Forge's chair. "He gave me the once over this morning, thought he was going to do to me what he did to Forge. What was it like with you?"

Ed briefly told him what had happened. "Interestingly, he's very keen to know about Bismarck."

Biting his lip in a show of uncharacteristic worry, Allen leaned closer and spoke very softly. "And there's another strange coincidence. I've been waiting in Kojo's office all morning and he's not arrived yet either. Incredibly unlike Kojo not to come into work, the man works like a Trojan, first in and last to leave."

"Perhaps the stress has got to him at last."

A quick shake of the head. "Not Kojo. I reckon somebody else has got to him."

"What? You mean Chiri?"

"Perhaps. Kojo's wife is from Bismarck's family, Kojo relies on Bismarck, they're almost blood brothers, though you wouldn't know it; took me a while to work it out."

"Chiri said nothing about Kojo. It was Bismarck he was after."

Allen shrugged. "I think events are moving quickly. Chiri's flushing the game ahead of him, and maybe Kojo's bolted from cover." Allen jumped out of his seat and walked to the door. "You bring both trilobites with you, Forge's and Dave's."

"Where are we going?"

"Best place to be at the moment is probably at my house. I'll grab my stuff, be ready in a few minutes." He threw the door open and marched out.

Ed opened his briefcase, fished out the trilobites and then swapped them with ones on the shelf, carefully noting down the nearest volume labels. Then, opening the door, he moved down the walkway and waited for Allen to arrive.

Before long there was the echoing clump of feet and Allen's ginger, sandy hair appeared around the corner. "Got the trilobites?" he asked as he drew near.

Ed opened his bag for Allen to see. Satisfied, Allen took off down the stairs to the car park.

Allen's place turned out to be a blue-painted hacienda surrounded by high breeze block walls. Geckos cantered between baking concrete paths and short grass to compete for the best spots to catch passing insects. Orchids and blousy tropical flowers grew in the shade of towering trees. When Ed stepped from the pickup he found the air did not fry the inside of his nose. Instead, his senses were assailed by the sweet smell of tropical fruit. Far off, like a distant reminder, there was the sound of ill-maintained vehicles, horns and street traders, but here in the garden it was tranquil.

"Do you own it?" Ed asked.

"'Course not. Lomax does. It's one of the properties the mine maintains for long term contractors, comes with its own hot and cold running chambermaids." He winked and moved off to the front door.

Inside, the house was tiled in glazed blues and whites

which gave the space a natural coolness. A living room was accessed from a corridor in which there were African wall hangings and wooden carvings.

"I'll get some beers," said Allen and disappeared into a kitchen which was decorated in exactly the same style as the rest of the house but with a number of added modern amenities, including a cooker and a washing machine. The living room had a sofa, some chairs and a table but was otherwise bare of decoration. A shelf on the far wall contained photographs and pictures, one was of Adzo, Allen's PA at the exploration offices. Picking it up, Ed couldn't avoid smiling. "You dark horse," he said.

A giggle echoed from the kitchen. "A man can't live on geology alone. She insisted I put her picture somewhere visible." He walked back into the room and handed Ed a beer. "I think it's a territorial thing. I'm off limits to any other woman."

"She's beautiful."

Allen grunted. "She's been very nosy lately, wanting to know where I am and what I'm doing."

"Who's the other one?" Ed asked pointing at the largest picture on the shelves which showed a woman with sandy hair, the same age as Allen. The style of the clothes and the age of the cars in the background suggested the picture had been taken a number of years previous.

"Me sister."

"Another stunner," Ed said.

A ferocious knock at the door made them both jump so that Allen's hand slipped and his beer slopped onto the table. Cursing, he stood up and went down the corridor that led off the living room. There was a moment's pause as he looked through the spyhole, then the bolts were thrown back and the door flung open.

"T'is yourself, you can leave your pups outside, I don't want me best tiling messed up. Adzo'll give me a row."

Ed put the picture of Allen's sister down and turned to look at the corridor.

"We're having a beer, would you like some?" he heard Allen say.

Chiri's sullen voice answered in the negative and then his scarred face appeared, framed in the corridor. He looked up at Ed through his cold, dark eyes before scanning the rest of the room. He addressed Allen. "We're looking for Bismarck, you were the last to see him, you picked him up from the geology offices."

"That's right. I dropped him off in town."

Chiri's eyes met Ed's, there was glinting suspicion. "What business did you have with him?" This to Allen.

Allen looked across at Ed and gave him a wink. "Chiri's checking up on me. I've already answered all his questions, but he likes to ask again and again."

Chiri walked through into the kitchen then he came back into the sitting room. "He's here. I'm sure he is." He walked down another corridor and Ed could hear him opening and slamming doors. "My men are searching the grounds. Bismarck is now a wanted fugitive." Giving Ed a final, dead-eye stare, he walked down the corridor that led to the door. Allen walked after him and shot the bolts as he left. There was the sound of several pickups driving away.

"Looks like the fox has slipped the hounds," Allen said when he returned.

"What'll you do if Bismarck turns up here?"

"Ask him what he did with his cut of the money, and what trilobites have to do with anything."

Ed sat back in his seat and sipped his beer. "How long since you saw your sister?"

"Not since I was about ten."

"The picture looks like it was taken in the last ten years or so."

"It was taken exactly ten years ago; Lomax tracked her down as a favour to me."

"Why?"

"I asked him, I suppose."

"I mean, why was it necessary to track her down?"

"My parents were killed in a car crash when I was ten. We were fostered by American families. She went to live in Boston and I went to New York. We lost touch. That picture was taken when she went to Ireland for a visit."

"I'm sorry."

"Dad was catholic, mum was protestant. Nobody wanted to know us or look after us; we were separated. Eileen was a bit older than me, by about three years. I was ten, an annoying younger brother."

"And you haven't spoken since?"

"She's chief of some strange religious sect, strictly no contact with outsiders."

Ed was about to commiserate again, but he shut his mouth before the noise of his words could make their way from his throat. Noise was all it would be.

"You haven't asked yet," said Allen abruptly

"About what?"

"That thing that's been on your lips ever since we first met." He smiled and took a swig of his beer before leaning back in his seat. It was almost as if Chiri had never arrived and walked around the house.

"Which is?"

"Why I'm here in Lomax, o' course."

"It's true," said Ed reluctantly. "You're attached to quite a few different stories. Terrorism, murder, robbery, fraud…"

A cackle. "A rumour only needs circulation to survive."

"So which rumour is true?"

"The one about being wanted by Canadian authorities I made up meself, but I think it was Miriam who made up the one about the IRA. What other rumours have you heard?"

"What is the truth?" asked Ed, unwilling to play Allen's strange game.

"The truth is that I was invited here by Lucky Lomax to find out if there was fraud in the exploration section. After Tremendous Resources bought those exploration prospects Lucky got suspicious. He knows the main shareholders of that company to be even dodgier than himself. He suspected Chiri of major wrongdoing."

"And what did you find?"

"Nothing. If there was fraud it was elsewhere in the mine, not at exploration."

"How could you be so certain?"

He shrugged. "You get a sense for these things. Chiri's an evil thug with the guile of a shithouse rat. Nevertheless, I came to the conclusion that there was no fraud and it was down to Chiri's incompetence. But just in case, I advised Lomax he needed a man inside the mining geology section. That was the only other place it could have happened."

"And Lomax sent in Greg? Is that what you're saying?"

"That's correct. But until the last day or so I had no idea how far Greg had got. When he disappeared, I thought he'd gone off with Bernie and was lying low in Accra; I didn't think he'd bust the ring."

A feeling of creeping nausea came to Ed's stomach. "You know what you're saying, don't you?"

"I'm afraid I do," replied Allen.

"You're expecting me to believe Bismarck is responsible for Greg's disappearance. "

"Who else would it be?" asked Allen.

"Chiri and his mates are the cold-blooded murderers around here, not Bismarck."

This time Allen leaned across in his chair. "You know how it is in these gold camps, we've both been in them long enough. For God's sake, you must realise that people will slash their grandmother's throat at a single gleam of the yellow stuff. Put yourself in Bismarck's shoes; a straight choice between ruin and poverty or fine houses, enough food and his children educated at the best schools in England. Would you stay your hand?"

"Bismarck is no criminal."

"Did I say he was a criminal? He's simply siphoning money away from those who have too much. Lucky Lomax is only rich because he was rich to start off with. Would you be scratching around in the arse end of Africa for a measly few thousand if you'd been born with millions under the pillow to start off with? Of course not; you were born in Liverpool, in a working class family who had nothing to leave you but a few words of wisdom."

"And let's be honest," continued Allen, "the money Lucky Lomax inherited is almost certainly dirty. That family made its money way back when, on the backs of the poor, because the Lomax's just happened to own the land that had coal underneath. Bismarck is no more criminal than Lucky Lomax, the only difference is that Lomax has the law on his side and he's rich enough to make sure it's enforced."

"I don't understand..." replied Ed.

"Just 'cos I work for him, doesn't mean I like him or

what he stands for. I'm like you, I just want to get this sorted and get the hell out of here, away from Chiri. I think it's very likely that the situation is going to deteriorate very badly."

"Why?"

"A little bird told me that Bismarck is involved with the miners' union, he's one of their main organisers. Secretly o' course."

"That explains why Chiri is so keen to find him, then. It's political."

"Could be. But he's very angry. More than you'd expect from a simple bit of politics. In any case, Chiri doesn't care about the union; his patch is exploration not mining. What he cares about is that he's been made to look a fool by Tremendous Resources of London."

"But Forge and Golf Club would never work for the union against the mine."

"No," agreed Allen, "but they might work with Bismarck and Kojo. The potential for making money would be too much to resist." Allen rose and went back into the kitchen. "More beer? I can put a sandwich together as well, Adzo keeps a store of stuff in the fridge."

FORGE'S TESTAMENT

In the afternoon Ed insisted on returning to the office, against Allen's better judgement. He was sure that the answers he needed could be found there, and it was no good skulking around hiding. In fact, as he pointed out to Allen, it would look much more suspicious to Chiri if they remained closeted together. Besides, he needed time and space to think about what Allen had said.

Climbing the stairs and entering Forge's office once more it occurred to him that Allen was the only western contractor of any long-standing in geology or exploration who was unscathed. He pondered whether there was any significance to this fact or if Allen was just one of those born survivors who had an unerring knack of knowing what to do and say and where to place themselves.

Then, with a shrug of his shoulders, he settled down in Forge's seat and set himself to try and hack into his computer. If challenged, he would simply say that he was trying to find clues about family members who may need to be contacted.

Forge's user name should be relatively easy to guess

because it was simply first initial followed by the surname, but breaking Forge's password would be more difficult. Dave Smith had discovered that the password was always a trilobite followed by a 01. For a moment he pondered why Dave Smith would have revealed the secret behind Forge's password to Bernie and whether this indicated something important about their relationship.

Shaking his head, as if removing moths, he tried to discern which trilobite Forge had used as his password. There were a myriad of different trilobite specimens sitting on his desk, each with a unique name which Forge probably knew off by heart. Trying 'Paradoxides' on the basis that this was the only name he could remember, he was not surprised to see a rejection message.

Standing, he paced up and down the office and then he looked out of the window. The queue of Galamsey had gone and the lads with Kalashnikovs sat in the shade of their blue scout cars talking quietly. Scratching his head, he turned and glanced at the shelves that lined the wall behind Forge's desk. The fossil he had rescued sat next to the one he had bought from Clarissa for $200. Perhaps Forge had used the species name of these specimens as a password.

Walking swiftly across the room he went to his bag and put his hand inside for Forge's will on the off chance that this document had some clues about the identity of the fossils. He'd put it in one of the side pockets and now, with an increasing sense of panic, he realised that it wasn't there; and neither were the swapped trilobites. Heart sinking, he checked in every other pocket before fully opening the bag to do a full visual check; no fossils and no will.

"Allen," he breathed. The trip to his house must have been a ruse to get Ed off his guard so it would be easier to steal the fossils. Throwing the bag on the floor in disgust he tried to think why Allen had removed them. Maybe he wanted them for the same reason Ed did, for leverage with Chiri and Bismarck and whoever else was operating in the murky pond. As he sat down on his small stool another reason occurred to him, which was that Allen might be working for one of the sides.

A small smile curled at the edge of his mouth as he wondered how long it would take Allen to discover that the trilobites had been switched. Looking around at the array of fossils in Forge's office he decided it may take him quite a bit of time.

Letting his gaze roam free as he tried to calm himself, he noticed that at the very end of Forge's book case was a huge volume on the identification of fossils. There were no footsteps on the walkway outside, everything was quiet, so he jumped up and grabbed the book.

A cursory glance showed that the book had virtually every type of trilobite that had ever been found. Forge's trilobite was quite common, it had a classic morphology and he felt that it would not take long to locate some likely names. After five minutes' frantic search he discovered a large photograph labelled Calymene that displayed a specimen identical to Forge's. Thinking that this was too easy he read the detailed description of the thoracic and glabella sections until he was finally satisfied that he had discovered the correct name. Replacing the volume on the shelf he made his way around to Forge's computer and typed in the username and then calymene01.

Username and password not recognised.

Cursing, he tried again, certain that if Forge had chosen a trilobite name at random then Dave would never have been able to guess the password. This time he put in Calymene01 with a capital C and to his delight the screen went blue and the words 'waiting' appeared. Holding his breath, he watched the little circle continue to turn until eventually, after what he thought must be minutes, the screen started to say 'Welcome'.

He was in.

As the desktop icons appeared, gradually filling in with colours and his head spun with joy at his own cleverness, he wondered what he would do now. 'Look for something that would shed light on events in the mine over the last year would be a good start,' he told himself.

Thinking that the lack of sound on the walkway outside was strange, he went over to the window to check that nobody was around. Maybe they were all out at meetings or they had all been scared off by Chiri on the rampage. Walking back to the desk he sat down and decided that he should look for files that indicated strange activity on or around the dates when crucial events occurred such as when Greg had disappeared. Finding the search function, he typed in a search for files created or modified between today's date and two weeks before Greg disappeared, the matter of a little over a month ago.

After remaining blank for a few seconds, the search window started to fill with results and eventually stopped when it showed fifty documents. Scanning the list carefully, he found five or more which had labels indicating that they were not spreadsheets full of drilling information. He determined that he needed to read each of them in date order, earliest to latest.

The first contained minutes of a meeting in which the appointment of Ed had been discussed. It was interesting to see his name in black and white; Kojo had demanded that it was Forge and Dave's job to look after him. A shrewd move given that all three appear to have been equally involved in whatever had been going on at the mine.

The second document was minutes of the meeting where Ed himself had been in attendance and Allen had produced his miraculous Burgess Shale trilobite. This was where there had been a discussion of the prospects that the mine had sold off for peanuts to Tremendous Resources. The details of this meeting were extremely vague because Ed remembered that Forge had been distracted.

The third document was minutes of a meeting in which the massacre of the Galamsey had been discussed. Chiri had been present and had been vocal that they should say nothing to visiting members of the press. There was an agreement that they should carry on as if nothing had happened. It was mentioned that Ed was ill in hospital with malaria.

The sound of the angry drums in the jungle came back to him, and Chiri sneaking into his room in the dead of night. With a shudder, he remembered the smell of roasted meat and chilli and the flash of lightning that illuminated Chiri's staring eyes. Clenching his teeth, he warned himself that he needed to keep active and focussed if he was to survive.

The fourth document concerned a meeting in which the disaster that had put the Lomax 'A' shaft out of commission was discussed. There were contingencies for how they would maintain underground production using the auxiliary shaft. Jeremy had attended this meeting and he had suggested that the disaster was a blessing in disguise because it would allow them to put in more modern technology, and what's more they could get the insurers to pay for it.

Yet again he felt his teeth clench as he remembered

the screams of the dying and then saw the charred bodies pass by as they headed down to the bottom of the shaft. Their death was a business opportunity for the mine, but there was no indication that there would be any compensation for the families. He felt the pendant of Uncle Edryd around his neck and wondered what the company minutes looked like after the Gresford disaster.

The fifth document was the most recent. It had been written on the afternoon before Forge had been attacked. Ed knew immediately when he opened it that this was something different. For one thing it was not minutes of meetings and for another it was a copy and paste from an email sent to Jeremy. It occurred to Ed that Jeremy had just been made Mine Manager at the time and this must have been one of the first emails he would have received.

At first the email congratulated him on his decision to take over the reins of the mine. Presumptuous and crawling with his language, Forge indicated his wish for a firm hand on the tiller. From this point the email became a lot stranger, it mentioned a company named Russell, Russell and Beadle, a firm of City lawyers with whom Forge was in communication about a financial matter. He said that he would be, 'forwarding certain information to this company in the event that his interests were not protected.'

Ed held his breath. There was no indication in the email about the nature of the 'certain information', but this looked very much like Forge was threatening Jeremy. Thinking he must be mistaken he re-read the email again and concluded that he had not misinterpreted Forge's meaning.

Loud footsteps on the boards outside caused him to quickly shut off the screen and rise from Forge's seat so he could face the door. If it was Allen, he had decided that he was going to confront him with the missing trilobites.

But it wasn't Allen, it was Bernie, accompanied by Chiri and his acolytes; he could hear their voices, recognised the stamp of their feet. Leaning across he pressed the off switch of Forge's computer and listened with satisfaction as the sound of the CPU fan shut down and saw the hard disc light disappear.

A door further up the walkway slammed; they must have entered Bismarck's office. He could hear them thumping about, smashing glass. Going to the shelves, he grabbed a volume which sat alone at the end of the row and then retreated to his own desk and opened it, pretending to look busy.

After several minutes waiting, hearing his heart thump against his chest, a painted face with blonde hair appeared at the door and grinned at him. Ed tried grinning back but found that all he could manage was one of his sliding smiles. To his surprise, when she opened the door and walked in she was followed by several of Chiri's acolytes.

"Said I'd catch up with you today; I want to see about those recordings you have."

Thinking that her cover was completely gone, that there was no way she could pretend any longer that she was just an honest journalist, Ed dived into his bag and then searched his drawers to find the USB stick with the recording of Bismarck. Finally, after much huffing and puffing he held it up for her.

"Funny," she remarked. "I looked in your drawers this morning and couldn't see a thing."

"Couldn't have looked hard enough," he said shrugging.

High heel boots banging on the floor boards, she made her way across the room and whipped the USB stick from his hand. As she turned to leave she hesitated and looked back at him. "Where's Forge's trilobite, the one he left for Golf Club?"

"You'll have to ask Allen, I went to his for lunch and when I came back it was gone from my bag."

"Tchah," she said loudly. "You better be tellin' the truth. I'll talk to Allen, where is he, why isn't he at work?"

"Gone into town on business; he didn't want to tell me where."

Another grunt indicated that Bernie was less than happy with Ed's performance. Not deigning to say anything more she stomped noisily from the room with USB in hand, clumped up the walkway, and then Ed heard the door to Bismarck's swing open and closed. There was a muffled conversation with Chiri, and then silence.

Realising that he had only moments to find out what Forge intended to send to Russell, Russell and Beadle he pressed the on switch of the computer. As the CPU fan whirred he determined that once the computer booted he would do an extensive search of Forge's sent folder. To his surprise the computer started up in no time and he found that within a couple of minutes he had logged back in. Quickly locating the email programme, he clicked on the sent items and was able to find a message addressed to a man named Cecil Walesby which had a short paragraph instructing the recipient to send the attached document to solicitors in London in the event of Forge's death or disappearance.

There was much in the email and document to digest, including a description of a secret syndicate meeting that had taken place in London two years ago, about the time that Bismarck visited Britain, he mused. But there was no time to investigate in more detail, at any minute he would be invaded and interrogated.

Soon the air was thick with the sound of the laser printer as Ed printed off multiple copies of the email and attached document. Looking quickly at the contents and realising he needed to make sure he kept one safe, he found a hole punch in Forge's top drawer. He inserted the document into a drilling volume closest to the Claymene specimens before forwarding the email to his own email account.

Heavy feet banging in the next room was followed by a door opening, more clomping along the walkway and finally a heavy hand pushing his door open so that he was invaded by Chiri and Bernie and a host of acolytes.

"Any use?" Ed asked.

"Plenty," said Bernie. "I don't suppose you know where Bismarck or Kojo can have gone?"

"No," he replied with a shrug.

"And you say Allen stole Forge's trilobite?"

"That's correct; it must have been around the time Chiri stormed into his house and demanded to know where he could find Bismarck, for the umpteenth time."

"You won't mind if Chiri searches will you?" asked Bernie coming fully into the room.

"Not at all," said Ed, standing up. "The trilobite was in my bag, along with Forge's will." He placed the bag on the table for Chiri to search.

Bernie looked at him with wide eyed puzzlement. "You really are useless at this sort of thing; why on earth did Lomax employ you?"

Ed shrugged. "I have no idea, why employ a man known to have had a nervous breakdown and fit for nothing except gibbering in a corner…I agree."

Giving him a quizzical look as if this was not the expected response, she opened her mouth to ask a question, but Chiri butted in first. "Nothing in the bag and nothing in the drawers."

"Search him," she said.

Before he could be manhandled or pushed, Ed lifted his arms above his head to enable a quick search. He felt Chiri's hands glide over his sides and pockets before being declared clean.

"Seems the chickens have flown the coop," he said. "Perhaps Allen has taken the trilobites to Bismarck and the pair of them, with Kojo, are racing away to start a new life together as bone idle rich."

In the silence after Bernie had turned her back and stormed from the office, followed very quickly by Chiri and his acolytes, Ed reflected on how she was now the one issuing orders for Chiri to follow. Doubting whether she had managed to catch Chiri with her feminine wiles, he wondered how else she could have got him to follow her instructions. There was no doubt in Ed's mind that she was now in charge of the hunt for Bismarck and Kojo.

For a dizzying moment he fought the compulsion to run after them waving Forge's email and shout that he knew the names of Tremendous Resources of London secret shareholders. Opening and closing his hands in an effort to bring himself under control he realised there would be a time and a place to make the contents of Forge's email public, but now was not the time; he needed to wait.

Settling himself for his lift home he dipped into the reams of drilling information contained in the volume which he had pulled from the shelves. For a few moments he was confused by the presence of handwritten serial numbers and descriptions of fossil parts. Blinking, he realised that this was not drilling information but a catalogue of Forge's trilobites. Flipping the cover shut again, he saw that the volume was completely unlabelled. Out of curiosity he riffled through each page and saw that Forge must have photographed his entire collection of trilobites; each trilobite was named and had been given its own catalogue number. Smiling at this latest evidence of Forge's obsession he stood up with the intention of putting the volume back on the shelves. But then he hesitated and sat down again thinking that it would be useful to check out what Forge had put on the pages where he had documented Calymene. The book was ordered alphabetically and there was even an index at the back showing the page numbers, so it took only a few seconds to find Calymene. There were four specimens, each on successive pages and each with a description of where Forge had bought it.

His mind was so full of information that he didn't immediately realise that he had just seen something else of real significance. It was like looking at your own reflection in a distorting mirror and trying to recognise prominent distinguishing features; he was learning too much in such a short space of time. Diving back into his desk drawers he retrieved Greg's notebook. Turning to the back page he saw Alice, her face extended to appear like a snout, a hungry, leering look in her eyes, and underneath her, serial numbers. They were exactly the same as the numbers in Forge's catalogue.

Walking over to Forge's shelves, he lifted both Calymene specimens and found they had the same serial numbers as in Greg's notebook and Forge's catalogue. Both had been bought in London the day after the Tremendous Resources shareholder meeting took place, as had the other two specimens of Calymene, current whereabouts unknown.

Feeling his head begin to swim again at this further evidence that the trilobites were significant, his mind turned to Allen and his vehement denial the previous night that Dave's fossil could have any significance. It must have been an attempt to buy him some time by throwing Ed off the scent.

A further check of the windows showed that Bernie and Chiri had disappeared, probably off to Engineering to speak with the Chief Engineer and his harridan wife, Miriam. Unable to believe the progress that he'd managed to make in the last half an hour he decided once again to examine the documents Forge had sent to Cecil Walesby, his business contact in Britain.

Hands shaking slightly, he unfolded the paper and he stared blankly for a few moments unable to take in what was plainly a record of a Tremendous Resources shareholder meeting. Present in the room were Jeremy, current Mine Manager, Bismarck, Kojo and Forge; there was also a man named Snodgrass.

The amount due to the shareholders after selling their stake to Lucky Lomax was put at one hundred million pounds. Remembering the picture of Bismarck smiling on the lawn outside some Cambridge University college, Ed realised the reason for his happiness.

Going back to the window, Greg's notebook in hand, he felt no elation at the thought that he was getting closer to discovering why Greg had disappeared. Bismarck and Kojo had plenty of motive for wanting Greg dead, as did Forge and the others. But for Ed, Chiri was still the chief suspect; he had the manpower and the attitude to kill. And yet he was not on the list of syndicate members present at the meeting. Could Chiri be a secret shareholder in the same way as Dave Smith and Golf Club? Anything was possible if the current Mine Manager was part of the conspiracy.

Had a crime had been committed at all? If the Mine Manager was involved, then perhaps Lucky Lomax was as well. In which case who were the victims? Looking down at the notebook, at the pictures of Alice, anger flared inside him, Greg had presumably been trying to lever himself into the syndicate when he died.

Looking down from Forge's windows he noticed a familiar pickup pull into the car park. Allen's face peered up at him through the windscreen. For a moment he thought of retreating from the window and pretending not to have noticed, but instead he decided to wave. Maybe it was because Allen appeared friendly on the surface, or maybe because he wanted to know what story Allen would spin about the trilobites. Whatever the reason, he grabbed his bag and headed down the steps. As he approached, Allen swung open the door and there, lying on the passenger seat were two trilobites. After looking at them for a second Ed lifted his gazed to Allen.

"Why?"

A shrug of the shoulders. "Because you wouldn't have let me look at them otherwise," he replied. "And I wanted to have a close examination away from you anxiously bobbing up and down."

"Where have you been?"

"I went back to my own home to examine them."

"And?"

"You getting in? Put the bugs back in your bag."

They set off through the mine gates and met the bumpy road that led into the town. Fresh rain in the night had created large, muddy puddles and the pickup moved in a series of skids and slides. The view of the township from the pickup was beginning to become familiar, he was starting to recognise the same children and the same women standing outside their houses.

"Chiri and Bernie arrived today," he said after a while.

"Ohh?"

"I think they might be looking for you right now."

"When are they not? Why am I so popular this time?"

"They were looking for Forge's trilobite and I said that you had taken it from my bag. Seems like Bernie has taken over from Chiri as the chief inquisitor."

Allen looked around in surprise. "Go on."

"Just that," replied Ed. "She was telling Chiri to do this or do that, and Chiri was obeying as if they were orders. I think we can ditch the notion that she's a simple newspaper correspondent."

"Oh, I never thought that," Allen chuckled.

They turned the last bend at the end of the town and spotted the compound with its guards patrolling the perimeter. Allen manoeuvred through the gates, careful not to splash mud on the lads with Kalashnikovs. "No sign of Chiri or his acolytes," said Ed looking around. "I'd rather not meet them tonight, not until they've caught Bismarck or Kojo." He jumped from the pickup and slammed the door. "What are you going to do?"

"I'm going to hide," said Allen and kicked the pickup into reverse.

THE KIDNAP

He'd consumed a bit too much beer, not enough to knock him out, but sufficient to wake him up with a raging thirst and a headache. Lying back on his pillow he listened intently, feeling distinctly warm and uncomfortable and searching his mind for the reason. He thought back to Forge's room, with the blood on the floor and the smashed trilobites, Forge lying in his hospital bed all but dead, Clarissa selling Dave's trilobite.
The air conditioner had stopped working, that's why he felt so warm. Its buzz and gurgle had been a constant refrain since he'd arrived in this steamy part of Africa. Now it had stopped and the room was warm, like a sauna, no wonder he'd woken up. Turning his head, he looked across to the air conditioner and saw that a light shone through the grill and there were vague shapes moving about on the other side. Groggily, he realised a gang was attempting to steal his air conditioner. But he had ensured it had remained turned on when he went to bed, he wasn't like the others who found real difficulty sleeping with the noise. The thieves must have somehow worked

out how to isolate the electric motor. Propping himself up on his elbows, the drowsiness suddenly gone he started shouting, "Oy, I can hear you, I'll get the guards." A frantic whispered conversation came from outside as Greg threw the covers off his bed, jumped up and started to throw on clothes. "I warn you, I'm armed," he said.

A boot thudded against the air conditioner carapace, breaking the plaster where it had been screwed into the wall; it fell with a clang to the floor. Three men stared at him with expressions of uncertainty on their dark faces as they wondered whether Greg was lying about being armed. Then one of them dived through the hole and Greg pelted across the room, reached for the door and flung it open.

A man dressed in green with a towel over his arm was on the other side. Ed did not stop to wonder why he had decided to wait outside his room in the middle of the night. "Thieves breaking into my room," he said and tried to push past. The man moved to block his exit, then threw the towel from his arm to reveal a two-foot-long machete. He swung it so that the end of the blade arrived quickly and accurately under Ed's chin. Then he advanced into the room, forcing Ed ahead of him, swinging the door closed. Ed turned to see a second man had made his way through the wall to join the original interloper.

The intended scream caught in his throat when he felt a sharp pain in the back of his head. Collapsing to the floor, face first, the three men fell on him, gagging his mouth and expertly pinning his arms and legs. When his senses returned and he began to struggle to free his limbs a knee was placed in the small of his back causing pain to shoot through his body.

Like bush meat, he was attached to a long pole and lifted off the ground. Struggling hard so that the pole bent like a spring, he forced the men carrying him to stumble. But more men joined to help as he was transferred through the hole to waiting hands. Once out in the fetid atmosphere of an African night, he was carried to a waiting pickup on the other side of the perimeter fence (a hole had been cut through which he was inserted).

He was placed onto the flat bed, the doors of the cab shut quietly and he heard the sound of an engine starting. Far off the mournful wail of a siren started, calling the morning shift to work. Five thousand men would soon be walking through the main gates of Lomax gold mine.

Further struggle hurt his back and his head so he started to force himself to relax. Why hadn't he grabbed his gun when he'd first heard the noise? As he sank his head onto the hard metal floor and braced himself against the bumps of the road, he knew he'd never have used it, and if he had he'd probably be dead by now. Time would tell if a quick death would be preferable. A tissue smelling of some strong surgical spirit was thrust over his nose and mouth so that he couldn't breathe. He began to feel drowsy, he struggled, but strong hands held him still, he couldn't escape the cloying fumes. He tried holding his breath, but a sharp blow to his stomach caused him to gasp and he took in more of the fumes. He was getting weaker, blackness was invading the edges of his sight, he could no longer resist the fumes. The struggle was too much, his body went limp and he submitted himself to the dark.

Waking, he saw blackness and smelled putrefaction. Choking and coughing on the foul atmosphere, he realised it was hot; hotter than was bearable. Sweat dripped from his brow and into his eyes. Rubbing them, he opened his lids as far as possible, to maximise the intake of light. There were small slats of illumination above his head, probably floorboards.

This must be a cellar, or an underground room. Standing, he felt his feet sink into soft earth, felt warm, foul liquid slosh around his ankles, soaking his trousers and socks. The putrid smell increased so he brought his sweat-soaked shirt over his nose. The thought of the fluid in contact with his skin made him retch and he tried to shut his mind about where the water may derive.

He was parched, like he hadn't drunk for a week. Sinking back on his bed he put his head in his hands. Who would come and see him? Would they be his jailer or his saviour? What if nobody arrived and he was left in this stinking shithole for the rest of his life? Was this the sum and substance of his remaining life?

Panic surged through his body, making him light-headed. Lying down, he curled up, careful not to place his stinking boots on the cover. This was where Greg had ended his days, he knew it. And now he was about to determine the exact details of what happened to him. Putting aside his panic, he thought of Alice, the woman over whom he and Greg had fallen out. He remembered hating Greg for his competitiveness, his charm and his bravado.

Why had Ed agreed to come back to Africa? Was it just to get back in Alice's favour? Was this all about throwing his hat in the ring now Greg had disappeared? Whatever his motivation, principled or selfish, he was still going to die. A shallow grave off the beaten track, far out in the jungle would be his last resting place. Perhaps he would share the same space as Greg. How ironic that he would inhabit the same space as the man he had come to bury.

He heard the faint shuffle of feet. They got louder, and

then arrived directly above his head. "Oy," he shouted. "Over here. Help." Listening intently, he heard a door creak open and saw a shaft of brilliant daylight shine through the slats between the floorboards. "I'm down here. I think there's a trapdoor."

Tramp, tramp, tramp. A man was silhouetted through the slats. "You're nearly there," Ed said, willing the man to be his saviour.

The figure lifted the edge of a trapdoor and Ed put his fingers through, but quickly withdrew when he felt an intense pain. A package dropped through the gap, landing on the ground with a liquid squelch. The trapdoor slammed and the man shuffled off again so Ed was plunged back into darkness.

Bending down, he lifted the package from the sticky mud and quickly undid the wrapping. It was a bottle of water and a torch. Unscrewing the cap, he glugged several mouthfuls of delicious, cool water before turning on the torch. In its raking light he saw what he expected; earth walls, a planked ceiling and a filthy floor. Interestingly, the wall next to the bed was wooden and had a drawing. Squelching his way back over to his bed, keeping the torch beam trained, he saw an attempt to draw the Disney caricature of Alice in Wonderland. This one lacked the wolf's snout and prominent canines but retained the big eyes and nurse's uniform. Sinking down on the bed, he hung his head and pictured Alice, the real Alice. She wasn't blonde with blue eyes like the Disney Alice, but she had that innocent and vulnerable manner that was irresistible. He found a piece of charcoal next to the bed, no doubt washed into the hole from surrounding streets. Picking it up he realised he was touching something last held by Greg's own hand.

Closing his eyes, he tried to send himself back to his

farmhouse in Wales. He could visualise the sweep of the views, the small fields and hedgerows, the mountainsides covered in trees with sparse grazing on the upper slopes. There'd be nobody to mourn him and send somebody after him if he never returned.

Hours passed. He must have slept, because the sound of shuffling footsteps woke him, and this time there was an extra pair of boots. The thin light of dawn shone through the slats so Ed was able to see two men looking down at him. Neither spoke as the trap door was flung open.

On standing, Ed found his legs wobbling like he'd just walked up a mountain, or been forced to squat down for hours. Drafts of cool air rushed through the open door bringing a wholesome balm into his cell. A voice called out. "Ed?"

"Hello?" He replied, watching as one of the silhouettes bend down. "It's me, Bismarck."

"Bismarck?" Why was he here? "Have you come to rescue me, Bismarck?"

"That's right," he said. "Come, you must leave this place."

A rope ladder dropped into the room. None of this made sense. But he wasn't going to argue, Bismarck was offering him a way out. Grabbing the rope ladder he climbed, one rung at a time, legs of clay shaking, until he thrust his body onto the dusty floorboards of his prison ceiling.

"We must be quick," said Bismarck.

Gripping Bismarck's hand, Ed rose to his feet and stood upright, eye to eye. "What's going on, Bismarck. Why are you here?"

"Come, we must go. Please."

"Where are we going? To a new cell?"

"No, we are escaping. Getting you away from here. Chiri is coming, we must escape."

"Chiri?"

Walking away from the trapdoor, Bismarck gestured over his shoulder. But Ed stood his ground, looking around. He saw a small room with a bar at one end, a few stools dotted here and there, and behind the bar was light flooding through a door. When Ed did not immediately follow his lead, Bismarck tutted, took his hand and pulled him across the floor, out into the fresh air.

Despite being low in the sky, the sun's glare burnt through Ed's eyes. Putting his left hand up, he looked down at the ground and allowed Bismarck to lead him by the right hand across dry compacted earth with sparse patches of yellowing grass. Looking up as he walked, he found that his eyes grew used to the light. He made out a ring of corrugated iron huts and people standing and watching in silence. He managed to open his eyes further so he could understand who these people were and what they wanted. His senses, already taut to breaking point, sharpened even more when he smelt the rich aroma of cigar smoke.

Bismarck stopped, still clutching Ed's hand, grip tightening. Through eyes that were now used to the light Ed saw a familiar helmet-shaped head. Herman the Helmet was blocking their path with several of his men. He had donned his full length silk, paisley dressing gown and had a thick cigar wedged defiantly in the side of his mouth. Speaking in Twi, he delivered an order in such a commanding voice that Ed quailed. Bismarck responded calmly in a voice that he used when ordering men in the underground. Herman attempted to interrupt once or twice, but Bismarck over-rode his objections. Eventually, an urgent tug on his hand indicated that Bismarck was ready to leave and once again they were on the move.

Despite keeping his head low, Ed could see out of the corner of his eye that they were approaching an alleyway that led from the patch of earth through the ring of houses. A boy stood close to the entrance, legs apart, hands outstretched in the universal action of a gun. "Bang, bang, bang."

Walking straight past the boy, Bismarck entered the alleyway. It grew dark, and shadowy corners appeared in which Ed was sure men waited, machetes in hand. Then they emerged out into a wide open space, deserted except for a few trees. A wind blew dust devils and rustled the leaves. Tyres suspended from branches swung backwards and forwards. No other noise, no other people and no other movement.

"I've been here before," said Ed. "It was quiet then as well."

Listening intently to the lack of sound, he began to hear a low growl on the gusty wind. Bismarck began to run, gripping tightly to Ed's arm. They headed for a line of corrugated iron huts fifty metres away.

The low growl began to resolve itself into the rattle of heavy engines, and the high pitched phut-phut of rotor blades. A white helicopter zoomed over-head, skimming the top of the shacks that bounded the edge of the open area, creating pressure waves of noise, and causing the ground to reverberate.

Without stopping, Bismarck dived into the nearest dwelling and hauled Ed after him. Inside was a sparsely-furnished room with a dusty dirt floor and a startled family of four sharing the same bed. A baby in a cot next to the wall started to cry and a man rose looking menacing. But after Bismarck produced a gun from his pocket the man retreated.

Ed noticed the gun was the same as the one given to him by the Mine Manager. It occurred to him to ask if they were standard mine issue or whether Bismarck had acquired it from the kidnap gang.

"Who are they?" asked Ed gesturing outside. By now, a scout car had arrived and heavily armed men dressed in fatigues were jumping to the ground.

"They've come for us."

Even through his clogged brain this did not have a ring of truth. "I don't understand…"

"They're Chiri's men…"

"I just saw a picture of Alice, drawn by Greg."

An uncertain look entered Bismarck's face. "What d'you mean?"

"The cellar where I was kept, Greg was kept there as well."

A gleam of understanding replaced the uncertain look. "Yes."

"You knew and you didn't tell me," said Ed, feeling anger growing in his chest. "You knew all along that it was the union who had kidnapped him, and yet you told me nothing." Then, without thinking of the consequences of declaring his knowledge, he ploughed on. "Greg tried to muscle his way in on your scheme, didn't he?"

Bismarck opened his mouth to try and make a denial, but Ed was certain now and determined to press home his advantage. "You decided to get the union to take care of him, which means that the union is involved in the scheme as well."

More scout cars arrived in the clearing outside the hut, and Bismarck took a very hasty look. He hesitated, unwilling to commit himself to an answer. Finally turning to Ed he said, "Those are Chiri's men. They know you have the trilobite…"

"But…"

"Where is it?" asked Bismarck.

"Or was it that you told the union that Greg was about to inform the mine of your secret role as the union organiser?"

"The trilobite. Where have you put the trilobite?" He shook the gun. "Where is it?"

"So you tricked the union into behaving as your own private muscle. And Greg was put in the hole, and that's where he died. A man couldn't survive more than a few days in there."

"You have it. I know it," said Bismarck.

"So why did you have me kidnapped? And why rescue me?" A movement out of the corner of Ed's eye attracted his attention. Another scout car had arrived and more men were jumping to the ground. They were all gazing in their direction, and a few were advancing.

Bismarck was momentarily distracted and Ed took his chance and grabbed the gun. There was a loud crack as the trigger was pulled and dust flew up from the floor. The advancing men dived to the ground before starting to fire indiscriminately into the shack. The occupants of the bed, stunned by the initial gun shot, started screaming. Ed and Bismarck fell to the floor, the gun forgotten. Bismarck rolled to the edge of the room.

The firing stopped abruptly and Bismarck jumped to his feet. There were shouts from outside and strident voices demanded that they come out with their hands up. Without a glance, Bismarck ran to a door at the other end of the room, pulled it open and dived through. Simultaneously, a boot kicked in the door next to Ed and men carrying Kalashnikovs entered. They looked first at the screaming woman and children in bed, and then spotted Ed lying on the floor. One of the men stepped forward and gestured that Ed should stand with his hands up.

Drawing himself to his feet, Ed felt that he best move as slowly and deliberately as possible. But the closest militia man mistook his exaggerated movements as an attempt to distract his attention. There was a push and then a threat to hit him with the rifle butt. Recoiling, Ed fell back to the floor, close to the gun recently knocked from Bismarck's hand. A look of panic in the man's face caused Ed to raise his hand in an act of reassurance, but it was too late. A boot connected with his rib cage, and then he heard, rather than felt, the gun zip through the air and connect with his head.

As the light faded he felt his body yanked from the room, outside into the bright sunlight.

AT LUCKY LOMAX'S RESIDENCE

A vision of a day on the beach came to him borne on a warm breeze that touched his cheek and inveigled its way up his nostrils. He opened his eyes to see mosquito nets and floor to ceiling doors with net curtains billowing like unrestrained sails. He had a vague memory of boots in the ribs and a rifle butt in the head. No wonder his brain felt like it had been shaken and then stuck back in his skull. Lifting his hand he found bandages around his head and then he touched his sore ribs. Bismarck had said they were both wanted by Chiri. He had demanded that Ed hand over Forge's trilobite.

After the militia had knocked him out they must have loaded him into one of their scout cars. He remembered banging his head against the metal sides as it bounced along the rutted roads of Lomax. Trying to raise his head a hand had restrained him, and then the banging had stopped and a needle had been shoved in his arm. He felt nervous at the thought of being handled by people while he was unconscious.

A roar close at hand could only be the sea breaking on

a shore. Throwing off his mosquito net and trying to stand, he felt his knees lock together and then a tightening in his muscles which might allow him to move forward. He was determined that he was going out of the large doors to somewhere he could see the sea. But after a few steps he tripped and fell, rolling onto his back. Looking about, he noticed his room was entirely wooden and full of beautiful carvings. It occurred to him that he might be in some sort of resort hotel, such as exist on the coast close to Accra.

Striped cotton pyjamas were not the beach attire he would have ideally chosen, but he was not proud. Picking himself up he made his way to the doors and stopped. There was short-cropped grass, a parkland of tropical palm trees, well-ordered flowerbeds; but no sea. Listening again he realised that the rushing was nothing more that the sound of wind rustling trees in the jungle on the mountain opposite.

Taking a tentative pace forward, he nearly fell over the large step that led down from his balcony on to the lawn. The grass felt good on the soles of his feet as he walked steadily across the hundred metres of lawn until he reached a place where forest trees plunged down into a steep valley. Turning to look back, he saw a large building with iron verandas and floor to ceiling doors. In the background was a shanty town, and off to the right a huge winding tower; he was at the Mine Manager's substantial villa.

He touched black despair, his mind visualising the squalid hole in which Greg must have died. There was no way anybody could survive in such conditions for long. If he ever got out of this, he would be sure not to tell Alice the whole truth of that dreadful place.

The knowledge that Ed probably owed his life to the

timely arrival of Chiri and his acolytes made him feel dizzy and disorientated. He decided to head back to his room.

On arriving he found a woman dressed in the green livery of the mine. She smiled at him and said it was nice to see him out of bed. "Mr Lomax requested that if I found you awake to tell him immediately."

"I'm about to go back to sleep. Either that or throw up."

Lying down on the bed he dreamt of a day in which a letter had arrived from Alice. It lay on the table like a time bomb. Then a letter from John Williams Consulting arrived which he opened, thus becoming aware of what Alice's letter might contain.

He had written back to her, it felt good to write the words and imagine her reading them. He imagined her sitting at her breakfast table, tea in one hand and letter in the other, like he had seen her on so many occasions.

"Mr Evans?"

Opening his eyes, he saw the dark shape of the maid clearly visible through the mosquito netting. "Mr Lomax is keen to meet with you. I've brought your clothes. Dinner is in an hour." The noise of the wind was cut off as she shut the outside door. "He is most insistent. He needs to go home tomorrow."

"Who else will be there?"

The maid shrugged and then moved away into the gloomier parts of the room. "I will come and take you there in thirty-five minutes. You should have a shower and a shave."

Tiredness coursed through his body as he rose from the bed. He noticed that his rucksack had been brought from the compound and dumped in the corner of his room. No sign of the bag containing the false trilobites and Forge's last will and testament.

Grabbing a towel he went into the bathroom and switched on the shower. The water came through under pressure, massaging his skin and awakening him. He even managed to wash part of the hair not covered in bandages. Emerging several minutes later, he felt refreshed and reborn. As he entered his bedroom, he noticed that the balcony doors were partially open and the noise of the wind was back. He closed them before walking to the bed and sitting down, an uneasy feeling in his stomach. He had the sense that a poisonous snake had entered the room while he had been washing. It was a snake that smelled of Eau d'Cologne and who was dextrous enough to open doors. He lifted his head slightly and stared into the gloom.

Standing in the corner was Jeremy, brilliant white teeth glowing and with a gun pointing at Ed's chest. A sneer grew on his perfectly-tanned face as he stepped forward so his features were better illuminated. "I've come to collect you," he said, putting the revolver back beneath his jacket.

Ed stared and then started to rub his hair with the towel, slow and deliberate. He fixed his gaze on the spot where the firearm had disappeared and wordlessly picked up his clothes and walked back into the bathroom.

As he dressed, he heard Jeremy moving around the room, heard him stop outside the door and clear his throat. "Allen has arrived. Chiri picked him up this afternoon. You two need to have your story synchronised or else…"

Jeremy must be standing directly outside, so close that his nose must be pressed against the wood. On instinct, throwing open the door, Ed leant forward and grabbed Jeremy into what could have been a loving embrace. He reached around and removed the gun, pushing Jeremy backward at the same time, then shut the door and locked it.

He finished dressing before putting his ear to the door and listening intently. There was the sound of wind coming through opened balcony doors but little else. Opening the door, careful not to let any part of him show in profile, he tumbled out onto the floor and rolled before standing up. The gloominess was impenetrable after the brightness of the bathroom. Switching on the room light he turned quickly to check nobody was lurking in shadowy corners, but Jeremy had fled.

He marched from the room, following Jeremy through the balcony doors, out into the night. He had no idea where he might find Lomax but expected he would not be difficult to locate.

On reaching the car park he saw a curvaceous figure climb from a pickup and make for the main doors. He was not surprised to see her after the way she had assumed control from Chiri in the pursuit of Bismarck.

Feeling inside his pocket for Jeremy's gun he walked swiftly after her, into the bright lights of the reception area. She crossed the squeaking polished wooden floor into the reception room on the right where Ed had met Jeremy and the previous Mine Manager only a few days previous.

The creak of the tinder-dry floor boards meant it was difficult to move without drawing attention. He stood still and listened to Bernie's voice wishing that Jeremy would hurry up before that Scouse drongo arrived. Moving quickly inside, wincing at every squeak, Ed pulled out Jeremy's gun from his pocket and slipped it into the drawer of a beautifully crafted writing table. Then he followed Bernie into the room.

In the largest leather chair furthest from the door was a sleek, silver-haired man with bright blue eyes that gazed from beneath overhanging brows. Folds of skin that dropped from his neck were partially obscured by a bright pink paisley neckerchief. Lomax looked much older than his official pictures but there was still something vital about the man. When he opened his mouth, Ed was not surprised to hear a commanding baritone voice. "It's the man himself."

Bernie's face fell. "You gotta be kiddin' me," she said in apparent embarrassment. But no blush reached her cheek.

To the right of Lomax sat Allen, his chair turned slightly away from where Ed stood. Moving his head, he looked directly at Ed, the dancing brown eyes serious.

A man dressed in the same khaki uniform as Lomax, medium build with short-cut ginger hair, made his way across the room with the easy grace of a gymnast. Ed put his palms out to him. "I'm not armed." Flicking Ed's arms into the air he did a professional body search before stepping away and nodding to Lomax.

"Take a seat, Ed," commanded Lomax. "Simon, pour him a drink."

The ginger-haired man walked across to the decanter at the edge of the room. "No thanks," said Ed, stepping towards the nearest wall. "And I'll stand if it's all the same to you."

Lomax looked surprised at Ed's defensive attitude. "Don't mind Simon, he searches everybody who comes near me. He's very protective."

"Where's Jeremy?" Ed asked.

Lomax turned to Simon. "Good point. I'm sure I'll be safe in present company. Go and find him."

Nodding at his employer, Simon scampered from the

room and into the hallway where his progress was marked by a rhythmic squeak of floorboards. "A very dedicated employee," remarked Lomax. "I wish all of my officials were so attentive to their duties."

They waited in silence. Even Bernie and Allen had nothing to say; it was if the presence of Lomax had temporarily robbed them of speech. Feeling the reassurance of his back against the wall, Ed felt prompted to ask a question. "Where's Chiri?"

Looking at Bernie, Lomax raised an enquiring eyebrow.

"He's coming," she replied.

"Excellent," said Lomax. "I feel that we will soon be able to get to the bottom of what's been going on here." Glancing at Ed, he pointed a finger at Allen. "I've had a report of course, but I feel more explanation is required and Allen thinks you're the man who knows most."

Ed gave an exasperated sniff. "I doubt I know half of what Allen keeps to himself."

Smiling, Lomax put his hand down behind his chair and produced Ed's bag. "It's you who have the trilobites and Forge's will. Perhaps you'd like to explain their significance." He dipped his hand inside the bag and produced the two fossils, then looked up, his blue eyes focussed on a spot several centimetres behind Ed's head. "I'd heard about Forge's trilobite complex, and now it seems that we all have a fascination with these strange critters. Everybody's falling over themselves to find these two. I wonder why?"

"No idea," said Ed.

Twirling one of the trilobites in his fingers, Lomax continued. "Allen says that you and he received one from Forge and the other from a seamstress down at the compound who claims that Dave Smith said it was worth a lot of money. Allen thinks we may be labouring under a misconception about what a seamstress would think was a lot of money. Nevertheless, it's interesting. A shame Dave isn't here to tell us exactly what he meant by 'a lot of money'."

Ed agreed.

Frowning, Lomax placed the trilobite back down on his lap. "Dave sent me a supposedly anonymous note via Chiri saying that he had information which he was willing to trade. He was disgruntled and he wanted a bigger share of the syndicate winnings. Jeremy sent Chiri 'round to do the bargaining but when he arrived, Dave was already dead."

Squeaking floorboards announced the arrival of Simon. "Not in his room," he said. "And the maid hasn't seen him either. Not since he headed across the grounds to Mr Evans' balcony doors."

All eyes turned to Ed again. "Don't ask me," he said. "He came into my room when I was having a shower, and threatened me with a gun."

"Threatened you with a gun?" said Lomax, as if this was inconceivable. "What the hell would he do that for?"

"Enjoys the power I suppose," said Ed. "I disarmed him and then he ran off."

"What did you do with the gun?" asked Simon.

"Left it in the room," Ed lied.

"We shall have to see what he says when he arrives," Lomax concluded. "In the meantime, I need to know what's been going on." He stood up and walked to the whisky decanter and poured himself a stiff measure before returning to his seat. "Allen assures me you've discovered quite a bit since you arrived and I want a full confession."

"Allen knows more," replied Ed. He glanced at Allen

and saw him gazing out through the window and into the darkened grounds.

"That's not what he says," continued Lomax. "He's convinced you're in possession of all the facts whereas he knows nothing."

"He knows far more than I do about everything that goes on in this mine."

Lomax clicked his tongue impatiently. "Allen is a trusted employee. I agree that he's being very reticent and I was most surprised when Chiri finally ran him to ground as he was preparing to flee."

"Perhaps he wants to avoid Forge's fate," suggested Ed.

For the first time, Bernie decided to join the discussion. "You know, Mr Lomax, I think you should give a little. I mean, none of us knows everything. Seems to me Ed might be frightened to tell you what he knows because of what happened to Greg. Perhaps you can trade information, gain his confidence. It might also get Allen to talk as well."

"What the hell for? I'm paying good money to them for information. I shouldn't need to trade," he said loudly.

Bernie nodded her head and fell silent. However, her words had the required effect because Lomax sighed and put down his whisky glass. "In case Allen hasn't explained why I employed him, I'd better fill you in." He shifted in his chair and crossed his legs. He still had a disgruntled look on his face, as if information was being forced from him against his will. "A few years ago Jeremy came up with a plan to sell off some of our less valuable assets such as exploration prospects which showed very limited signs of gold mineralisation and capital equipment which was running out of its useful life. It was a nice piece of work, fully costed and with a fancy report from some highly expensive City consultants." He smiled to himself and picked up his whisky glass again. "I naturally agreed. I mean who wouldn't if you were offered several million quid for doing nothing."

"Anyway, everything went fine initially. Chiri was asked to recommend ten exploration prospects to be sold off to the highest bidder. At the same time, we ear-marked some old bits of kit to do with the processing side of the operation. We did a massive fire sale and, as Jeremy predicted, I was now several million quid better off."

"But then the rumours started to circulate that some of the prospects we sold were not as barren as they appeared. In fact, one company named Tremendous Resources had struck lucky. I was naturally a bit disappointed and sent an angry missive to Jeremy, who then went and kicked Chiri and assorted others at the mine. All went quiet again, until another rumour surfaced about a second prospect that had yielded a sizeable gold deposit, then a third, then a fourth. All owned by Tremendous Resources. I ordered an investigation, a full audit of all the decisions taken."

"At the same time, I did a bit of digging myself and discovered that Tremendous Resources was one hundred percent owned by a man named Snodgrass, a great tub of lard who lives his life in a cheap hotel in the middle of London. He's a very creepy individual with his fingers in many pies. He's what's known in the trade as a fixer."

"And what d'you think he was up to?" asked Ed.

"Any number of things. He could have been fronting for a politician wishing to make money while they're also in government, or acting on behalf of a rival businessman wanting to discredit me. The point I'm trying to make is that when I saw that he was involved, I realised there was something criminal happening. The share price of Tremendous Resources had gone from a few cents a share to hundreds of dollars. I had no alternative but to enter the market and buy all of the stock I could lay my hands on."

"How much?" asked Ed.

"Nearly one hundred million dollars US."

By now, all eyes were on Lomax, including Allen who had stopped feigning disinterest. Whistling his astonishment, Ed looked at Allen again. "And that's when you came in?"

"Precisely," said Allen. "I was sent here to find out if it was an inside job and whether the money was recoverable. When I arrived and saw how Chiri ran his operation, I naturally assumed he was the weak link. He was pants at the job, more interested in consolidating his position and intimidating his rivals than doing the job for which he was employed. But having a gut instinct was one thing, actually getting proof that it was him was entirely another. And Lomax wanted proof, for some reason."

"So I started to look hard at the data which had caused Chiri to recommend the sale of these prospects to Tremendous Resources. It all looked above board, and I even told Lucky Lomax he had the unluckiest Exploration Manager in the world." He wrinkled his nose and shook his head at this point as if to show disbelief in his own naivety.

"But Lucky Lomax got back to me and said that was nonsense. How could a man be that unlucky? What we needed was somebody from outside the company, to have a look at mine procedures. Everybody knew I was in Lomax's pocket so it couldn't be me. Besides, by then I was fairly certain that the problem was not in Exploration Services but in Geological Services, somewhere close to Forge.

"Lomax managed to find Greg, and installed him in the offices where I suspected the fraud was taking place. Greg dug around for quite a time and decided that Forge had far too much control. Over the years he had gathered the various strings of the Lomax mining operation to his hand until he had become like a spider at the centre of a web, able to feel all the vibrations. He had managed to control the flow of information around the mine to such an extent that he saw drilling results before Chiri, before the Chief Engineer, even before the Mine Manager. He was able to edit information before it became public knowledge.

"Even so, he could not be operating alone. I became fairly certain that he was at the centre of any conspiracy, but who were his co-conspirators? We reported back to Lomax who said we should determine who else was involved before he'd act.

"Greg went after Bismarck. He was getting close to him, he'd even managed to make himself an honest broker between the mine and the union; it was known that Bismarck was a union organiser. Lomax had been on the edge of giving him the sack with the rest of the union hierarchy but Greg had told him to hold off until he'd established Bismarck's involvement with Forge and the potential conspiracy.

"Of course, the involvement of Bismarck indicated that the conspiracy went far beyond a few greedy individuals. If the union was involved, then perhaps the Galamsey were involved as well. We were suddenly in a much more difficult situation.

"Then, when Greg was getting close to the heart of

the matter, he disappeared. Worse still, he had managed to encode all of his information in a form that was completely un-readable. For a long time I wondered why he had done this, and I was drawn to the conclusion that he had lost trust in everybody around him, including me.

"I was all for getting Lomax to sort out Forge and Bismarck and then to reorganise the mine management structure. At least we could cut off the head before any further damage to the mine had been done. But Lomax insisted that we should wait. He asked a few friends in London who suggested that the best person to pick up the trail would be somebody who knew Greg well. He would be able to make educated guesses about how Greg would have reacted in a set of circumstances. That was why you were approached.

"One of the first things which you found of significance was the modified data from Rusty Lion. This was further confirmation that Forge's office was at the centre of wholesale modification of data."

Bernie had been listening intently and nodding at various points. "I was meant to be Greg's contact. All information about the mine should go through me. We established a system where he would encode information using biblical quotations. He kept hinting that he was getting to the heart of the matter but somehow he never quite delivered. On the day when he disappeared, he sent a fax to my office which was clearly encoded but with no indication of the key. He wanted money for that information.

"That was not part of the arrangement. Lomax was paying him to infiltrate the group and provide information. We were not going to negotiate separately for every piece of information he unearthed. Then we heard from another source, Dave Smith, that Greg was trying to negotiate a piece of the action for himself. He was using the threat of revealing all to Lomax as a way of getting a cut of the money made by the syndicate."

"So now you know as much as the rest of us," concluded Lomax, whose eyes twinkled with excitement. He gave Ed one of his piercing stares and waited for him to unload. But he soon realised from Ed's expression that he was far from happy. "What's the problem now?" he asked.

"Everything we've heard so far is largely a fabrication."

"I don't follow you," said Lomax.

"I'm saying that far from being the work of a few rogue individuals, modification of drilling data was, and still is, company policy, that you are responsible for defrauding your own company." There, he'd said it now, for better or for worse. He felt giddy, like he'd just lost his balance at the top of a cliff. "That's why Allen was trying to escape, and it's why Greg decided to encode all of his findings. He was looking for a way out without having his throat cut. When he realised that the union and the mine were in this together, he decided to try and negotiate with the union. It was a lot safer than negotiating with the company, and their main enforcer, Chiri."

"What nonsense," said Lomax. "Why would I defraud my own company?"

"Give me my bag," said Ed. He knew that he might be handing over his own demise, but he was in too deep and he had to follow this all the way to the bitter end. He remembered Taid's advice that nobody ever died from telling the truth. Well, Ed was about to put his grandfather's advice to the test. He found Forge's email and thrust it at Lomax, who took the proffered piece of paper, confusion clouding his otherwise clear blue eyes.

"Where did you get this?" he asked.

"I hacked into Forge's email and printed it off."

As Lomax skim-read the document, his eyebrows progressively rode up to his receding hair line. Then he addressed his bodyguard Simon. "Find Jeremy, and this time don't come back until you've found him." As Simon moved quickly to the door, Lomax called after him. "Expect trouble."

Lifting his eyes from the document, Lomax looked at Allen. "I still want to know why you were escaping," he said. "Are you part of this conspiracy as well?"

Shaking his head, Allen suddenly smiled, and the dance returned to his eyes. "When I realised that Ed had been kidnapped, I forced my way into his room and saw that the air conditioner had been removed. The same had happened to Dave Smith when he was killed and Greg when he disappeared. I decided that it was likely that Bismarck and the union had taken him. I put the word out that I needed to speak with Bismarck or Kojo."

"You put the word out?" asked Lomax. "You mean you have the means of tracking them down?"

"That's right," replied Allen cheerfully. "But I wouldn't say I have the means of capturing them, just talking with them. We spoke on the union's phone number."

"And?" asked Lomax.

For a moment, Allen was reluctant to say, but then he shrugged his shoulders. "I told them that Ed had Forge and Smith's trilobites."

Silence.

"You did what?" asked Lomax, an angry hue flushing his cheeks. The famous Lomax anger was beginning to surface.

Once again, Allen shrugged his shoulders. "I told them that Ed had the trilobites. It was the only thing I could think of which might save his life. If the union knew it had the means to access the money from the syndicate, they may decide to spare him."

"It worked," said Ed. "Bismarck came for me alone and pretended to rescue me from that hell hole. He tried to convince me that Chiri was after us both, and then asked where Forge's trilobite could be found."

"You were lucky they didn't just knock ten bells out of you," remarked Lomax.

"That's more Chiri's style," said Allen.

"Oh really?" retorted Lomax.

"Look what he did to Forge," said Ed.

"That was the union," said Lomax. "In case you've forgotten, Chiri was besieged in Exploration Services."

"And what about Golf Club?" asked Ed.

"The union as well," said Lomax. "Where the hell is Simon and Jeremy?" He stood up and started to prowl the room angrily. "Continue," he ordered Allen, "You still haven't provided me with an adequate reason for why you decided to leave."

Sighing with exasperation, Allen looked straight into Lomax's face. "Until Ed's miraculous rescue, I was the only white exploration contractor who wasn't dead, dying or lost. I think that's a good enough reason to leave, don't you?"

"You could have come up here, got protection from me," said Lomax.

Allen folded his arms in an uncharacteristically defensive gesture and shook his head.

By now, Lomax had stopped pacing the room, he was directly in front of Allen, looking down at him, the colour rising in his cheeks, an angry outburst was due. "Tell me what I should think," Lomax breathed through his teeth.

However, it was Ed who provided the answer. "Because Bismarck, or Kojo, must have told him that they had been following orders from you. Presumably Jeremy and Forge had convinced them that you had created Tremendous Resources of London as a way of stripping assets away from Lomax Gold Mine."

Turning on him, his eyes gleaming, Lomax began to shout. "And why should I do that?"

"To enrich yourself, of course," replied Ed equally loudly. "So you can hide assets from the tax man, so you could deceive the markets and the local government."

By now Lomax's face was flushing red like an angry cuttlefish, and no doubt he would have produced one of his famous rants had the noise of squeaking floorboards not signalled new arrivals. Simon entered the room, followed by Jeremy, armed with a small revolver.

"Everybody out into the hall," Jeremy shouted, waving his gun around excitedly. He marched across the room, rounding everybody up like a sheepdog, pushing Lomax when he refused to move. Then he grabbed Ed's bag with its trilobite contents.

They all trooped out into the hallway, floor boards squeaking. Ed positioned himself next to the drawers in which he had put the gun. He opened it slightly, enough for the gun to be exposed.

Jeremy ran out of the room and shouted for them to stop. "We're all going to wait here, where I can see you," he said, waving the gun and the bag around. "Put your hands behind your heads."

"You're not going to get away with this," said Lomax as he lifted his hands into the air.

"We'll see about that," said Jeremy.

From outside came the unmistakeable sound of a gas

turbine engine. The helicopter was starting up. As Jeremy marched to the door and took his eyes off his prisoners, Ed nudged Simon with his elbow, who turned to look at him. He flicked his head to indicate behind him, "drawer," he whispered through the side of his mouth.

"I need a hostage," Jeremy said.

His eyes travelled up the line and landed on Lomax. "I think I'll take the big fish." He motioned with his gun for Lomax to move, but Lomax stood his ground. "MOVE," he shouted. His eyes were round and staring, mad with adrenaline.

Lomax moved forward. "It's over," he told Jeremy. "There's no use continuing on with it. We've discovered exactly what's been going on. My people will get to Snodgrass. You'll be looking over your shoulder for the rest of your life."

Smiling madly, Jeremy continued waving his gun agitatedly. "GET A MOVE ON," he shouted.

As Lomax walked past, Jeremy's eyes followed. Diving into the drawer containing the gun, Simon turned to shoot, but Jeremy was quicker.

Alive to what was happening Lomax shouted, 'Stop,' before pushing Jeremy hard in the back so that his first shot went up into the ceiling. With a shout of rage, Jeremy grabbed Lomax and hurled him at Simon and both fell heavily against the chest of drawers. By the time they'd regained balance, Jeremy had gone, bag in hand, and was racing to the helicopter. Simon ran through the door but quickly dived inside as a shot came through the doorway.

The noise of the helicopter increased, and the thut of its rotor blades indicated that it was ready to leave. In desperation, Simon rolled out of the doorway onto the floor and let off a volley of shots. More shots were returned making it clear that he had missed. Simon continued to return fire, but after two shots he stopped and rolled back into the hallway.

The turbine increased in intensity, Allen walked to the door and peered around the corner. "It's taking off," he called. Ed followed him and looked up in the sky to see tail lights disappearing into the distance.

"Off to Accra to catch the next flight," commented Allen.

"Not if I can help it," said Lomax, and he rushed back into the drawing room where his voice could be heard on the phone talking to somebody from Head Office in Accra, demanding that they get the police and army to intercept the helicopter when it landed.

"Won't go to Accra," said Bernie, who broke her prolonged silence. "He'll have gone over the border. Probably catch a flight to Liberia and then on." Ed looked at her quizzically, and then she explained. "If you have enough money it's easy to disappear in Africa. You never know," she said reflectively, "Greg might turn up yet."

The thin light of dawn was beginning to break when Ed made his way up the wooden steps to Forge's drilling office. Unlocking the door and stepping inside he looked around at the winking trilobites on the shelf. Walking across to his desk he reflected that it had been a long night.

The two Calymene specimens stared down, innocuous and blithely uncaring about the fuss they had created. Smiling to himself, he put his feet on his desk, opened Forge's catalogue of trilobites and waited; it wouldn't be long until Allen arrived.

Sure enough, several minutes later he heard the heavy tread of boots making their way along the walkway. When

Allen appeared at the window he looked surprisingly chirpy for a man who'd been up all night and had been held at gun point. On opening the door, he gave Ed one of his roguish smiles. "Just heard Forge has been moved," he said. "Apparently his insurance covers evacuation to Britain. Someone at Head Office in Accra looked up the details. You never know, in a proper hospital, he may survive, but I'd say it'll take him a while to recover. I doubt he'll be asking for his old job back."

"What about you?" asked Ed. "Are you going to head home or are you staying?"

"Where's home?" replied Allen. "Here's home for now, and Lomax wants me to stay on and sort out the mess. After that, who knows? I'm sure Lomax will have something interesting for me."

"You not thought about branching out on your own? Having your own exploration company?"

"Naah," Allen replied. "I've tried that and it was a disaster. Besides, Lomax pays me well and I should be able to retire in a few years. Spend the rest of my time on a beach somewhere with a local girl to look after me in old age."

"Sounds nice to me," said Ed. "Warmer than my old cottage anyway."

"What are you going to do?" asked Allen. "I expect Lomax will be generous. You'll have a bit of money to come and go with."

"The cottage needs complete renovation," Ed said yawning. "Most of the money will go on that. I'll have to find work eventually, but not in Africa."

Smiling, Allen walked across to the desk to shake Ed's hand. "I've got to go and find Chiri. Tell him all is forgiven." He paused in mid-shake. "You going to see Alice?"

Ed shrugged his shoulders in a sign that he wasn't sure and didn't care either way. In fact, he knew he would be heading across to Liverpool at his first opportunity. She was an itch that could not be scratched away very easily.

"The power of love," said Allen departing into uncharacteristically philosophical waters. "It's one of the things I remember my dad saying when somebody asked him why he'd married a Catholic."

"I don't think…" Ed began, but Allen held up his hand.

"I envy your strength. You still want her, despite the rejection. I've never been able to love anybody like that. You go and make her your own, and no pussyfooting around or she'll be off again. I didn't save your life so you could moon around like some jilted teenager. Faint heart never won fair lady." Advice delivered, he turned and walked to the door.

"Golf Club's trilobite," Ed called after him.

Hand on the door handle, Allen froze as if he'd been zapped then looked around very slowly. "What trilobite?" he asked. But Allen's confident mask had slipped and it was obvious he knew exactly which trilobite Ed was talking about.

"The one you took from Golf Club's room in the bin full of beer mats," said Ed.

"What about it?" he asked, not bothering to deny it.

"Lomax'll be watching your every move."

Allen gave a nod of his head before walking out through the open door. The sound of his boots receded along the corridor, and once again the office was plunged into silence.

Chancing a last look around Forge's office, Ed gathered up his few belongings. Most of his stuff had been in the bag that Jeremy stole, except for the most important items which were still perched on the shelf. Amidst all of the chaos last night, he reflected that he had not managed to tell anybody about the significance of Calymene. Thinking that maybe he would keep that secret close to his chest he went to sit down in Forge's plush, comfortable seat.

Yawning again, he found a pen in Forge's desk, and some writing paper. It would be nice to know who had the fourth Calymene, he decided. Hesitating for a moment, letting his tired thoughts bubble to the surface, Bernie's painted face swam across his eyes. Yes, he reflected, Bernie almost certainly had the final trilobite, all the rushing about issuing orders was a show to throw everybody off the scent.

Before he made any decision about whether to tell Lomax about Calymene and his suspicions about Bernie, he would sit down and write a letter to Alice.

RETURNING HOME

Edryd huddled into his warm jacket and climbed aboard a bus that would take him into Liverpool city centre. The bus was full so he gripped one of the floor to ceiling bars and rode the motion as it bounced along the road. He looked at the passing houses, noting the miniscule changes that had occurred since his last trip into the city. Eventually he alighted in Aigburth Vale and then walked up the hill to where Alice lived in a large house converted to flats that overlooked Sefton Park. He dipped his hand in his pocket and produced a piece of Lomax note paper on which her address was written. He found his feet taking him into a large wooded area close to a lake. Small yellow primroses poked their heads out of the grass and the trees were starting to break into bud. If spring had reached Liverpool, his own patch of Welsh hillside would not be far away from throwing off the yoke of winter.

Exiting the park and joining a nearby road, he looked carefully at each of the houses until he found one that matched the address on his note paper. Taking a deep breath, he walked up the path through extensive, leafy vegetation to a large wooden door with stained glass windows. Ringing the bell for flat number 1 he was surprised to find that the door was opened instantly by a woman with dark red hair and big brown eyes. She wore a nurse's uniform, complete with apron and was in the middle of putting on a long khaki coat. Staring, he tried to reach for a smile; it appeared and then disappeared, like the moon passing behind clouds.

"You look as if you've seen a ghost," she said.

"Perhaps I did."

Silence.

"You got my letter?" he asked.

"I did. You better come in. I'm already late for my shift." She walked down the hall to her kitchen. "How long have you been back?" she asked.

"A month or so." He knew what she was thinking. "Sorry it took so long to write, I had a bout of malaria. I've been feeling wasted."

She stopped and turned around, professional concern registering in her soft brown eyes.

"I'm much better though, apart from the bruises on my bum where they stuck the needles."

She nodded and disappeared behind the kitchen door. The hall and kitchen smelt of flowers and apricot, Alice's favourite scent. It took his mind back to the small place they had shared together only a few short years before. He wondered if there was a smell she associated with him, his awful socks perhaps. He felt unsure that he had done the right thing by turning up on her doorstep, unannounced.

The colour schemes in the hallway and the kitchen had been thoroughly thought through and even the cups on a natty little sideboard perfectly complemented the wallpaper. Ed was the only thing out of place, with his dark overcoat, big black boots and five o'clock shadow.

"So, Greg died because he disturbed thieves," she called.

Coughing nervously, he moved across the kitchen threshold. "There'd been a lot of thefts of air conditioners at the camp and I think he surprised the gang. They probably panicked and killed him and then they took his body." He poked his head around the door and saw her standing by the sink arranging a pot of tea and some cups. There was a small area set aside which had a table and chairs. He noticed the letter he had written was on a windowsill and he was gratified to see it was well thumbed.

"And what have the police done to catch the criminals?" she asked. "What about the mine? What have they done? Surely they'd be interested in finding who killed one of their employees?"

How to convey the chaos of the Lomax mine? How could he explain why the disappearance of Greg and the murder of Dave Smith had been treated as an inconvenience rather than as a crime to be solved. "They did investigate, but they have such limited resources."

She handed him the tea. "Would you like a beer with that? Or some whisky? I have some in the cupboard."

"I thought you'd never offer," he smiled.

"And there was no suggestion he went off with another woman?" she said, lacing his drink with whisky. "You said there were many local women that hung around the contractors' compound."

A mistake to add that to the letter. "James Allen questioned them all very closely. They were adamant that none of their number had disappeared at the same time."

The late afternoon gloom had been growing. She decided to flick the wall switch and then offer him a seat.

"I need to go in a few minutes. You should have warned me you were coming and I could have laid on a better welcome."

"You never answer your phone," he said reproachfully. "Anyway, I came on impulse."

"Your sister told me you'd taken yourself off to your grandad's place. Can't say she was very sympathetic. She thought you were completely crazy. Said she tried to persuade you to get somewhere near her where she could keep an eye on you."

He shrugged and pretended not to care. "It's where I like to be. Perhaps in a few years when I've done the place up a bit I can move on somewhere there's a few more people around."

"How're your nerves?"

He forced himself to smile, to keep the friendly atmosphere bumping along. The month since he had arrived back from Africa had been the loneliest he could remember. "And what do you think? Am I mad to live up there?" he asked.

There was a pause while he took a sip of his tea. The whisky had a strengthening effect on him, allowing him to feel more in the moment. He glanced sideways and saw Alice's strip lights reflect a glassiness in her eyes. She rose from her seat and placed a hand on his shoulder. It felt warm and comfortable. "Of course not," she said.

He put his hand on hers and felt electricity.

"It's just that if I'd known you were suffering I would have been more forceful… tried to stop you I mean."

She withdrew her hand and sat back down, crossed her legs. "I loved Taid's place." She paused for a few moments and looked away out of the window. "Somewhere detached from the world where you can retreat and pull up the draw-bridge." Then, fixing him with a piercing stare, she leant forward. "He didn't really die at the hands of air conditioner thieves."

Ed took a few swigs of tea and then shook his head.

"Then how did he die?"

"By mistake; at the hands of a friend." He stood up. "I'm going home. Take a couple of days off and come and visit me. It'll take at least a day to explain."

Alice rose as well, her hands buttoning her coat. He could tell she was desperate to ask more questions but was finding it difficult to put her thoughts into words. "Did he suffer much?" She hesitated at Ed's quizzical look. "I mean was it a good death? Did he die in a lot of pain?"

"I think he probably died of dysentery and dehydration. There's no way of really knowing."

"How can you know he's really dead then?"

He was now standing at Alice's open door, looking out at the expanse of Sefton Park. "I talked to the people who buried him. He's dead." Turning, he gazed at her so he could have a last look at those beautiful brown eyes. Then he glanced at a shelf that ran the length of her hallway. Several flowery plates looked down at him. He remembered Alice's passion for collecting, that she had an unerring knack of knowing what would look good.

But there was also something else which his mind couldn't quite see even though his eyes lingered. Alice had stopped buttoning her coat and was looking at him, surprised that he was staring past her shoulder. "What is it?" she asked trying to follow his line of sight.

Blinking several times to make sure he wasn't seeing things he transferred his gaze to Alice. "You started collecting trilobites now?" he asked.

Shaking her head, she attempted to walk out of her front door, but Ed stood his ground. "The trilobite," he said quietly. "Where did you get it?"

Her face started to colour, she gave Ed a push, forcing him out of the doorway and onto the front step. But Ed twirled around and jammed a foot in the door. "Where did you get it?" he asked. His voice was even lower, whispering rather than speaking out loud.

Stepping back, startled by his sudden change in demeanour, she let the door swing open again. He marched inside and quickly grabbed the trilobite off the shelf. It was virtually identical to the two in his possession; Calymene. He glanced at the base and saw a serial number; it was the next in the progression on Forge's list. "Did Greg give you this?" he asked.

Tears once again pricked the edge of her eyes. Had he frightened her with his earnestness, was she afraid of him? He supposed his faint scars made him look ferocious. Trying to soften his face he stopped his direct stare into her eyes. "It's important," he said.

Perhaps she recognised his attempt to restrain his enthusiasm, or the fact that his voice had become less like a snake's hiss and more like the cooing of a dove. Whatever it was, she visibly relaxed. But an answer to his question was still unforthcoming.

"This is why Greg died," he said, holding the trilobite up for her to see. "When did he give you this? What did he say about it? Did he give you any instructions?" A thought that she might be part of the conspiracy raced into his mind. Did she know what had happened to Greg all along? Had she let him go into the lion's den for a reason other than her concern for Greg? In which case, what had she expected Ed to find?

He felt a wave of vulnerability enter his body that was so strong that he began to tremble. Alice must have sensed the turmoil in his mind, must have realised why he had suddenly recoiled. She took a step towards him, concern etched in her eyes. "Yes, he gave it to me. It arrived in a box over a month ago." She grabbed his hand and hauled him through to the kitchen. "He said in the note I was to keep quiet about it, tell nobody I had it." She dropped his hand and searched through a drawer. "Look, this is the receipt left by the postman, it arrived after you left for Africa." Sensing that Ed wasn't listening, she grabbed him by the shoulders and began to shake him.

But Ed was miles away, he was seeing the stinking cellar with the portrait of Alice on the wall, the smell of raw sewage was in his nostrils, overpowering the sweet smell of Alice's apricot blossom scent. Then he saw Forge in the hospital fighting through the pain to tell of the location of a trilobite, the partner to the one which he was now holding. He looked down at it and then in a trance he looked up at Alice who was shaking him ever more vigorously. She guided him to a chair, took out her mobile phone, rang somebody, took off her coat.

Brandy was forced into his hand and he felt her arm around his shoulders. The fire of the spirit allowed his thoughts to become lucid, allowed him to recognise that Alice could not be involved. He remembered Greg's notebooks with the wolf-like Alice, Greg's affair with Bernie.

With his new found certainty, he began to talk about what had happened. When he had finished, Alice looked pale. She took a swig of her own brandy and then pursed her lips.

"So what exactly is the significance of these trilobites?" she asked.

"I think they're calling cards, but maybe not in the way you think. I'm not absolutely certain of their significance myself. Their owners died rather than reveal their location, or their significance. I found them by pure luck." He licked his lips and looked across the garden and then coughed. "Until now I'd have sworn that Greg had never received one. He was playing both ends against the middle and the syndicate bumped him off rather than give him a share. But your trilobite shows that might not be the case."

"But Greg said in his note that he picked it up at the airport, a quirky present for me; an ornament." There was an edge of pleading in her voice. He could sense her eyes on his face even though he was deliberately looking away from her.

"An ornament he didn't want you to display," he said. The implication flitted around the room like a moth around a candle flame. "Between us we have three of the four trilobites."

"And what do we do with them?"

Ed shrugged. "As to that I have no idea. Perhaps they're nothing but a bit of silliness dreamed up by men who had too much time on their hands."

"But surely you must have some idea?" she said.

He looked at her again. "I couldn't even guess. It can't be a simple matter of presenting them to the right person and receiving payment, cash on delivery. It would be too simple to circumvent, the opportunity for corruption would be too great for any of the syndicate to contemplate."

"Did Allen have anything to suggest?" she asked.

"Nothing. What about Greg?" he asked. "You mentioned a note that came with the trilobite. Perhaps the note contains a clue."

Removing her arm from around his shoulders she rose to her feet and walked to a cupboard in the kitchen.

Stretching, she reached into the back and brought out a padded envelope. She shook it and a piece of paper dropped into her outstretched hand.

A week later, Ed headed for Horncastle in Lincolnshire, a town which was miles from the nearest motorway with no rail link and buses that ran only occasionally. He was alone, Alice had decided that she could not afford to take time off from her job and had stayed in Liverpool. He'd been disappointed, but the thought of their new found partnership energised him.

There were dangers, he had explained. Lomax would be watching, so would Jeremy. Both knew the significance of trilobites. "And Jeremy might have guessed there's something amiss with the trilobites he stole. He'll know I switched them, and then what? My best chance is to recover the money and approach Lomax, throw myself on his mercy, try and strike a deal." It was thin, and he could tell by the look on Alice's face that she was frightened.

Arriving late at night, he booked himself into a small guest house. After a late rise and a huge breakfast he wandered about the town centre looking at various bric-a-brac shops which were a feature of this rather nice market town. There were some shops which specialised only in old furniture, others which were notable for china and pottery. The range of second hand paraphernalia of all vintages was staggering.

At mid-morning he decided to sit in the market square and have a cup of coffee out of a paper cup. He was disappointed; there was nothing in this town which fitted with what Greg had described in his letter to Alice. Perhaps Greg had wanted to send Alice on a wild goose chase. The strange wolf-like Alice sketched in the back of Greg's notebook floated through his mind. 'She should've married Ed,' that was what Greg had told Allen. 'There were three people in the marriage.'

He still had several different places to visit, he thought, but he didn't hold out much hope; none of the other shopkeepers had heard of anywhere that dealt in fossils and minerals. He pulled out Greg's letter and read the instructions again. "The shop is small and located between the main road and the river."

From where he sat he could see a small bridge clogged with traffic and pedestrians. The road over the bridge led out of town and during his cursory search he had not seen any shops that way. Finishing his coffee, he crossed the busy road that ran through the town and made his way along the pavement.

The bridge spanned a small canalised water course clogged with supermarket trolleys, plastic refuse and soggy chip wrappers. In the shade of the bridge span there was a shoal of healthy-looking fish jostling for position in the fast flowing water. For a moment he watched the flashes of silver and thought of Taid, the fisherman. Then he lifted his gaze to examine the surrounding area in more detail.

Opposite was a small shop with a sign that indicated that the proprietor was named Hardacre. There was a display in the main window consisting of old cake tins, a sherry decanter, an ivory chess set and, in pride of place, two trilobites. Feeling his heart thump against his ribs, Ed meandered across to the shop as nonchalantly as possible and gazed at the display. He pretended to look at the sherry decanter but all the time he focused on the trilobites. He recognised them as the ones he'd swapped back in Forge's office, grabbed by Jeremy when he'd snatched Ed's bag. Without turning them over and seeing Forge's carefully crafted serial numbers, he couldn't be absolutely certain, but in his mind there was no doubt.

Entering the musty interior of the shop he pretended to examine several shelves that were full of sherry decanters. Then he browsed through boxes of old magazines before looking at examples of ancient board games in their bashed and dog eared cardboard boxes.

Finally, he approached the counter where a man of over sixty sat reading a book, feet up against a one bar electric fire, hot water bottle clasped to his mid riff. He was portly and had a round face with comb-across hair. He didn't look up as Ed approached

"The sherry decanter in the window," he said, "is it for sale or just for show?"

The man looked at him as if he'd gone mad. "Everything's for sale in here."

"So if I wanted to buy it I'd have to pay you?"

"Certainly not," he said. "I am just the enabler. People rent space in the window to place items they wish to sell. That's my only involvement."

"So if I wished to buy the decanter?"

"You take a business card," said the man indicating a small rack. "Next to the door for any passer-by."

Ed followed the man's pointing finger and saw a metal shelf screwed into the wall in front of the door. "So anybody could come along and take one, even in the dead of night?"

"If they so wished, yes they could get a card under cover of night."

"And how much would it cost to place items in the window?" asked Ed.

"£10 per calendar month, £100 for the year."

"Thank you."

He walked out and made a show of looking through the cards on the shelf next to the front door, pretending to look for the owner of the decanter. He guessed that the decanter belonged to a Mr Walesby of Horncastle, he was also the owner of the tin box and the chess set. The other set of cards identified a vendor known simply as "Snodgrass" and gave as his address, The Penzance Hotel in central London.

Once again Ed felt his insides contract with excitement. Lomax had mentioned a man named Snodgrass. He was a fixer, do anything to anybody as long as the price was right. He was a friend of newspaper men and politicians, knew a lot about those who mattered, enough to make him untouchable. He'd been responsible for convening the one and only meeting of the Tremendous Resources syndicate at his hotel. According to Lomax he was, 'as ugly on the outside as on the inside, small eyes almost closed because of an excess of flesh, corpulent as an over-fed pig carrying a litter of piglets.'

The thought of Snodgrass made Ed shudder and fight the desire to replace the card back on the stack. This was not a man he wanted as his enemy. Then a little voice inside spoke up, 'Snodgrass is your enemy whether you like it or not. Once you found the truth and forced the syndicate's hand he became aware of who you were.' He put the card in his top pocket.

Alice insisted they visit the Penzance Hotel together. Arriving in the early evening they entered the lounge bar and gazed disconsolately at faded simulation chip board, a red carpet and red fake-leather cushioned seats. Strip lighting left nothing to the imagination. "Like a Liverpool suburban pub when I was a kid," said Ed under his breath. Alice sniffed slightly and then agreed.

Around the edges of the room were young men dressed in red, green or brown velvet suits. They sat in small groups, flowery cravats around their necks, ironed handkerchiefs in their top pockets. A few scowled at one another, others flicked their hair back in affectation and some shouted greetings at fellow velvet-jacketed men who were arriving behind Ed and Alice.

"Is it some kind of fancy dress party?" said Alice in a low murmur. "Except they've all come dressed as the same person."

Shrugging, Ed turned to the bar and waited to be served. The barman was dressed in a white jacket with a purple velvet bow tie. He was much older than the clientele, balding and a black moustache and beard. "Just come into town," Ed told him. "Is this a good place to eat?"

The man frowned and then stroked his moustache. "There's better," he said in a surprisingly high voice. "Down the road."

"Two gins and tonic then," said Ed.

The barman walked off to find glasses and left Ed and Alice staring at the mirror behind the bar. "This place gives me the creeps," she said.

Alice had been adamant she wanted to come here despite his warning that nothing of any use would arise from the trip. "What d'you want to do when we get there?" he'd asked. "Beard him in his lair? Fix him with a glare? Announce that you were once married to a man who he arranged to have killed?"

"I want to fix him in the eyes," she had said.

In the mirror, Ed saw several men enter, one of them clad in charcoal grey, enormous, like a great balloon on legs, his ears perched on ripples of fat that bulged like an over-inflated tyre above a tight white collar. Ed felt his breath catch in his lungs, 'corpulent as an over-fed pig carrying a litter of piglets'.

"Snodgrass," he whispered.

Alice turned, but Ed remained looking at the reflection, his attention had been taken by a man walking with Snodgrass. Slightly older than the other young men in the bar, skin tanned, a beautiful suit from the same charcoal material that Snodgrass wore, somebody hailed him and he turned to reveal an aquiline nose, high cheek bones, a paisley cravat.

"Jeremy," Ed breathed at Alice. On the run from Lomax's avenging agents, and here he was walking about town as if he owned the place, a special guest of Snodgrass. Ed's insides contracted in loathing` as he watched the man lift a languid arm to casually acknowledge the greetings of lesser men. Like an overbred pooch, he assumed an entitlement wherever he went, that he had a right to expect other men act deferentially, it was part of his birth right.

The barman put gin and tonics on the counter and proffered his hand for the required money. "We've changed our mind," Ed said in a flash. He grabbed Alice's arm and pushed, but Alice resisted. "Move," he said. "They'll recognise me, they'll likely kill me." What the hell was he doing here? Somehow he had never believed he would see Snodgrass in all of his flesh.

Alice continued to struggle. "Let me go," she said. "He's in here. I saw him."

"He certainly is."

They were soon outside in the cold London air where she tried to shake him off, but he managed to pin her against the wall. "Stop it," he hissed, so quiet that only she could hear. "Greg's dead, at the hands of those men in there. He tried to muscle in on their bit of enterprise, they'd kill me too if they found me in the bar."

***

A week later, Edryd stood on a patch of hillside above his cottage and watched trees sway in the valley below. The wind was frigid and cut like a knife, pin-pricks of moisture collided with his face, a prelude to something more substantial. The sparse, wind-blown trees of the high hills hissed, black-faced mountain sheep scattered across the steep slopes bleated pathetically.

Sniffing the wind, he found very little that assaulted his olfactory senses, except the sweet smell of rain and closely-cropped sheep pasture. He sniffed again and found an undertone of old wood smoke from the kitchen fire.

From the front of the cottage a rutted and worn track wound down the hillside and disappeared beneath a coppice. It was his only connection to the outside world, except for the landline, which, like the electricity, was intermittent at best.

Wandering down the small slope he entered his kitchen which was by far the biggest room in the house, and the one he tended to use most. An old wooden table in the middle of a flagstone floor was piled high with groceries. Next to it were a couple of threadbare comfortable chairs and against the far wall was a Rayburn belching out heat.

Glancing above the Rayburn, he saw two trilobites, side by side on the mantelpiece, impassive as always, their gaze fixed on the cupboards on the other side of the room. Even if he was correct about their significance, to attempt to cash them in would be suicidal. "Water, water everywhere but not a drop to drink," he told them.

He lit candles to keep out the late afternoon gloom. The wind that came through the bottom of the door and through the window frames caused each flame to flicker. Strange shadows appeared on the ceilings and walls which, when combined with the faint bubbling from the stew on the stove, gave the kitchen a touch of the occult.

From quite close he heard a diesel engine. The sound of the wind must have masked the vehicle until it was quite close. He quickly made his way out of the door and looked down the sloping farmland. Snow was beginning to fall in sweeping curtains, but he was able to make out a large blue vehicle making its way ponderously towards the house. It was Alice's most recent acquisition, an old diesel four by four. She'd passed the difficult part, where most people gave up.

"Rayburn's on the go," he said as she arrived. Her ashen face gave a weak smile as she stepped out of the car. Fat flakes of snow made a polka dot of her black woollen overcoat. "We'd best get in," he said opening the kitchen door so she could enter a surprisingly warm and atmospheric house shimmering in candle and firelight. "The electricity's down," he added by way of an explanation before shutting the door on the wild wintry weather.

For ten minutes they talked of the weather, the traffic, the price of fuel. She refused to sit down or take off her coat; she stalked the kitchen ringing her hands, gazing out at the snow and then at the fire. Once or twice she walked over to the mantelpiece and gave the trilobites a hard stare.

"Sure you don't want whisky in your tea?" he asked. "It might settle your nerves."

She thought for a few seconds and then held out her cup. Smiling, Ed unscrewed the top of a small bottle and poured a generous measure then added a splash to his own.

"Have you reached a decision?" she asked.

He sipped some tea and felt the fire disappear down his throat. "I have no choice." Not after seeing Snodgrass in his hotel, he thought.

Nodding, she hovered close to where he sat, the warmth of the Rayburn making her coat steam. She threw it off to reveal jeans and a simple pullover. "You must have come straight from work, you've gotta be tired," he said. "We can talk about this in the morning."

She brushed off his concern with a flick of her head. "Why don't you have any choice?"

He sighed, he didn't want to talk about this now, not yet, not until she was relaxed. "The remaining members of the syndicate'll know they have the wrong trilobites by now."

"You mean Jeremy and Snodgrass?"

"They'll soon be coming for me; us. I have to act, now."

"You could always just take the trilobites to Lomax and explain what happened. Apologise for not telling him the truth. Throw yourself on his mercy."

"Lomax doesn't really believe the story about the trilobites. When I told him he could barely keep the scorn from his voice. Telling him the same story over again won't make any difference. On the other hand, if I can go to him with something more substantial, then he'd have to listen. He's the only man with the resources to counter Snodgrass. He might bring enough influence to bear, particularly if I'm able to demonstrate Snodgrass's complicity. It might stop a lone gunman in the dead of night."

"Is Snodgrass so evil?"

"Ask Greg."

"So Lomax is our only hope," she said. And either it

was the whisky working to calm her nerves, or Ed had finally convinced her, and she began to relax. "That's settled then. I'll have that glass of wine now."

As he poured, she walked over to the trilobites on the mantelpiece again. "We'll have another discussion tomorrow, see if we still feel the same. But for now I'd like to pretend that none of this ever happened, no more trilobites. It should be like just before you went on that last trip and went missing. Is that possible?"

He picked up his glass. "Here's to forgetting."

"But we're not keeping the money are we?" she asked. "It's not ours to keep."

"The money belongs to Lomax," he agreed, "even though he doesn't need it. A hundred million's loose change to him, ready cash to lose behind the sofa."

For a long while there was silence, both lost in their own thoughts. Alice was still pale, despite the wine, the fire and the prospect of having Ed's thick mutton stew. Ed thought it was tiredness from working long shifts at the hospital and the stress of waiting for the knock on the door from unwelcome visitors. As for Ed, he felt a sense of elation, like he had passed through darkness and into the light.

He'd have to trust that Lomax was a man of his word. Ed had already been in contact with him, and with Allen. He'd described the shop in Horncastle and how the trilobites should be left in the window. Lomax had been sceptical, Allen had been curious; both had agreed they needed to rent space in Hardacre's premises.

So, Mr Walesby's decanter, chess board and biscuit tin had been purchased at a fair price, Snodgrass's trilobites had been moved to the back, and there would soon be four new trilobites displayed prominently, three supplied by Ed, and one by Allen. If anybody wished to negotiate a price for them they would have to take one of Lucky Lomax's business cards from the shelf outside the shop.

It would soon be a waiting game. He didn't want to tell Alice the whole details. The less she knew, the more dependent she was on Ed, and at this point in his life he needed her. If she knew that it was no longer just her and Ed against the world, would she walk out on him? He wasn't willing to take the risk. When he had word from Lomax that he needed to take the trilobites to Horncastle, he would tell her.

But with no electricity, the house phone not working, no mobile reception and snow falling in blankets, it looked like no message would arrive for several days. Any pang of guilt at his deception was overwhelmed by the realisation that for the time being he would not have to share Alice with anybody, living or dead.

Was Greg dead? Did Ed really believe he'd died in that stinking cellar? The image of a face, distorted by a mirror floated into his mind. As Snodgrass had walked into the Penzance Hotel bar it had appeared from behind a partition; it had stared at Alice, and then lifted its eyes to look into the mirror, directly into Ed's eyes. It was a furtive face, with blonde curly hair. Alice had seen it as well and that's why she'd struggled when Ed had forced her out of the bar. When she'd shouted that she had seen him, Ed had deliberately misunderstood her meaning. He was dead, that was what she needed to believe; that was what Ed needed her to believe.

ACKNOWLEDGEMENTS

Thanks go to Andrew Williams for his encouragement, and his confidence that my experiences in African mining would be of interest to a wide audience. To Suzanna Wadeson, Director at Doubleday Books and Phil Rankin (Phil the Shelf) who were so positive about an early draft of Dead Man's Gold when I appeared on BBC Radio Wales. Christian Huenfhausen for his excellent cover design. TeamAuthorUK: Susan Miller for editing and ensuring that this book saw the light of day and Phil Burrows with his help with my website. To Richard Sayle, English teacher at Bishop Heber, Peter Read and Ray Pinder for their encouraging reviews of early drafts of scripts.

ABOUT THE AUTHOR

Mendus Harris has been writing conspiracy thrillers for the last ten years. His latest books are based in a fictional gold mine named Lomax and draw on his extensive experience as an exploration geologist. Very few people appreciate how a large gold mine in Africa functions and those that do may not be keen for the truth to be told.

His writing conjures images which are redolent with the sights and sounds of West African gold mines, the characters who inhabit them and the political conflicts which can threaten to rip them apart. Here is an author who has been there and seen that and has a view on what he has experienced.

Contact:
mendusharris.co.uk
davidmendusharris@gmail.com
www.facebook.com/authormendusharris

COMING IN 2017…

Wolf Man –
Book 2 of the Lomax Gold Mine series

Ed returns to Lomax Gold Mine after a plea from Allen, his friend and mentor. The major financial fraud discovered by Ed on his last visit has caused the new Mine Manger to throw the mine into turmoil. Ed is tasked with auditing all the mine drilling along with Billy, a new employee who Allen has fetched from Papua New Guinea.

Ed discovers that Allen and Billy share a secret past after he investigates the death of a white drilling contractor (who has apparently been murdered by the miners' union in revenge for the Mine Manager's increasingly draconian regime). A story of Cold War espionage and betrayal emerges amid the shanty town of Lomax which threatens to destabilise the local balance of power and tip the mine into chaos.

COMING IN 2017…

Ice Bound –
Book 3 of the Lomax Gold Mine Series

At the behest of Lucky Lomax, wealthy tycoon and owner of Lomax Gold Mine, Ed undertakes a hazardous journey to the wilderness of Canada's eastern coast where he joins an exploration crew prospecting in an isolated corner of the Labrador sea.

They are stranded on a remote island after an enormous storm tracks south down the Davis Strait and cuts their line of communication. When the crew investigate the best way to escape they spot a man on a remote hillside. At first they take him for a lone adventurer out in the wilderness trapping and shooting game, but soon his malevolent intentions become clear.

As the days pass, the morale of the crew disintegrates and a story of a cruel conspiracy emerges that gradually comes to explain the presence of the man on the island. Events at Lomax Gold Mine reverberate, even here.

When Ed returns home he is determined to put a stop to those who have dogged his steps for so long. It's kill or be killed.

Made in the USA
Charleston, SC
06 December 2016